FIGHT FOR ME

FIGHT FOR ME

BOOK 2: THE TATE CHRONICLES

K. A. LAST

www.kalastbooks.com.au

For everyone who has helped along my writing journey: there are too many of you to name, but know that I am grateful for each and every one of you.

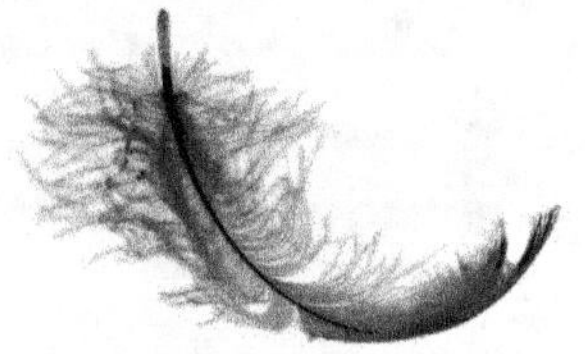

Good things of day begin to droop and drowse,
Whiles night's black agents to their preys do rouse.
William Shakespeare – *Macbeth, Act III, Scene II*

1

SETH
The In-Between

I tumbled through the darkness, fighting something I couldn't see. When I tried to unfurl my wings, the scars on my back burned with the painful reminder of what I'd lost. My body twisted, enduring the relentless torture. I stopped. For a moment I was suspended in time, not moving with it or through it. Then everything moved around me, forming a powerful vortex that sucked me further into blackness.

When I came out the other side, thin tendrils of blue celestial fire bound my wrists and ankles. My feet pressed against a solid sheet of black, and millions of tiny lights filled the sky.

A beautiful angelic face—one I'd come to loathe—split the darkness. Her laughter echoed around us before falling away into nothing. Angelica stood before me, dressed in her impractical white linen. She emanated light and glory.

"I'm going to have *so* much fun with you," she said, a sweet smile touching her lips.

I didn't answer. I didn't want to give her the satisfaction. Instead, I held her pale blue gaze for a moment, before turning away and staring at the floating lights.

"Pretty, aren't they?" Angelica said.

"Where are we?" I asked, attempting to hide the fear in my voice. For the first time since I'd renounced my god and fallen from Heaven, I was scared. Not of Angelica, but of what she could do to me, and to those I loved.

"I think you know where we are. In a place you should have been a long time ago … Be thankful you're not still in here." She held up my creation ring—an angel's wing swept around the black onyx stone at the centre. A trace of blood marred the silver band.

"Why did you strip me?"

Angelica sniggered, and closed her fist around the ring. "You got in my way," she said. "And you stripped one of my closest friends."

"Then why didn't you bind me and send me into oblivion with the others?" I concentrated on the lights bobbing in the darkness.

"Oh, don't worry, I did bind you. But now I need you to do something for me."

"You're letting me go?"

"Not exactly. Everything comes with a price; you should know that by now."

I clenched my fists in an attempt to control my anger. I'd almost forgotten how infuriating Angelica could be.

Even when we were on the same side, when we'd been friends so long ago, she'd still annoyed me.

"What. Do. You. Want?" I struggled against my restraints.

Angelica walked towards me and didn't stop until our noses almost touched. "I want you to get me that ring. You're the only one who can free her."

"No chance," I said.

"Then your friends will pay."

Angelica conjured an orb of white light. She balanced it on her fingertips, twirled it until it got bigger and flattened out. With both hands, she moulded it roughly into a square, and with a flick of her wrist the makeshift screen stuck itself to the blackness, like a magnet. The kitchen of a terrace house came into focus. The place was a mess. Upturned chairs littered the floor. The table had been split, and the lounge slashed. Blood stained the walls. Angelica twirled her finger again, and the picture rewound, like an old VHS tape. I leant forward, staring at the moving image.

Charlotte and Josh battled with Angelica and some other angels I'd never met.

Angelica won.

Charlotte managed to flee, but Josh lay crumpled in a heap at Angelica's feet. If it had have been anyone else, maybe I'd feel sorry for him, but Josh was one of my least favourite people.

"Is he dead?" I asked.

"Not yet," Angelica said, smiling.

She clicked her fingers and Josh appeared beside me, like she'd shone a stage light on him. Celestial fire also bound his wrists and ankles.

He glowered at me.

The feeling was mutual.

Before we had time to verbally rip shreds off each other, Angelica conjured another orb. She hurled it at Josh and it landed in his chest, penetrating his body until it filled him with light. When the light went out, Josh was gone.

"What have you done to him?" I searched the darkness, but all I saw were the floating lights of fallen souls.

"Watch." Angelica pointed to the screen.

Josh lay on the side of a busy highway. A familiar huge steel bridge loomed over him. It had been a while since I'd stepped foot in Wide Island City.

Angelica clicked her fingers again and the screen fell away, breaking into glass-like shards before disappearing into the darkness.

"What did you do?" I gritted my teeth.

Angelica shrugged. "He no longer has any memory of anything that occurred in the past. Only his future is waiting for him. And think of the destruction he can cause, now he doesn't know who he is."

"You are unbelievable," I said. "You're supposed to be one of the good guys."

She laughed. "The time will come when I'll need you to unlock Annie's ring. Then, and only then, will I restore Josh's memory. You'll be staying here until then."

"What if I couldn't care less if he remembers anything?" I said.

"Then I will spend the rest of my existence making Grace's existence a living hell."

I was beginning to understand where all this was

coming from, but I wanted Angelica to admit it. I took a deep breath and stood perfectly still, levelling my stare with hers. Then I attempted to get inside her head, and discover what was really going on. Her block was strong. She walked back to me and smiled her sickly sweet smile.

"What do you really want?" I asked. There had to be more to it than unlocking Annie's ring. She needed me for something else, the desperation in her eyes proved it.

"I want you to suffer," she whispered.

"Why?" I yelled, making her flinch and step back. "Because I protected her? Because we almost defeated you?"

Angelica threw her head back and laughed. Her shoulders shook and she spread her arms wide. "Do not be fooled into thinking you could ever defeat me."

"Then why?" I asked again.

We stared each other down, neither of us wanting to be the first to look away. This time, I shoved my way inside her head, but she pushed me out with enough force to rock me on my feet.

"It's Grace, isn't it?" I finally asked. "Why do you despise her so much? What did she ever do to you?"

Angelica smiled. "It's actually your fault, really. I hate her because you love her."

2

JOSH

Four months later, early Thursday morning

Lilith found me in a ditch on the side of the highway, covered in filth and soaked with rain. I should've been dead. Actually, I was dead, just not in the conventional way.

I don't remember becoming a vampire, and I can't recall anything before Lilith. She seems to think I have amnesia by choice, but why would anyone *want* to forget who they are? When your memories are screwed, what do you live for? How do you go on when you don't know if there's anyone out there looking for you?

The driver's licence in my pocket told me my name was Joshua David Chase. My eighteenth birthday was a little over a month away, so I was forever frozen at seventeen. I came from the small country town of Flats End near Hopetown Valley, but what I was doing so far from home was a mystery. The only other things I'd had, apart from the clothes on my back, were my phone and a silver ring. On the inside of the band was an inscription, one word: *Grace.* I couldn't remember anyone called Grace. I couldn't remember anyone at all.

I've called Wide Island City home for about four months, and I was glad to have Lilith show me the ropes. She'd taught me everything I knew about my kind. Who would've thought there would be so many rules when it came to being a vampire? She knows where to go, who to talk to and who to eat. When your food source walks around on two legs you kind of have to keep a low profile.

Vampires are killers, and I know that's what we're designed to do—it's how we survive—but each time I take a life it's like I lose a piece of myself. Lilith thinks that's crazy; we're made to drink human blood. We're creatures of the night, your worst nightmare, like Freddy Krueger only prettier.

Lilith gets a kick out of tormenting her subjects, but watching her do it makes me feel sick. The taste and smell of human blood is undeniably enticing, and when the frenzy takes over nothing else matters. You're in the moment, thinking it's so good you can't possibly get enough, but when you come out the other side, the blood leaves a foul aftertaste in your mouth—the taste of death.

From my seat on an alcove step halfway down a deserted lane, I watched as Lilith's long raven hair fell over her face. She had one thick, crimson streak in her fringe, as red as fresh blood. If I didn't have vampire eyes, the rest of her would have been hard to see in the dim light. Dressed entirely in black, she blended into the night.

Lilith knelt beside her latest victim, a pretty blonde

girl, probably about sixteen, and lowered her lips to the bare skin of her neck. The girl's eyes glittered under the moonlight, awash with terror. For a second I was excited, perched on the edge of the step, mesmerised by the scene before me. The girl screamed, splitting the night air and tearing me out of my trance.

Disgust engulfed me.

No one would come to help, even if they did hear her. In the city so many people surround you, but you're in fact completely alone.

Lilith laughed. Blood so dark it was almost black stained her lips, and I shuddered as it trickled down her chin. In that moment I hated her, and myself. I hated that she was all I had, and that she was all that I could remember.

"How does this not bother you?" I jumped up from the step.

"Josh, honey, don't get so worked up. What does it matter now, anyway? She's dead." Lilith stood and dropped the girl, whose head hit the asphalt with a thud.

I cringed and said, "Someone somewhere is going to miss her."

"Come on, baby, don't start with that again."

Lilith reached out and took my hand. She twirled herself in front of me and spun into my chest. We danced a few steps, face to face, down the lane. Lilith was tall; her long hair fell past her shoulders and her skin was pale, almost white. Her eyes were dark and haunted, accentuated by the eyeliner she applied every day. A small diamond stud twinkled in her nose, and a simple black velvet choker with a tear-shaped ruby hanging from the centre adorned her neck. A pink flush crept into her cheeks.

"Don't you get it?" she said. "We can do whatever we like. We are more powerful than any of them out there."

Lilith used to make the rules—not that everyone followed them—and she had been the leader of the city vamps for a long time. But I soon learnt that I'd stumbled into some sort of war. There was one vamp in particular I couldn't quite get my head around. He'd had a good shot at killing me once, but Lilith had gotten in his way.

Lucas was another of the city leaders. He and Lilith had some sort of history, but she never let on what it was. She never told me much of anything, really. Sometimes she was too secretive.

Lilith pressed her body against me then pulled back and ran her hands up my chest and over my shoulders. Unable to resist her, I nipped her on the neck and pulled her to me. She moaned as I ran my tongue over her smooth skin, finding her mouth. Her kisses were always intense, and I licked the points of her fangs. With vampire speed I pushed her up against the wall of the building, and she giggled. Lilith liked to play rough.

Amidst the passion and the heat, there hung a sadness I couldn't shake. Right then, Lilith was everything to me, but there had to be more to my existence than killing the homeless and the runaways. There had to be more to life than hiding out in abandoned buildings by day, and roaming the city streets by night.

"We should move on." I pulled away. She leant against the wall and sucked her bottom lip, her hair awry and her mouth smeared with blood. "If we stay still too long, they'll find us." Other vampires were not the only things we had to contend with.

The buildings around us muffled Lilith's laugh. "They don't scare me, Josh. They make it more interesting."

The angels and the hunters we were running from—although Lilith wouldn't call it running; more like avoiding—had been on us most of the time we'd been together. I wished they would leave us alone.

I watched Lilith for a moment as she headed down the lane, away from the city noise. I didn't know how old she was, but she looked around nineteen.

With one last glance at the dead girl on the ground, I followed Lilith up a rickety fire escape and onto the roof of an abandoned warehouse. When I looked over my shoulder, I caught a quick glimpse of something in the lane below—a flash of white.

The girl had been following us for a while, but no matter how hard I tried I could never catch sight of her face. I paused to stare at the spot where I thought I'd seen her, and willed her to come back into view.

"What's the matter, baby?" Lilith came to my side and peered over the edge of the building.

"It's nothing." I took her hand and led her across the roof.

The arch of the steel city bridge loomed in the distance, and the night darkened as the moon tucked itself behind a cloud. We were in the bad part of town where everything was either rusty, broken or beginning to fall down. It was the way we liked it, though—so many places to hide with no chance of being discovered.

"We need to get you something to eat," Lilith said. "Sorry I didn't leave you any. She tasted too good."

I leapt over the next laneway onto the opposite roof, watching as Lilith did the same. She soared gracefully through the air and landed beside me.

My phone vibrated in my pocket, and I pulled it out. The name 'Dad' flashed on the illuminated screen. I couldn't even remember my own father. The first few times he'd called after Lilith found me, I'd answered in the hope it would spark a memory. I'd gotten nothing. The sound of his voice was like any other human's. I'd pretended I was okay so he would leave me alone. After a while, I stopped answering. Our conversations never amounted to anything, so I didn't see the point. I hit *end* and shoved the phone into my pocket.

"Your father again?" Lilith asked. "And you still don't remember?"

I moved away from her and ran the length of the roof then dropped to the ground. I wasn't in the mood for the you-must-remember-something lecture. A tall chain-wire fence stood across the small city back street, and I climbed up and over it with ease. Lilith fell into step beside me.

Wind buffeted us as a passenger train rattled past; the lights inside turned the windows yellow against the grey metal carriages. I hunched over, stuffing my hands into the pockets of my dark jeans, and walked the path of the train tracks. The gravel crunched under the weight of my boots.

Being a vampire was something Lilith didn't think I was very good at. *You think too much,* she'd said to me once. Apparently I need to follow my instincts, but sometimes my instincts tell me this is all wrong.

Another train whooshed past, and the wind made my shirt billow out behind me. Lilith was right; I needed to eat. There was only so much of the burning in my throat I could handle. I stopped, tilted my head to one side and listened. Lilith's glistening eyes locked with mine and she smiled.

"Go on," she said.

The sound of long, deep breaths came from behind the bushes that lined the railway fence. Slowly, I walked over and pulled a branch back. The leaves rustled. Snores came from the pile of dirty rags and newspapers that lay at my feet. It wasn't the most appetising meal, but it would have to do.

As I sank my teeth into the homeless man's neck, I wondered if this was where I was meant to be.

3

GRACE
Late Thursday afternoon

The girl behind the register smiled at Archer, and I resisted the urge to roll my eyes, or stick my finger down my throat and mimic gagging. Every time we stocked up on groceries Amy had to flirt with Archer. She gushed at him. Yes, my brother was nice to look at, but after a while it got old. I tapped my foot in frustration and Archer threw me a dirty look.

"What are you doing for the holidays?" Amy asked, oblivious to my annoyance. "Tomorrow's the last day of term, right?" The checkout beeped as she scanned our items—slowly.

"Not much," Archer said. "We'll probably hang out at home."

"What about you, Grace?" Amy looked at me with her friendly brown eyes, and I scolded myself for being so impatient. "Will you be seeing Josh?"

Ah, Josh. I wished I'd be seeing him, but unfortunately there were a few minor problems, including the fact that he didn't want to see me, and that he was now a vampire. Okay, maybe not quite so minor.

Some stuff had happened at the beginning of the year that left me a little jaded. I fell in love, broke some rules, and my best friend died. Finding my way past the pain and betrayal had not been easy, and I wasn't sure I'd completely recovered yet. It wasn't a very fun time.

"He's been working pretty hard, so I'll probably let him be," I said.

Amy smiled. "Long-distance relationships must be tricky."

Yep. They were even harder when there was no relationship. When Josh had left, the story was he'd dropped out to go and work in the city. It took a few weeks for the initial shock to die down. When you're the captain of the school soccer team and a pretty good student, people tended to notice when things were tough for you. I'd taken a trip to the city to try and get him to come home, but that hadn't gone down so well.

"Hey, what ever happened to that Seth guy?" Amy asked. The checkout beeped again as she scanned a tin of tomatoes. "I haven't seen him around for ages. Weren't you friends with him, Grace?"

Amy looked at me with seemingly innocent eyes, but her thoughts didn't match her pretty face. *I bet you wanted more,* I heard her think.

I didn't react to her silent stab. After years with the ability to hear everyone's thoughts I'd become used to controlling my reactions. I shut her out. If she was going to be nasty I didn't want to hear it.

Besides, when it came to Seth, I probably wouldn't have used the word friend. Enemy, arch-nemesis and pain-in-the-butt sprang to mind. We'd been very close friends a long time ago, but that had changed when he'd made the decision to shut me, and his entire family, out of his life. Seth's a fallen angel, and sometimes I'm ashamed to admit that so am I.

At one point Seth and I might have been on the right path to becoming friends again, but then everything exploded in a massive cloud of *no, Grace, you can't ever be happy so don't even try.* Seth had fought by my side, stood up for me and helped me when I needed it, only to be taken away. Angelica, another former friend and Angel of the Light, had captured him and trapped him in his ring. I desperately wanted to find him, but I had no idea where to start looking. Angelica hadn't shown her face again, so I couldn't even have it out with her, and there was no chance I could ask the Council. They don't talk to the fallen.

Archer clicked his fingers in front of my face. "Earth to Grace? Amy asked you a question."

"Sorry, um … *Friend* isn't really the right word," I said. "Besides, I haven't heard from him, so I can't comment."

I spoke to Archer silently to try and get things moving a bit. At the rate Amy was scanning items we'd be there until midnight. *Can yet get her to hurry up?*

Come on, it's the only time I get to watch her flirt with me, Archer said.

Why don't you ask her out?

You know why, now shut up.

Archer's face split into a wide grin, and Amy blushed.

"I need to go to the newsagent." I pinched Archer's arm. *I'll meet you in the car.* "See you next week, Amy."

Archer was a big boy; he could push the trolley by himself. And I didn't want to be there any longer in case Amy started asking about Charlotte. She was a touchy subject. Her story was similar to Josh's, only she'd gone back to the city because she didn't like country life.

The automatic doors whooshed open as I approached, and the frigid outside air smacked me in the face. I hated this time of year. The cold and rain made me cranky—I was definitely a summer person. With my head down against the weather, I fumbled in the pocket of my red woollen coat for the car keys. I didn't see the man until it was too late. My shoulder connected with his arm and I dropped the keys. Some papers slipped from the man's fingers. They fluttered to the ground, landing in the scattered puddles.

"Grace, honey, I'm so sorry. I didn't see you coming." Mr Chase put a hand on my arm. "Are you all right?"

"I'm fine." I crouched down and helped him retrieve the leaflets.

Josh's features blurred as the ink ran through the wet patches of the paper.

"What's this about?" I forced myself to tear my gaze away from his face staring at me from the flyer.

"He won't answer my calls. It's been weeks, and I'm worried," Mr Chase said. "Have you heard from him?"

"I'm sorry, but no. Josh and I had a bit of an argument, so we decided to keep our distance for a while. But as far as I know, he's fine ... or at least, he was."

16

I balled the wet paper in my hands, throwing it in the bin behind me and grabbing my keys from the ground where they'd fallen. I took a good look at Mr Chase, and didn't like what I saw. He had purple blotches under his eyes and looked as if he hadn't shaved for a week. Josh's mum had passed away when he was young, and now Mr Chase had to deal with the possibility of losing his son as well. A possibility that was too real.

"He stayed in touch at first," Mr Chase said. "Then the calls grew further and further apart. He sounded strange. Our conversations were short ... and now he's not answering his phone. All I get is voicemail."

"And the police are involved?" I looked at the wad of flyers in his hand, and Mr Chase nodded.

They'd never find him. Josh was either dead, or he didn't want to be found. "Have you been to see him?"

"Yes, but no one answered the door." Mr Chase handed me one of the dryer leaflets. "The neighbours said there hadn't been anyone there for a while, and the police found nothing suspicious. Please, Grace. If you hear from him, let me know."

"Sure, no problem." I attempted a smile, but it felt more like a grimace.

Mr Chase went into the supermarket and I watched him disappear behind the sliding doors. Tears stung my eyes when I looked at Josh's picture. I hadn't been lying when I'd told Mr Chase we'd had a fight. I'd followed Josh soon after he'd left in the hope of bringing him home. He hadn't wanted to see me, and in the heat of our argument, we'd done something we shouldn't have, even though we both wanted to.

I'd never in all my existence been that close to someone, and instead of it fixing the rift between us, it had only made things worse. I'd left without a resolution, because Josh was adamant he didn't want anything to do with me until I'd sorted out my issues with Seth. How? That was the ultimate question. How could I sort things out with Seth when I couldn't even find him?

"What are you doing?" Archer's voice made me jump.

"I bumped into Mr Chase. He had these." I showed him the piece of paper.

"Oh. I thought you knew where he was."

"I did, but it looks like I don't anymore. Mr Chase said he's not answering his phone."

Archer pushed the trolley towards our black Defender, and I fell into step beside him. The rain had reduced to a fine mist that blanketed everything, and by the time we'd packed the car and clambered in I was shivering from the cold. I cranked the heating up and rubbed my hands together.

"Well?" Archer searched my face. "Are you going to call him?" He turned the key and the engine roared to life.

"Do you think I should? He made it pretty clear he didn't want to speak to me until I'd sorted things out with Seth."

"And do you think that will happen any time soon? Come on, Gracie. The worst he can do is hang up on you."

Archer was right. One phone call couldn't hurt, just to see if Josh was okay.

I pulled my phone out and swiped the screen then found his number in my favourites list. It rang a few times before going to voicemail. Josh's familiar voice travelled to my ear and my heart lurched. It had been too long since I'd heard him speak.

I left a quick message asking if he was okay, and for him to call me back. If he didn't, I'd try again in the morning. We may not have been on the best of terms, but something was wrong. I couldn't wait for the problem to resolve itself, and if he hadn't returned my calls in twenty-four hours, I was going to go find him.

4

JOSH

Early Friday morning

After drinking my fill from the homeless guy I'd felt better, but not for long. The satisfaction had quickly worn off, only to be replaced with self-loathing. It wouldn't be long before the cycle repeated itself.

Lilith walked silently beside me.

My phone vibrated in my pocket—an all too familiar feeling. I'd been ignoring it, and I'd switched it to silent because I was getting sick of hearing the ring tone. Maybe it was time to switch it off. When I took it out, the name on the screen made me stop. I expected to see 'Dad', but instead it said 'Grace'. My thumb immediately went to the ring on my right hand and twirled it around my finger. The call went to voicemail, and for the first time I actually wanted to listen to my messages.

I swiped the screen and found the voicemail icon,

raising the phone to my ear. The recorded message was the most beautiful voice I'd ever heard.

"Josh, it's Grace again. Where are you? Please call me back. I'm worried."

It was sweet and melodic. And I could have sworn I'd heard it before, but I couldn't remember anyone called Grace.

"Who was it this time?" Lilith asked.

"Wrong number." I shoved my phone into my pocket and kept walking.

There was no way I was going to tell Lilith a girl named Grace had called. I was tired of trying to explain or justify things I knew nothing about.

Lilith returned to her silent state until we reached our hideout. We snaked through the underground tunnels and the city's sewer network, doubling back a few times to make sure we weren't being followed by an angel or a hunter.

In the darkness of the tunnel I found the latch on the trap door and flicked it open. The hole brought us out into the basement of an old, abandoned terrace house. When we'd first moved in the furniture had been covered in sheets, and there was a thick film of dust on every surface. Lilith said she'd known the previous owners. I was curious, but happy to have a place to stay, so didn't question her.

At the top of the basement stairs was a U-shaped kitchen. This room we'd left pretty much untouched, for obvious reasons. I hadn't even bothered to take a look and see what was behind the old-fashioned timber cupboard doors. A large green glass fruit bowl—empty, apart from a layer of dust—sat on a delicate crocheted doily in the middle of the bench, and a rusty toaster had been pushed into the corner by the sink. The old fridge looked as if it had seen better days. It wasn't running, and I had no idea what was inside. I'd never needed to open it.

The rest of the house looked as if it had years of stories to tell. The furniture was elegantly beautiful. Queen Anne-style chairs and tables filled the lounge and sitting rooms, while canopy beds furnished the two bedrooms upstairs. Ornate patterned carpets covered the timber floors and the china cabinets were full of porcelain knick-knacks and glassware. Once we'd tidied the place up as best we could, everything still looked old, but at least it was clean. It puzzled me why the terrace had been left fully furnished, as if one day someone was here, and the next they were ... gone.

Lilith crossed the sitting room to the large arched window overlooking the street. She adjusted the heavy velvet curtains before the morning sunlight could creep through the crack in the middle. Then she systematically went around the rest of the house, checking all the windows as she did every morning, even though we never opened any of them. It was quite depressing, really. Okay, we would burst into flames if we came into contact with *direct* sunlight, but no natural light sucked.

I flopped down into a wing chair by the fireplace, sighed and closed my eyes. This was the part I hated the most, waiting out the day. It would be easier if I could sleep. Lilith could, but for some reason I couldn't. No matter what I did, or how many times I tried, sleep never came for me. And as much as I was grateful we had somewhere to spend the daylight hours, I couldn't wait to get outside again. There was something about confined spaces I didn't like. Being inside suffocated me.

"Would you cheer up?" Lilith said, sensing my mood.

She flicked on the lamp beside me then knelt at my feet. She laid her head in my lap and wrapped her arms around my waist. Absentmindedly, I stroked her hair and twirled it through my fingers. Lilith lifted her head and I stared into her charcoal eyes. I wondered what colour they'd been when she was human. She had a perfect heart-shaped mouth and she knew how to use it. She gently picked up my hand and kissed it, but I wasn't in the mood. I sighed again and pulled my hand away.

"You can talk. You've been in a mood yourself," I said.

"Fine." Lilith got up and walked to the doorway. "If you want to brood, that's your choice. I'll be upstairs." Her ebony hair spun in an arc as she turned away, and she was gone before I could reply.

I sank into the chair and prepared myself for the wait ahead. Each new day seemed longer than the last, and the waiting got harder every time. For what seemed like the millionth time I wished I could follow Lilith upstairs and stretch out on the bed beside her, but it would be no use, so I settled back as best I could.

My eyes had been closed for about ten minutes and I'd been concentrating on keeping as still as possible— something I liked to do to pass the time—when I heard a noise. It took me a few moments to realise someone was knocking on the front door. I couldn't help wondering who on earth it could be.

With a little hesitation, I rose from my chair and

walked the length of the narrow hallway. My head was telling me to let it alone and ignore whoever it was, but my curiosity got the better of me. I reached out to turn the dead bolt and the knock came again, this time a little more forcefully. The front of the house had a balcony on the next level, casting a shadow over the entrance, so I'd be safe from the sunlight. I flipped the bolt across, turned the knob, and pulled the door open a crack.

What I saw on the other side was nothing short of astonishing. A girl, tall, slender, and very beautiful, stood on the front step. Her eyes were black, and her wavy hair softly framed her face. A hint of red accented the golden strands. Her skin was pale but luminous, and seemed to glow. My instant reaction was to widen my eyes to take in as much of her beauty as possible, but I kept my composure and scowled at her instead.

"Can I help you?" I asked.

"I ..." She faltered.

I looked her straight in the eyes. There was something very familiar about her, but I couldn't place it.

"Do I know you from somewhere?" I opened the door a fraction more.

The girl seemed to hesitate, and a small frown crossed her face. She tilted her head to the side and stared at me for a few moments. I don't know what she was searching for.

"Um, no," she finally replied, raising her hand to her face. "I think I'm lost. Which way is it to the train station?"

I pulled the door open enough to step onto the threshold. The sun had risen a little farther and the day was awash with dull morning light. Lilith would be angry if she knew I'd gone outside while the sun was up, even if

I was protected by shadows. The girl hadn't shifted when I'd moved towards her, so we stood close enough to touch. Again, I thought I could feel a familiarity about her, but I couldn't quite place it.

I gave the girl simple directions. "Walk to end of the street, turn right then first left. That street will take you there."

"Thank you," she said, and placed her hand on my arm.

I flinched. I hadn't meant to, but her touch triggered a feeling inside me. I tried scowling a little more to scare her off. It bugged me, not knowing why she was so familiar, or how I knew her. My mind was full of blank spaces, like someone had thrown a sheet over the contents to hide them. I had a feeling we had some sort of distant connection I couldn't quite put my finger on.

"You don't know who you are, do you?" she asked.

"What?" Anger coursed through my veins. I was sick of people questioning me. "Who do you think you are, asking me that?"

"Sorry," she said. "My mistake."

The girl stared at me as if waiting for a reply, but what did she want me to say? I didn't know her.

My phone vibrated in my pocket and the buzzing broke the silence. I didn't move to answer it. It was probably my dad again; he hadn't called for a few hours.

"Are you going to get that?" She raised her eyebrows.

"It won't be anyone important."

"Right ... thanks for the directions."

From the shadow of the balcony, I watched as the girl elegantly descended the stairs to the street and walked in the direction I'd told her. Her hair rippled around her shoulders, the light glinting off the golden strands. She had a grace I'd never seen in another human before, and that was when it hit me. Why had I not wanted to sink my fangs into her? Why had she not stirred the burning in my throat? Usually when I stood in such close proximity to any human my senses started roaring. I could smell the victim's blood and sweat, and usually their fear.

This girl had not smelt human, but she couldn't be like me. Maybe she was an angel or a hunter, but all the ones I'd met had wanted to kill me within the first minute, sometimes less. They had a knack for seeking out and dusting vamps. Puzzled, I watched until she turned the corner.

"What are you?" I asked, staring at the place she'd been a moment before. I decided to make it my new mission to find out.

5

GRACE

Friday morning

The wind assaulted me as I jumped down from the Defender, and I wrapped my arms around myself in an attempt to thwart the chill.

"I hate this time of year." Archer huddled close to me and we walked through the front gates of Hopetown Valley High. "Maybe we should start chasing the summer."

I grunted and rubbed my arms—I really wasn't in the mood for light chitchat. All I wanted was to get through the last day of term.

I'd tried calling Josh another four times with no success. His twenty-four hours would be up by the afternoon. The seconds stretched into minutes, and I hoped he'd call soon to save my sanity. Somehow, I didn't think he would.

My gaze drifted over the entry to the girls' dorm as we passed. Since Emma's death, I hadn't set foot inside.

I couldn't bring myself to go near her room. Someone else occupied it, and the thought of another person using Emma's space made me sad. I had too many memories of our friendship and time inside that room, and it hurt too much. I missed her.

We quickened our pace and walked around the dorm into the main yard. With Josh fresh on my mind, my thoughts drifted back to all the things that happened that first week of our final school year. The day Josh left felt as if it had only been minutes ago. Every time I thought of him my lips burned with the memory of his kiss, and the way he'd held me. What we'd done before the heated words of our argument in the city. His eventual hostility cut me to my core, but I couldn't blame him. I'd abandoned him when he'd needed me most. Every time I closed my eyes I saw the way he'd looked at me—not with the beautiful blue eyes he'd once had, but with the black ones that came after he was changed.

Actually, when I closed my eyes I saw a lot of things I didn't want to: Emma's scared face when Matthew bit her and killed her; my fingers pressed into Josh's neck, covered with his blood; Charlotte's glistening fangs as she bit into his wrist; Seth's cheeky smile, his furrowed brow, the way he looked when he was angry with me, and his wings turning to mist when Angelica stripped him.

So much had happened that had caused so much pain, not only for me, but everyone close to me as well.

A light drizzle fell as we made our way to the cafeteria. I pulled the hood on my red coat over my head and hunched my shoulders, shivering against the cold. When we finally walked into the cafeteria, a warm wave of air hit my face and I felt as if I could breathe properly again.

"What do you want today?" Archer asked.

"Nothing. I don't think I can stomach it."

"Come on, Gracie, you have to eat." He frowned.

"I'll be fine." I waved him off and went to sit at our table by the window.

The noise level lifted as more and more students rushed in to get out of the weather. I watched the clouds as they finally let go and rain poured down in a sheet. It hit the glass and trickled along it, forming tiny rivers that ran into each other.

Archer pulled me from my reverie when he dumped his tray on the table, making me jump. Ryan joined us shortly after and both boys sat across from me, staring.

"What?" I stared back.

"Arch filled me in on the Josh news. Are you okay?" Ryan asked.

"Oh. My. God! I'm a big girl. I'm fine."

"You don't look fine. Did you get any sleep last night?"

"No. But I don't need to sleep much anyway."

"You still need to sleep a little," Archer said.

"We're worried about you." Ryan picked at the edge of his tray.

It should have been the other way around. I was the Protection Angel. I should be doing all the worrying.

Since Emma's death, Ryan and I had become good friends. They'd only just started dating before she'd died, but he'd crushed on her for years so it messed him up pretty bad. It messed us all up, and we kind of fell together over a common experience. He'd become like a second brother to me, only more breakable.

"His mug shot is probably being plastered all over town as we speak," Archer said. "Didn't you say Mr Chase had a pretty big stack of flyers?

"Like I said, I'm fine. I've … moved on."

"No you haven't." Archer pushed a plate with a piece of toast on it in front of me. "Eat. It will make you feel better."

The last thing I felt like doing was eating, but I picked up the toast and had a bite to humour him.

I took my phone from my pocket and checked it for the millionth time that morning. If Josh had called back I would've heard it, but I couldn't help checking anyway, in case I'd missed him.

"Still no go on the call back?" Archer asked as I set my phone down on the table.

I shook my head and stared at the screen until it blinked off. "I tried calling again this morning, but it went to voicemail."

"Stop thinking the worst. The fact his phone is even ringing and not going straight to messages is something." Archer raised his eyebrows. A goofy grin spread across his face and he crossed his eyes.

I almost spat my toast out. "You look like an idiot."

"Ah! But you smiled," he said. "You don't do that enough anymore."

"I'm. Fine."

I wasn't. There was something seriously up with Josh, and I wanted—no, *needed*—to find him. I probably needed to find Charlotte as well. She'd mostly left me alone when I'd gone to the city to see Josh. They'd been staying together, and I was glad he had someone, but not so glad it was her. She'd lied, and I'd been stubborn. But the biggest part of not being fine was Seth. We had so much to resolve, and I couldn't do that by myself. He needed to be present for any resolving to happen.

I'd been hanging around Hopetown Valley going through the motions, slaying vamps almost every night, set to auto-pilot, in the hope that an answer would jump out from behind a tree and tackle me. It would say, *Hey, Grace, Seth is over there. He's been there the whole time.*

No such luck.

Another tray slid onto the table and Abigail West plonked down beside me. Abby and I had a bit of a love-hate relationship, although we'd grown closer since Josh left. Abby felt sorry for me and thought we had something in common. Josh had dumped both of us—at least, that's what had happened in her eyes. If only she knew the whole story.

When Abby didn't say anything after sitting down, I dragged my gaze from the window and looked at her. Her green eyes were puffy, and she dabbed at the corner of them with a tissue. She nervously ran her hand through her platinum blonde hair, twirling a piece around her finger.

"Okay, Abby, out with it," I said. "What's wrong?" I already knew from reading her thoughts that she was worried about Josh.

Archer hid a smile behind his hand and Ryan rolled his eyes. Abby didn't notice. Most of the time, she was too engrossed with herself to see what was happening around her.

"Have you read this morning's paper?" she said.

"I don't read the paper." I also didn't watch TV or listen

to the radio. My iPod was well used.

Abby reached into her skirt pocket and pulled out a newspaper clipping. With shaky fingers, she unfolded it and spread it out on the table. I leant over to read the headline.

Local Flats End Teenager—MISSING. Have you seen this face?

The article had been cut from the Hopetown Valley Gazette. The same photo of Josh that was on Mr Chase's flyers stared at me. I picked it up and my heart sank further into my stomach. I handed the article to Archer. He sat back in his chair and held the paper so Ryan could also see.

Archer looked up once he'd finished reading and met my eyes. "This is pretty serious, isn't it? It made the local paper ..."

"What's happened to him, Grace?" Abby grabbed my arm so tightly it hurt.

I felt like saying *how should I know,* but I bit my tongue.

"I'm sure he'll be fine," I said, knowing full well he was far from it.

"I went and saw him before he left for the city. He looked pretty sick. What if he got so sick he died? What if he's lying on the floor somewhere and no one knows?"

"Abby, he's not sick," I said. "Let the police do their job."

Something bad had happened. Okay, bad things had *already* happened, but I had a feeling this was going to be much, much worse. Abby was right in some respects; Josh could be dead. Once I'd had the thought, I couldn't let it go. What if he were dead, as in not vampire dead, but not-walking-around-anymore dead? What would I do?

Looks like we'll be taking a road trip. Archer stared at me as he spoke in my mind.

It hasn't been twenty-four hours. Josh has time to call me back.

And you really think that's going to happen?

Before I could answer, the first bell for the day sounded through the cafeteria. It sent everyone into a flurry of movement.

"Go to class, Abby. I'm sure they'll find him." I stood and shouldered my bag. "It's probably something really stupid like his phone is flat ... I wouldn't blame Mr Chase for panicking. Everything will be fine ..."

"What are your plans for the holidays?" Archer asked Abby as he rose from the table.

I smiled and sighed with relief when Abby followed him. He was trying to help take her mind off Josh. Archer didn't particularly like Abby, but she had grown on all of us this year.

"Jesse is picking me up after school; he's taking me out tonight," Abby said. "He seems to think now his little sis is eighteen, I need to be initiated."

"See?" Archer said. "Something to take your mind off things." He gave Abby a quick pat on the arm.

"I guess," she said.

I waited until Abby was outside before facing the boys. We were pretty much the last ones in the cafeteria. "Something really, *really* bad has happened."

"That's stating the obvious," Archer said. "Maybe ..."

I waited for him to continue, but he didn't.

"Maybe ... what?" I twirled my hand in the air. "I'll look in your head, so tell me before I do."

Archer shuffled his feet and adjusted the strap of his backpack. "Maybe we should call Charlotte."

"No. *N. O.* No. We are not calling her."

"Why?" Ryan asked. "If Josh is staying with her, maybe she knows something."

"I don't want her help." I scowled and headed towards the door. "I'll think it over today and we'll talk about it later."

"Okay, boss, whatever you say." Archer ducked out the door and made a run for it through the rain to the main building.

Ryan followed, leaving me standing in the doorway. I stopped for a moment under the eaves and braced myself for the drenching that was to come.

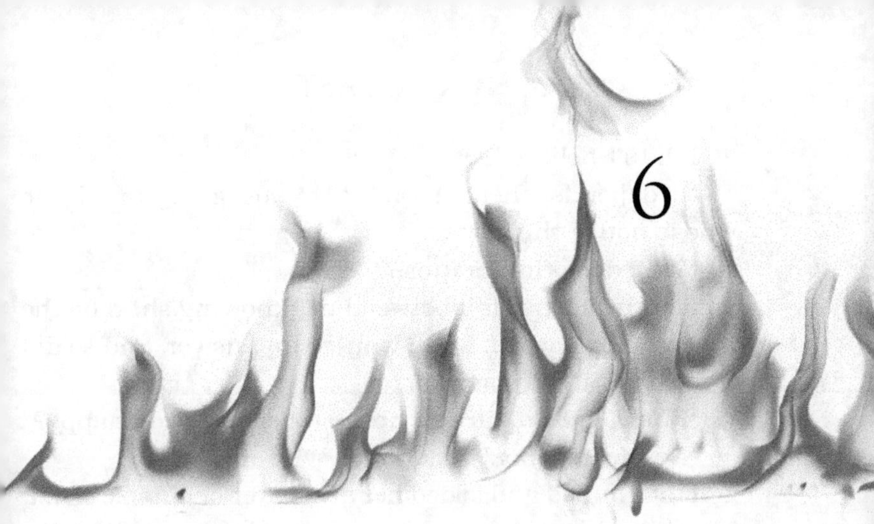

6

JOSH
Friday night

My encounter with the strange girl was fresh in my mind. I'd been sitting in the wing chair for several hours, racking my brain and trying to remember who she was. Sifting through my thoughts and memories was not a hard process as I didn't have that many to catalogue. I was certain she was from my past, but who was she?

"Are you going to tell me how you know that girl? I saw you talking to her." Lilith stood at the bottom of the stairs. I was so absorbed in my thoughts I hadn't registered that she was in the room. Was that jealousy I detected in her voice?

"You should've been sleeping," I said.

"It's hard when I sense someone who isn't welcome."

"Why should I tell you if I know her, Lilith? Do you?"

"No," she said quickly, her face darkening.

35

I didn't believe her.

"It depends, then," I said. "Are you going to tell me whose house this is?"

"Why does that matter?"

I let the silence fall between us, knowing she'd be the first to speak again. Lilith wanted an answer, and so did I. All I had to do was wait.

"Fine. I grew up in this house. There, are you happy?"

"No. Keep going." I motioned with my hand.

Lilith huffed and folded her arms over her ample chest. The pale skin of her cleavage glowed in the dim light.

"My parents bought this place in 1897. A year later, I was born."

"Wow. You're older than I thought."

Lilith pursed her lips. "Nineteen years after that, they died."

"How?"

"Josh! It was almost a hundred years ago."

I fixed a neutral expression on my face and simply waited for her to continue. Eventually, Lilith grunted and launched into her story.

"In 1917 I met a charming young man who courted me." A smile played at the corners of Lilith's mouth, but she wrapped her arms tighter around herself. "I asked him why he wasn't fighting the war with all the other brave young men. At the time he told me he didn't meet their physical standards for recruits, but that turned out to be a lie. He would take me to the theatre, and out dancing. He was a true gentleman, and I was a lady."

The snort I made didn't impress Lilith. The thought of her being a lady was rather funny, what with her long, sleek hair, dark eye makeup and pierced nose. Not to mention the large tattoo that spread across her lower back from one hip to the other. A labyrinthine weave of Celtic knots in the form of a bat. She was definitely not a lady.

Ignoring me, she continued. "But one night ... let's just say he changed me forever."

"Ah, your creator." I predicted what was coming next. "You killed your parents."

For a brief moment Lilith looked like a frightened child; in all the time I'd known her I had never seen her appear so weak.

"My parents, yes, and my twin sister. The war had taken care of my two older brothers," she said. "Josh, I helped wipe out my entire family." Her voice sounded surprised, as if this were the first time she'd actually thought about what she'd done. Lilith wrung her hands together, and the numerous silver rings on her fingers made a metallic clink. She looked at them then stopped and folded her arms again.

"Please continue," I said.

Lilith scowled. "I left the house pretty much straight away. Locked it up and didn't come back for a very long time. Being here now, it's hard. It brings back memories I'd rather forget."

"See, it's nice to have a history, to know your past. Isn't it?"

"How do you know that girl, Josh?" The frightened little girl was suddenly gone. Lilith stood tall and pushed her shoulders back. "You're very brave to step outside during the day. Is she worth dying for?"

"I don't know who she is. I've been sitting here all day trying to work that out." I got up from the chair. "And I get the feeling you already know anyway."

"That's right, you have amnesia," Lilith said, ignoring my last comment. "How convenient for you when a gorgeous blonde happens to knock on our door. I've worked hard to keep this place hidden so the angels and hunters don't find us."

Lilith stared at me with her coal-black, angry eyes. She did have a bit of a temper, which I found very attractive, and right then I felt like a fight. For so long I'd been wandering around aimlessly, knowing nothing about myself. I was even angrier still, now I knew a piece of Lilith's past. At least she had one she could remember.

"Obviously we haven't been careful enough then, have we?" I said.

"If I discover you've betrayed me—"

"You'll what, kill me?" I laughed. "I'm stronger than you, but you don't want to admit it because it should be the other way around. Isn't that why you helped me in the first place? What do they say, Lilith? The enemy of my enemy is my friend."

She glared at me, speechless. Finally, I'd put her in her place.

"Why didn't you kill her?" she said. "Let me guess. You didn't want to scar her pretty face."

"She isn't human."

"Then what is she?" Lilith came across the room, her long, black dress trailing out behind her.

I studied Lilith's face, so close to mine her breath brushed my lips. An overwhelming desire to kiss her washed over me, but I held back. I sensed she knew something about this girl, and she was holding out on me. If I'd learnt anything since I'd known Lilith, it was that I couldn't completely trust anyone, even her. If I played my cards right, I'd get the information I needed out of her eventually.

"I said I don't know anything about her."

"I don't believe you," Lilith said.

"And I don't believe you don't know anything about her either."

She moved to slap me, but I was too quick, catching her wrist in my hand before it could connect with my cheek. I yanked her to me and pressed my other hand into her back.

"I know that girl from somewhere. She's from my past, and I want answers." I leant forward and whispered in her ear, "And I'll be damned if I let you, or anyone else, stand in my way."

Lilith lowered her face and tried to pull away from my grasp, but I held her firm. The scarlet streak in her hair fell across her cheek.

"So what will it be?"

"What do you mean?" Lilith tried to pull away again.

"Are you going to tell me what you know? Because you do know her, don't you?"

She didn't reply, not with words anyway. Lilith stopped resisting and leant into me. She raised her head and her eyes glistened under the artificial glow of the lamp. I released her wrist, holding her tight with my other hand, and brushed the hair from her face. She flicked her tongue, licking my lip, before pressing her lips to mine.

I was powerless to resist her.

Lilith's kisses were hard and eager. She slipped her hands under my shirt and raked her nails down my back. I pulled her closer. Tilting her head back, I kissed the skin at her neck and ran my fingers up her bare arm. She had such smooth, perfect skin, and I relished the feel of it.

Something flickered in my thoughts, but when I tried to hold onto it, it was gone. The suggestion of a memory angered me and I pulled away from Lilith. I felt more impatient than I ever had; I needed to find the girl who'd shown up on our doorstep. I released Lilith and walked across the room to distance myself.

"We search for her tonight," I said.

"Who? The blonde girl? What makes you think you can find her?"

I studied Lilith for a moment, certain she was keeping something from me. "Jealousy doesn't really suit you." I smirked. My shoulder brushed hers as I walked to the door.

"I'm not jealous." Lilith laughed, but it was strained.

"Lead the way, then." I opened the door and motioned with my hand.

"Fine," she said through clenched teeth. "But we're probably wasting our time. Who says she'll even be out tonight?"

"This is Wide Island City, Lilith. Anyone worth finding comes out at night."

7

GRACE

The rain hadn't let up for most of the day, covering the ground in a soggy blanket. I'd spent every moment of it thinking about Josh, running all the possible scenarios through my head. Most of them I didn't like.

Now that the sun had gone down, his twenty-four hours were up, and I wasn't sure what to do.

My knees sank into the dirt at the foot of Emma's grave. I didn't care that I was soaked to the bone. I'd dry. All I wanted was someone to tell me everything was going to be okay—even if that someone was dead.

"I don't think I can keep doing this," I whispered to Emma. "It's been too long since you left. One day without you is too long … I miss you so bad. I want things back the way they were before Charlotte showed up … I want Josh … I want to find Seth. But how do I do all of that and stay sane? How do I keep going, Emma?" I reached out and touched the marble slab that lay on top of her.

After she'd died, Emma had come to me in the small family cemetery on our property. The memory of holding her in my arms for the last time was so overwhelming, I stifled a sob. She'd told me she hoped one day she'd be able to help me. I wanted that day to be now.

"Please, Emma. If you can hear me … do something."

The rain trickled down my cheeks and mingled with my tears. I stared at Emma's headstone, and at the butterfly engraved above the inscription. Its wings glowed and peeled away from the marble. At first I thought I was seeing things. Then the butterfly detached itself from the headstone and flittered towards me. I held out my hand and it landed on my palm.

I smiled.

The butterfly moved its wings up and down slowly, and the rain formed little droplets on their shimmery, white surface.

"What do I do?" I whispered.

The butterfly's wings stopped on the downbeat.

I waited.

Nothing happened.

The butterfly left my hand and headed back towards the headstone, melting into the stone where it became an engraving again. I sighed. There was no point getting angry. It was the best Emma could do, and at least she'd heard me; that had to mean something. If I knew my best friend like I thought I did, there would be no way she'd let something as trivial as dying come between us.

"I wanted to show you something." I reached into my top and pulled out the chain that hung around my neck.

"I finally had it made into a pendant." I held it up, watching the tear-shaped diamond glimmer in the dim light.

"This is all I have left of him." I tucked it back inside my top. "I need him back, Emma … He has to come back."

And I wasn't only thinking of myself. The rain ran over my hands as I opened a small, red velvet pouch. Seth had given me Annie's ring not long before Angelica took him. I wanted to free her, but I wasn't sure how.

At one point, my existence had been simple. I longed for that again, but I had to fix the mess I was in.

Emma and Pa had told me to follow my heart. To do the one thing that had gotten me into trouble in the first place. But which part of my heart did I follow? Did I want to know what had happened to Josh? Or would it be easier to do nothing? I had no leads on Seth's whereabouts, but I wasn't prepared to give up hope of finding him. Still, I couldn't turn my back on Josh again. If I wanted to find peace with anything that had happened, I had to start somewhere.

With a shaky hand I pocketed Annie's ring, and wiped the rain from my face. I pulled my phone from my jacket pocket. Josh's time was up. I hadn't had a missed call or a message from him all day. I stared at the screen and willed my phone to ring.

Nothing.

I had powers, but making people use their phones was not one of them.

It took a few attempts to swipe my wet fingers over the screen and get it to work, and when the ringtone echoed into my ear, my fingers ached from holding the phone so tightly.

After ten rings it went to voicemail—again.

"Josh, it's Grace." I paused and took a deep breath, sucking the raindrops off my lips. "I know you're probably sick of hearing from me, but I'm worried about you. Please call me back. I … want to hear your voice. I need to know you're okay. Your dad's worried. I'm worried. School let out today, so I'm going to come for a visit. I hope you'll be home when I get there. Whatever it is that's happened … I … I miss you."

I ended the call before I could say anymore. I'd probably already said too much. Now he knew I was coming, and I hoped he loved me like he'd said he did and wouldn't run.

"Okay, Emma. I'm following my heart. I hope you're happy." I stood up.

After bumping into Mr Chase and seeing Josh's face on the flyers, finding him was something I had to do. He was in danger, and I couldn't go on the way I had been. Going through the motions was not helping any. Now that he'd been reported missing, I was sick with worry. When I'd gone to see him soon after he'd left, I'd been searching for closure. I didn't get it back then, and I was hoping I would this time. I'd never told him I loved him.

Maybe I had to tell him.

Black mist swirled around me, and a second later I landed in the shed, next to the couch. Archer jumped in his seat at the kitchen table, and threw his butter knife at me. I caught it before it could stab me in the shoulder.

"You didn't go for the kill shot," I said.

"Gracie, you scared the crap outta me."

"Who else can get inside this shed that travels like I do?" I raised my eyebrows.

"Seth." Archer stared at me. "And every other angel

I've ever met."

"In case you've forgotten, Angelica locked him in his ring. And you can't kill Seth with a butter knife."

"No, but I can hurt him." Archer smiled.

I took my jacket off and threw it on the old church pew that sat against the wall of the shed, shaking the rain from my hair. Archer grabbed another knife from the drawer and buttered his bread roll. I snatched it on my way past. He grunted but didn't protest.

Ryan walked down the stairs from the loft and flopped onto the couch. "Have you heard anything?"

"I left another message before leaving the cemetery," I said. "You're not heading home for the holidays?"

"I convinced Mum to let me stay for the first week. Then I have to grace her with my awesome presence."

Archer chuckled and I shook my head.

"How's Emma?" Archer asked.

"You're itching for me to say 'still dead', aren't you?"

"You know me so well."

I took a bite of the bread roll and leant against the bench. "I saw the butterfly again."

"Like the one at the funeral?" Archer asked.

I nodded.

Silence fell between the three of us, and I chewed the bread roll. "I'm going to the city."

"You mean we're going to the city." Archer put his butter knife in the centre of his plate. It clinked against the ceramic.

Ryan ran a hand down his face and rested his head against the back of the couch. "This can't be good. You're looking for trouble. But at least you've already fallen.

That can't happen again."

"Ha ha. Funny." I threw a piece of bread at him.

Archer jumped up from the table and put his plate in the sink. "Your dinner's in the fridge," he said when he caught me eyeing it.

I pulled out a plate filled with honey mustard chicken, rice, and steamed vegetables. "Did you cook, Ryan?"

He rolled his head to the side and looked at me. "Is that a stupid question?"

"You're right, sorry. There's no way Arch could cook something like this."

"I *will* stab you," Archer said, his mouth pinching to hide a smile. "Now, when are we leaving?"

Ryan stared blankly ahead and sighed.

"We won't be gone long. I'm hoping only a few days," I said. Ryan didn't respond, and the air was thick with uncomfortable silence. "You know why I don't want you to come."

"Yes, Grace. Mortal danger, and all that. I get it. I'm the only one who's still human."

Archer cleared his throat loudly, and put his hand up. "Hey. Human over here, too."

"Yeah, with super powers," Ryan said.

"Aha! But still human."

Ryan chuckled and shook his head.

"Really, Ryan, we'll be home as soon as we find him," I said. "I have to know he's okay."

"And what am I supposed to do while you're gone?"

"Stay out of trouble?" I shrugged.

Apart from Archer, Ryan was the only one who hadn't deserted me, or been taken from me. Now, looking into his deep mocha eyes, I felt racked with guilt that *I* was the one about to leave him. He rose from the couch and ran his hands through his dark honey-brown hair. Usually it was a lighter shade, but a combination of the cooler weather and spending more time indoors had deepened its colour.

I set my plate on the bench and went to him. Ryan wrapped me in his arms and gave me a tight hug. Being this close to him, touching him, made it easier to hear what he was thinking. Ryan didn't want me to leave because he didn't trust Josh, not after what he'd done in the forest. I couldn't blame him, really; if my best friend turned into a vampire and then tried to eat me I'd be pretty pissed, too.

Ryan let go. "I'm coming with you," he said, not meeting my eyes.

"No. I won't let you."

"You're not his mum, Gracie," Archer said.

"He could get hurt."

"We could all get hurt." Archer shrugged.

"I don't want to put anyone else in danger," I said.

"Hey, guys. I'm right here. Stop talking as if I'm not in the room." Ryan met my stare. "I want to help. I admit, Josh isn't my favourite person right now, but helping you find him beats sitting around here all by myself."

I turned towards my brother. *I don't like this, Arch.*

He crossed his arms. *Ryan is a big boy. And have you ever considered that maybe he can help?*

How? We haven't taught him to fight.

He's seen us do it plenty of times, Archer thought.

That was true. Ryan had snuck out of the dorm at

school on several nights to come hunting with us. The first few times I'd been against it, but after a while he'd proved he could stay out of trouble.

We'll be on unfamiliar ground, I thought. *And watching it and doing it are two different things.*

Let it go, already, Gracie. Let him come.

Ryan coughed. "I know what you two are doing, and can you not? I hate that you're talking about me in your heads."

"She cares about you, dude," Archer said.

"He's right. I do." I smiled.

Ryan sighed.

Maybe having him with us wouldn't be such a bad thing. He was loyal, and he'd fight for the right reasons. I didn't want him getting hurt, but Ryan was old enough to make his own decisions.

"Fine, you can come. But you do what I say." I poked him in the chest.

"Yes, boss." Ryan saluted me. "You know, wherever Josh is, Charlotte won't be too far behind." Ryan glanced at Archer and he furrowed his brow.

"I can handle Charlotte," Archer said. *But I still think we should call her first,* he added silently.

I glared at him. *We don't need her help.*

Archer needed closure with Charlotte as much as I needed it with Josh, but I didn't want her to know we were coming.

"We need to pack," I said.

The sooner we left, the better.

8

JOSH

The bolt clicked as I pushed it closed on the inside of the trap door. Lilith was already below me at the bottom of the metal ladder. I descended quickly, missing the last few rungs, and dropped to the moist ground. A few steps forward and we were in a room like a bunker. Lilith reached above her head and pulled the light cord, switching on a naked bulb.

Wooden shelves filled with rusty tin cans lined one wall. Most of the cans had lost their labels or were decayed beyond recognition. A stack of crates sat in the corner under an old timber table. Lilith had said her father built the bunker himself not long after The First World War began. Her family had reason to be afraid. Even though they'd all been naturalised and her brothers fought in the Australian army, they were still of German descent.

We passed through the room and walked a little way

until Lilith's tunnel came to a door, meeting up with the sewer network. I hated the sewers; they were the most disgusting way to travel, but they were also a necessity when you wanted to move around undetected. I was glad when we reached the manhole that opened onto a deserted city laneway. To avoid being followed we tried to pick a different spot each time, and this one brought us out north of the city's main train station.

"Josh, baby, would you slow down? People will start to notice you," Lilith said.

She was right. A vampire walking really fast looked like a sprinter. A vampire running was a blur.

"Sorry." I slowed to a more human walking pace. Lilith gently stroked my arm. Running her fingertips down to my wrist, she slipped her hand in mine. Swinging my arm, she skipped around and faced me, forcing me to stop. We were on our way through the small park across the road from the station, and I glanced at my surroundings for the first time since coming out of the sewer. I liked the parks that dotted the city. Each was like a tiny oasis in a barren desert. They made me feel better, and I much preferred the open spaces to the confined concrete jungle.

Lilith leaned towards me and pressed her hips to mine. She stroked my cheek then grabbed my face and turned my head, making me look at her. Forcing her heart-shaped lips to mine she kissed me, and I wrapped my arms around her waist, giving in. Lilith had a crazed look in her eyes, the one she got when she was ready to feed, and they sparkled like diamonds.

I eventually pulled away. "When are you going to stop stalling and tell me what you know?"

Lilith pouted. "I don't know what you mean." She stroked my cheek again and I grabbed her wrist, squeezing it.

My patience was wearing thin. "Stop playing games, and tell me what you know about the blonde girl."

"Josh, you're hurting me." Lilith gritted her teeth.

"This is nothing compared to what I will do to you if you don't start talking," I said.

Lilith yanked her hand from my grip and stepped back, her eyes burning with unleashed anger.

"Trust me, it's better you don't know. There's a whole world out there you know nothing about. Get mixed up in it and you could die."

Laughter welled in my chest, so strong it felt like I would burst. "Do you have any idea what it's like not knowing who I am?"

"It's better than being dead."

"I'm already dead!" I said.

"But you still exist. I need you to exist." A crimson tear trickled down Lilith's face. "I can't lose you as well."

My hands curled into fists and I had the urge to punch something. Breaking things always seemed to make me feel better. I yelled and slammed my fist into the nearest thing I could find that wasn't Lilith. The park table shattered on impact, sending splinters of wood flying in every direction. A group of girls quickened their steps as they walked past, staring at their feet and avoiding our eyes.

"You want me to trust you?" I asked, wiping the blood from my knuckles onto my shirt. "Then start acting like I can."

Lilith licked her lips and went to speak, trying several times before she did. When she finally made a sound her voice was shaky. "You think I'm jealous of that girl, but that is so much the opposite of the truth it makes me feel sick. I don't want you to be involved with her because she ... she's the one who will change everything about our existence. And I hate myself every day, because I had a part in it."

"I don't understand. You're not making any sense."

"Of all the people in the entire world, why do you have to be involved with her?" Lilith laughed, but it sounded hollow. "You're not the only one who wants to find her. That girl is the most wanted vampire in this entire city."

"She's not a vampire." I frowned. "I saw her walking in the sun."

"Like I said. You don't know what you're getting yourself into." Lilith turned away and headed deeper into the park.

"You can't stop me from trying to find her. She's the only link I have to my past."

"There's something you need to see first," she called over her shoulder.

I shoved my hands into my jeans pockets and followed. I wanted to find the blonde girl, but without Lilith I'd probably end up walking in circles. She'd better not be leading me on a wild goose chase. Lilith was an expert at the art of distraction, and deception.

"Where are we going?" I asked when I'd caught up to her.

"The war memorial."

"Why, what's in it?"

"Not in it." Lilith turned her head and her steel gaze bore into me. "Under it. You think there are a lot of vamps in this city? You have no idea."

9

GRACE
Late Friday night

The last thing I expected was to have the police knocking on the shed door. In all my mixed-up thoughts and emotions, the possibility hadn't even entered my mind.

It took a while to get rid of them. I couldn't blame them for doing their job, but I wanted to get packed and on the road. After several questions, lots of note-taking, and two hours, they were finally out of the way.

The three of us pleaded ignorance, claiming we hadn't seen or spoken to Josh in months. I didn't need the police poking around in our lives. It had been bad enough when we'd had a social worker, even if she'd turned out to be an angel.

We stuffed a couple of backpacks with some clothes, and gave the shed a quick tidy up. Most of what we needed was already in the car, so we headed out the door. With my hand on the doorknob, I paused, scanning the ground floor of the shed. It looked as it always had, with its old mismatched furniture and makeshift kitchen. My heart ached as I looked at the threadbare rug and remembered the way Seth had kissed me on the morning of my eighteenth birthday. I didn't want to leave, not even for a few days.

"Come on, Grace." Archer gently put his hand on my shoulder.

I pulled the door closed and the click of the lock echoed into the night. My feet felt heavy as we walked to our Defender, which was parked under the carport at the far end of the clearing. Archer opened the back door and threw our backpacks in on top of a big gym bag and a suitcase. The bag held a few stakes, daggers and other odds and ends, while the suitcase hid two crossbows and the larger knives.

"Do we really need all this?" Archer asked.

"Yes, we do," I said. "The necessities: clothes, weapons, and more weapons. We have to be prepared."

"Why we can't mist to the city is beyond me," Archer said. "And I'm sure we don't need all of it, Gracie. You can mist back if we've forgotten something."

"Ryan hates misting; it turns his stomach. We're driving, Arch, end of story."

"Oh great, five hours in a car with you. I *can't* wait. Ouch!" Archer cried when I punched him on the arm. Laughing, I shook my head. He could be so annoying, but I loved him.

Archer was about to close the back of the car when headlights lit up the clearing. A blue Ute ambled across the grass and stopped alongside the shed.

"This can't be good," Archer said. "That's Jesse's car. Why are they out so late?"

"Jesse was taking Abby out for drinks, I think," I said.

Abby stumbled out of the car, her hands stuffed in her jacket pockets, and her shoulders hunched against the chill of the night air.

"What are you doing here, Abby?" I asked.

Jesse joined us and offered me an apologetic smile. "Sorry guys. She made me drive her here. She's had a bit to drink, and she insisted we stop on the way home."

Abby swayed on her feet, and eyed the bags in the back of the car. Archer slammed the door shut.

"You're going to find him, aren't you?" Abby asked, slurring her words.

"We thought we'd take a drive." Archer folded his arms and leant against the back of the car.

"I want to come."

"Abby, I promised Mum we'd be home," Jesse said, scratching his head.

"Josh is missing." Abby turned to her brother. "If Grace is going, I want to go." She sounded like a spoiled brat.

"Well, you're not going to the city without me. I won't let you."

"Believe me, you do not want to come with us," I said.

I peeked into Jesse's mind to see what the hell was going on with these two, and I was surprised at what I found. He was as worried as Abby. They'd grown up with Josh, and I was grateful he had so many people who cared about him. But he wasn't the same person now, and it wasn't a good idea if they found out how much he'd changed.

"Josh isn't who he used to be," I said. "He's … different."

"He may have chosen you ..." Abby lifted her chin, and took a wobbly step towards me. "... but he was with me for three years. You don't forget about everything you shared with someone for that long."

"You'll be in the way," I said. "I don't want you getting hurt."

"Why would we get hurt?" Abby giggled. "It's Josh. He wouldn't hurt us."

"You obviously didn't hear Grace the first time," Archer said. "Josh has changed."

Jesse laughed. "Are you kidding? We've known him all our lives. He's a good guy. And if anyone's in danger of getting hurt in the city it's you, Grace. You're tiny."

I didn't know Jesse very well. He was older so wasn't in school anymore. I took a few steps closer to him. There was no way he was going to get away with trying to intimidate me.

"Easy, Grace." Archer laid his hand on my arm. "Dude, don't tempt her. She'll knock you on your arse before you can blink."

"Grace is our little pocket rocket," Ryan said.

"You don't believe them? Try me." I stared at Jesse, willing him to react. For some reason, I wanted to prove a point. I didn't want them coming with us, or getting hurt. If I had to wound Jesse's pride to convince him to stay, then I would.

"I don't hit girls," Jesse said.

"You don't have to hit me, just try and grab my arm or something."

"Jesse did karate when he was a kid," Abby said.

"I doubt that will help." Archer smirked. He seemed

to be enjoying the show.

"This is going to end badly," Ryan said.

Jesse hesitated, and before he could act on the plan he'd been running through in his head—kudos to him for not wanting to hurt me—something stirred in the forest.

"Hold that thought." I jogged to the mouth of the path that led into the trees and listened for the sound of vampire footsteps. The faint rustle of leaves faded after a minute or so, but I didn't believe for one second they'd gone. And there I was, hoping for a night off hunting.

Gracie, please tell me it's not what I think it is, Archer thought, coming to my side.

The trees above my head stirred. "Get the others to the shed. It's exactly what you think it is."

Three vampires jumped at me and I landed heavily on my back. I couldn't tell if there were any more of them because I was covered in vamp.

Abby's scream filled the night.

There were arms and legs everywhere. Teeth snapped at my neck. I flicked the switch on my wrist stake and it shot out from under my sleeve, into the heart of the vamp on top of me. I spat dust from my mouth. Another vamp disintegrated beside me, but there was still one more trying to bite my neck. I jammed my thumb into its eye and it howled before exploding and covering me in more dust. Archer stood over me with a stake in his hand.

Abby was still screaming.

I sat up and brushed the ash from my clothes and hair. "Ugh. I hate dead vamp."

"A dead vamp is the best kind." Archer offered me his hand and pulled me to my feet.

I looked at Abby. "Would you stop doing that, please?"

She clamped her mouth shut and whimpered, wrapping her arms around herself. Jesse stared at me wide-eyed.

I scanned the clearing and the edge of the forest, on guard for another attack.

"I think there were only three," Archer said.

"Why didn't you run?" I turned to Ryan.

"I was ready to help if you needed me." He twirled a stake between his fingers.

Jesse stared at Ryan's hand, his mouth open. Great, now I had more explaining to do. I remembered when I went through the whole explanation thing with Josh, and then later with Ryan. Something told me Abby wouldn't take it so well. Jesse, I wasn't sure about.

Abby wrung her hands together and took a step back when I moved towards her.

"I always knew there was something weird about you," she said. "What ... were they? And what's that thing in Ryan's hand?"

"It's a stake, Abby. You drive the pointy end through the heart. Usually it's the most effective way to kill them," Archer said.

"Kill ... those people?" Abby looked at the dust that littered the mouth of the forest path.

You know, if Angelica hadn't erased their memories the night of our birthday party, we wouldn't be having this conversation. Archer clapped me on the shoulder as he walked towards the car. He opened the driver's side door and slipped the key into the ignition.

Yes, but they would also be dead, I thought.

"Look, guys." I stared at Abby and Jesse. Abby stumbled

closer to her brother, who seemed to be frozen in shock. "I don't have time to explain all this to you. All I can say is if you come with us, it's not going to be all that great."

"You're seriously considering letting them come?" Archer said, tucking his stake into the belt under his T-shirt.

"No. I'm advising them not to come. But if anyone deserves to know the truth about Josh, it's Abby."

Archer narrowed his eyes. "Why? Because they used to shag?"

"Hey!" Abby said. "I want to come because I care about him? I mean, who knows how long he has, right? Maybe he's stopped calling Mr Chase because he doesn't want anyone to know how sick he is."

"Abby, Josh doesn't have cancer," I said.

"But ... the last time I saw him he was so pale."

Archer ran a hand down his face and hid a smirk. "Oh, this is priceless."

"What does that mean?" Abby put her hands on her hips, and swayed a little.

"Archer, don't be a dick," Ryan said.

"What?" He raised his hands in mock defence.

"She's drunk. And you can't expect her to join the dots after a two-minute dusting battle," I said.

"During which you got your arse kicked, I might add."

"We're not going with them, Abs," Jesse said. It was almost quiet enough for no one to hear, but I did. "Abigail West." Jesse grabbed her hand. "Let's go. It's late and I'm taking you home."

"Jesse, I want to go." Abby's voice was like a whiny five-year-old's.

"Get in the truck." He pushed her gently towards his

Ute. "We can visit Josh another time."

Jesse was scared after what he'd witnessed, and he wanted to get away from us as quickly as possible. I couldn't blame him. There had been many times I'd wanted to get away from my life. Jesse also wanted to know what had happened to his childhood friend, and I listened to him weigh up the options in his head, convincing himself he'd take Abby to see Josh at some point. I only hoped it would be after I'd sorted everything out.

Abby finally relented and got into the passenger seat in a huff. She crossed her arms and pouted.

I grabbed Ryan's hand and pulled him to the Defender.

"You know they'll probably follow us," Archer said. "If Abby gets her way, she'll have Jesse driving her to the city first thing in the morning."

"Or she'll drive herself," Ryan said.

"She doesn't have a car." I shrugged.

"That wouldn't stop me." Archer turned the key and the car roared to life.

I sighed and settled into the seat, ready for the long trip ahead, but we didn't even get out of the carport.

A figure stood in the darkness at the mouth of the path that led into the forest. Shadows obscured his face, but I didn't need to see it to know who it was. His posture told me everything I wanted to know.

"Is that who I think it is?" Archer asked.

"Oh boy, here we go," Ryan said.

I didn't answer because I was already out of the car, but by the time I got to the edge of the clearing, he was gone.

10

JOSH

Early Saturday morning

The nightlife was pumping, and it took us longer than it should have to get across the city. Lilith was easily distracted by fresh blood, especially young blood. She also enjoyed the high that came with drinking from someone who was intoxicated.

I couldn't think of anything worse, and I wanted to have my wits about me. If I were smashed off tainted blood, who knew what trouble I'd get into?

We circled the outskirts of Dhye Park, the biggest in the city, making sure no one was on our tail. Lilith assured me the underground vamps wouldn't be too pleased if we led the angels or hunters straight to their lair.

The park was quiet, which was no surprise. All the action usually happened on the streets and, if you were a vamp, in the alleyways.

We dropped below ground into the service tunnels and joined up with the rail network. The train station below the war memorial was pretty much deserted, apart from a drunken guy asleep against the wall. I followed Lilith into the subway tunnel and through a door, which brought us into the tunnel wall cavity. We followed that, making a few turns and descending a couple of flights of metal stairs, before it opened into a small stone room lit with a naked bulb hanging from the ceiling. I'd lost all concept of direction. It was disorienting, but the air was damp and heavy which meant we were a fair way underground.

"Where's the power coming from?" I asked. "Aren't we too far down?"

Lilith chuckled. "We can tap into anything in this city. Power is never a problem."

The only door in the room was the one we'd come through. Before I could point out that we were at a dead end, Lilith went to the far wall and pressed her foot to a protruding piece of stone the same colour as the floor. The wall opened with a grating sound to reveal another tunnel on the other side.

Lilith glanced at me over her shoulder. "Let me do the talking."

"Sure," I said, following her into the tunnel. There was no way I wanted to get myself into trouble down there, especially since I had no idea how to get out.

We turned a corner and emerged onto a metal platform. It towered over a huge underground cavity. Several wide pillars rose up to meet the ceiling, providing small walls for the hundreds of vampires to lounge against. To our right was a metal staircase leading to the cavern floor.

Oil lamps burned in alcoves in the stone walls, cordoned off by metal grates, and casting shadowy light across the open expanse. Entrances to passageways dotted the walls at irregular intervals. The ceiling towered over our heads. Pieces of jagged stone stuck out all over the place, and the room looked as if it had been carved from the rock centuries ago.

Several vamps studied us as we descended the steps into the cavern. I understood what Lilith meant when she'd said I had no idea. I'd never seen so many vampires in one place before. The sea of dark eyes and menacing stares unnerved me.

At the far end of the large room was a raised area. Some parts of the rock had been carved away to make the platform, and in other sections flat rocks were piled on top of each other. In the centre of the makeshift stage was a throne. The back was shaped like a gothic arch, and the cross at the top made it look like a tombstone. Lounging on the throne, with one leg hanging over the arm, was a dark-haired, cocky-looking vamp. He had the kind of looks girls turned into puddles over. In comparison to the rest of the vamps in the room, he was a piece of quartz in a sea of stone.

I'd only met him once before, but I recognised him.

Lucas.

"He better not try to kill me again," I said.

Lilith shushed me. "He can hear you, you know."

The vamp sat up straight and smiled. "Lilith, so nice to see you. And you've brought your friend." He stood and descended the three rough steps to the main floor.

"Lucas, you remember Josh," Lilith said.

Lucas sauntered towards us. I didn't like the guy. He held himself like everyone was beneath him.

"Ah, yes. The vamp you found in a ditch and decided to take under your wing," Lucas said. "Why was that?"

Lilith scowled. "Do I have to have a reason? We need to look after our own, don't we?"

"Of course. Very nice to see you again, Josh." He looked me over carefully.

Other vampires around the room stopped what they were doing to watch. All eyes were on me, waiting for my next move. I clenched my fists and stood with my feet slightly apart, at the ready.

Lucas grinned. "To what do I owe this pleasure, Lilith? You don't come down here much anymore."

"I thought Josh should meet the leader of our city … properly," Lilith said.

Behind the throne, another stone door slid open. The grating sound echoed through the cavern. It seemed no one could come and go without being noticed. A vamp stepped through and made his way down the steps towards us. Lilith stiffened beside me.

"There's been another sighting," the vamp said when he reached Lucas's side.

"Hello, Cain." Lilith smiled her sweetest smile.

Cain grunted at her and faced Lucas.

"And let me guess, she got away?" Lucas folded his arms and stood at his full height. He was tall, and pretty menacing. I didn't like the thought of going up against him.

I glanced around the room and wondered how many other hidden doors there were, and how many vamps could burst through them at any moment, adding to the already populated space.

"You know she's fast, Lucas. And she's smart," Cain said.

"Of course she is. She's had hundreds of years of training to outsmart and defeat people like you," Lucas said.

"Then how are we supposed to catch her?"

Cain looked at me for the first time. He had the kind of face that would look angry no matter what sort of mood he was in. I didn't recognise him, but as soon as his lips curled back into a snarl, it was clear he recognised me.

"You," he said. "You're supposed to be dead."

I smiled with my lips closed. "Like I keep telling everyone, I'm already dead." My comment angered him further. Why was he angry with me in the first place?

"You've got a pretty smart mouth on you." Cain got right in my face. "Matthew ripped you up pretty good. After what that little bitch and her brother did to Tyler, you deserved it … If she hadn't have gotten in the way, Matthew would've finished the job before she dusted him, too."

"I have no idea what you're talking about. None of those names are familiar." I took a step back. Cain was way too close for comfort.

"Who turned you?" Cain said.

"Look." I raised my hands in defence. "I really don't know anything. I have no memory of my life before I met Lilith."

She slipped her arm through mine and gripped it tightly. We both could sense everything was about to turn bad.

Lucas frowned and narrowed his eyes.

Things weren't looking too good for me.

Lucas laughed. His shoulders shook, and his voice resonated off the walls. Most of the vamps in the room turned their complete attention to him. He laughed so hard he leant forward and rested his hands on his knees. When he straightened up, his features took on a seriousness again. I was definitely in trouble.

"Well, this is interesting," Lucas said. "Either you really don't know, or you're pretending to be ignorant. Which is it?"

"Shit," Lilith whispered under her breath.

I had never seen so much fear in her eyes—ever.

"I'm getting the feeling that maybe it's time for us to leave," I said.

"I don't think I want you to go anywhere." Lucas took a step towards me and that's when Lilith sprang into action.

She pulled on my arm and I had no option but to follow. She wasn't letting go. We raced across the cavern, Lilith practically dragging me, batting vamps aside on her way through. I punched one vamp in the face when he tried to grab my free arm. He flew through the air and smacked into one of the pillars.

We reached the right side of the raised area, and for a moment I thought Lilith was going to run into the wall. Before we could smack into it, she stamped her foot on a section of the floor and the wall opened. I had one second to register that this part of the floor was slightly different to the rest, and then we were in the wall and blanketed in darkness.

Lucas's angry cries penetrated the stone. "You will pay for this, Lilith. Come back."

"I don't care anymore," she said.

Lilith hadn't let go of my arm. She dragged me farther into the blackness. It was so dark, even my heightened eyesight couldn't make anything out.

The stone wall grated. "I'm coming after you, Lilith. You better run faster." Lucas's voice was closer, no longer muffled by the wall between us.

"I hope you know where you're going," I said.

"Of course I do. I've been a vampire a lot longer than Lucas, and this is my city. I know this place better than he does. Most days he forgets that."

We rounded a bend in the narrow passage then turned again. I trailed my fingers along the wall. It was so dark. We went down a set of steps and hooked to the right, creeping along another passage until we reached the end, which was covered with a metal grate. I hooked my fingers through the holes and looked into another tunnel. Light seeped through the darkness, enough so we could see what we were doing. Lilith grabbed my shoulders and turned me around so my back pressed against the grate. She cupped my hands so she could stand on them, and I lifted her off the ground. She searched the stone ceiling then slid her finger into a small hole.

Stone ground against stone as an opening formed in the ceiling. Lilith hoisted herself up and through it in one swift motion.

"What's with all the secret passageways?" I said.

"Would you get up here before Lucas finds us?" Lilith stretched her hand down and I grabbed hold, pulling myself into the space above.

The ceiling, which was now the floor, slid closed beside me. Lilith took off along the cramped passage and I thought we were backtracking, but what did I know? I had no idea where we were, and no hope of finding my way out.

Lilith stopped at a junction point and the familiar smell of sewer wafted to my nose. She had to be kidding—she knew how much I hated the sewers. When I looked out of the hole the passage made in the stone, I was greeted with my least favourite thing in the city—a sewer tunnel.

"Come on, pretty boy. Time to get your feet dirty." Lilith jumped out and landed in the trickle of muck below.

I stayed where I was and sat on the ledge of the passage, dangling my feet over the side. "I'm not getting in that until you tell me what the hell is going on."

Lilith kicked sewer water at me and scowled. "Can we discuss the reason for our fleeing once we've actually fled? Come on."

She turned and walked along the tunnel. I waited until she'd made it to an access platform before jumping down to follow, but my feet never touched the ground. An arm encircled my throat. Luckily, I didn't need to breathe. My feet scrabbled against the wall. Lilith heard the noise and glanced over her shoulder, her expression changing from annoyance to anger in a split second.

Lilith ran towards us and my attacker jumped, pulling us both out of the tunnel. I landed on my back in the sewer muck with the vamp on top of me. Curses flew from my mouth dirtier than the water.

"Don't you touch him," Lilith said, kicking the vamp.

Cain and two other vamps joined us. They flanked Lucas like faithful bodyguards.

Lucas stepped forward and placed his finger under Lilith's chin, raising it slightly. He looked her in the eyes and said, "Why did you run?"

I got to my feet slowly. If Lucas thought I was going to take off, it would only make things worse.

"Josh might have a history with Charlotte, and I figured you'd want to keep him. I'm protecting the only thing I have left … since you're so bent on taking everything from me." Lilith swatted his arm away.

Charlotte? Who was that? I wanted to ask, but I thought it was best to keep quiet.

"Oh, this is interesting." Lucas rubbed his hands together. "It seems Lilith has her eye on someone."

"Shut up," Lilith said.

Cain snarled and it drew my attention to him. Yep, I definitely didn't like the guy.

"And I don't want to take everything from you. I want you at my side," Lucas said.

"You want me as your slave, you mean." Lilith gritted her teeth.

"You're not even curious, what it would be like?" Lucas ran a finger down Lilith's cheek and I wanted to punch him. "You should be proud of me."

"I'm a lot of things, but proud is not one of them." Lilith took a step towards Lucas, and I had to stop myself from pulling her back. "You may have them falling at your feet now, but you know I could take you if I wanted to. I could walk in there and they'd be putty in my hands. This is my city, and you'd better not forget it."

For a second I thought I saw fear in Lucas's eyes. "Now, now, Lilith, we can play nice."

"I'd prefer not to," Cain growled, and I suppressed a laugh. Something told me laughing wouldn't be the best idea.

"All right, how about this?" Lucas clapped his hands.

"Since lover boy here knows our dear Charlotte, you can bring her to me. Then I might think about leaving your boyfriend alone."

"You *will* leave him alone," Lilith said.

"I'm not making any promises. But I am letting him go—for now. If you can bring Charlotte to me, he'll have a better chance. If you don't, well ... I don't need to tell you what I'll do to him."

Lilith clenched her hands into fists. "I don't like threats. Come on, Josh." She turned away and headed along the sewer tunnel.

I didn't hesitate to follow. There was no way I was hanging around Lucas any longer than I had to. I wanted to clarify exactly who Charlotte was, but I kept my mouth shut, waiting until we were well away from Lucas. He and his vamps seemed pretty eager to get their hands on her for some reason, and call it a hunch, but I didn't think those reasons involved them being friendly.

11

GRACE
Saturday morning

I'd made Archer help me search the forest for about an hour, but Seth had left no trace behind. Maybe I'd been seeing things, thinking he was there, wanting him to be, but he really hadn't been. But Archer had seen him, too. In the end, I'd given up and climbed back into the car, where Ryan had fallen asleep in the back. I did my best to push Seth from my mind, which wasn't easy. Since he'd gone, I'd spent half my time thinking about him. The other half, I thought about Josh.

We'd been driving for what seemed like forever. I wasn't used to driving long distances. Usually if I wanted to be somewhere, I orbed. My heart sank at the memory of orbing. I had to remind myself constantly that things didn't work how they used to. I misted—glowing balls of light would never surround me again. Now I was one of the fallen, I'd only ever be surrounded by darkness.

"Coffee break?" Archer said.

I rolled my head to the side and stared at his face, washed with the glow of light from the dashboard.

"Sure. But I'm having tea?"

"It's an expression, Gracie."

"I'm up for a stop." Ryan yawned from the back seat. "I'm hungry."

Archer pulled off the freeway and guided the car along the exit ramp to the service station. We parked in front of the café, and the crisp early morning greeted us when we got out of the car. The sliding doors to the café whooshed open as we approached, and I shivered at the too-cool air-conditioned interior. The buzz of voices welcomed us after so many hours in a car with my brooding brother, and listening to Ryan's snores.

We stood in line in silence, waiting to place our order. Archer's thoughts turned to Charlotte again, but that was old news. He was always thinking about Charlotte.

You're always thinking about Josh, he burst into my head. Sometimes, the twin connection thing was annoying. *Actually, on second thought, you think about Seth more.*

I frowned and turned my back to him, facing the counter. After I'd ordered an English Breakfast tea and some cinnamon toast, he grabbed a coffee, an apple and some yoghurt. Ryan went with fruit toast and water.

"What's the plan?" Archer asked once we were seated at a table by the window.

"Don't you have his address?" Ryan asked through a mouthful of toast.

I stared out the window at the cars coming and going.

It was busy for such an early hour, full of trucks refuelling at the service station, and families with cars packed to the brim, going away for the school break.

"Yes, I do." I turned my attention back to the boys. "I hope he'll be there, but we have to be prepared for the chance that he's not. Mr Chase said the place had been empty."

"Then what?" Ryan shrugged his question.

"Then ... I don't know. If something's happened to him, maybe someone will know something."

"Who, Gracie? The local vamps? I don't really like the idea of waltzing in and torturing the first vamp we see for information." Archer paused. "Actually, that sounds like a fantastic idea." He pointed his spoon at me, and yoghurt slopped onto the table.

"I was thinking more along the lines of his next door neighbour, but we can torture the vamps if you want."

Ryan laughed and had another bite of toast. "What if Josh doesn't want to be found?"

"I don't want to think about that right now." I nibbled my toast then set it down on my plate. All this talk about whether we'd find Josh or not had suppressed my appetite. But Ryan was right. It was a big city, one massive haystack with two sharp, pointy fangs in there somewhere. If Josh didn't want to be found, it was going to make everything that much harder.

Archer whistled through his teeth and I looked up, following his gaze out to the car park. A shiny red Porsche Boxster pulled in and a graceful, masculine figure stepped out. I liked red, and the shade of the car matched the top I was wearing perfectly.

"Who is this tool?" Archer said.

"One with a nice car." Ryan threw a napkin at Archer. "Clean up your mess."

As I watched the man walk towards the glass doors, I caught my reflection in the window. My delicate porcelain features stared back at me. No matter how many times I looked at myself, I still wasn't used to the change in my eyes. Before I'd fallen they'd been a perfect sapphire blue, like the stone in my ring had been, but now they were a lot darker, almost black.

A face appeared above mine in the window, surprising me. A pair of deep brown eyes, framed by short, messy blond hair, gazed at me. My heart beat faster because, for a split second, he looked like Seth. I wanted to smile, but when I realised whom it was I faltered.

An angel from my past stared at me through the glass, a smile touching his lips. I didn't want to look away, but I couldn't help it. I hadn't seen Michael for longer than I cared to think about, and the last time we'd spoken I'd told him I'd probably never forgive him for what he'd done. Even though he hadn't hurt me like Seth did, he'd still played a part, and I didn't know if, even after all this time, my heart was ready to forgive him.

When Seth had made the decision to fall, to leave me behind, Michael had known, and he hadn't tried to stop him.

He should have stopped him.

I stared at the table, wishing I were anywhere else but right there, with Michael walking through the doors and towards our table. I wasn't ready to face him, but it looked as if I had no choice.

Michael slid in beside me.

Archer raised his eyebrows. "And can I help you?" he asked, giving him the once over.

"I think the question is can *I* help *you*?"

"I highly doubt that," Archer said.

"Hi, Grace." Michael nudged my shoulder.

I had to admit it was nice being in his presence again. Michael and I shared a special bond I'd never had with another angel. He was like my protective older brother— even though I already had one of those—but better. He understood me, and everything I'd been through, right from the beginning.

I looked into Michael's eyes and couldn't help smiling. His eyes were filled with a divine light that only I could see and, as mad as I was at him, it was hard to stay that way. I realised I'd missed him.

"Hey, don't look at my sister like that," Archer said. "Who are you, and what the hell do you want?"

"To help." Michael placed his hand flat on the table, and a soft light glowed underneath it. The light burst upwards, falling around us in a dome.

I glanced around to see if anyone had noticed, but no one had.

"What did you do?" Archer asked.

Michael smiled. "Protective field. No one will know what we're talking about. They can hear us, but it won't be anything interesting."

"Cool," Ryan said.

Archer scowled. His attitude and nasty voice didn't faze Michael.

"I've been watching Grace for the past few months,"

Michael said. "There are so many angels—a lot of them never get to meet each other over the course of their existence, but Grace … everyone knows Grace. She's the one who defied Heaven to protect a vampire."

"If only it were that simple," I said.

"Yeah, I know." Michael laughed. "Charlotte was an angel. A vampire turned her, now her blood is all-powerful, yadda, yadda, yadda. She turned your human boyfriend, now he's a vamp with special blood, too. Josh isn't answering your calls, you don't want to think about Charlotte because she didn't tell you the truth, and now you're on your way to find them because you think something is wrong. Did I miss anything?" Michael sat back in his seat, a smug smile plastered over his face.

"No one can argue with any of that." Ryan looked at me across the table.

I sighed. "Actually, you didn't mention Seth."

Michael's smile fell away. "He's safe at the moment."

"Yes, but where is he?"

"Angelica took him to the In-Between."

"Why haven't you gotten him out?" I asked.

"I can't." Michael shrugged. "He's a fallen angel, and she's the Guardian. She's doing her job."

"You're an archangel, for crying out loud. Surely you can do something."

Michael shook his head. "Angelica has plans. She'll release him eventually. You need to be ready."

"You're an angel?" Archer interrupted. "I didn't think you were supposed to reveal yourselves to humans. Ryan is human."

"Ryan already knows about us," Michael said. "And

from what I've seen, I happen to think he's pretty cool."

I'm cool, too. Archer glared at me.

"That's debatable." Michael tapped my leg under the table.

"Don't stir him up, Michael. I don't want you two fighting," I said.

"You still haven't told us who you are." Archer's glare intensified.

"This is Michael. He's ... not supposed to be here." I turned to my old friend and pursed my lips. "Really? A Boxster?"

"Well, I can't exactly explode cloud dust here, can I?" Michael said.

I smiled.

"Gracie, come on. Who is this guy?" Archer said.

Michael laughed.

"Arch, he's kind of my old boss, but not the big boss. Michael is an old friend."

"We're still friends?" Michael leant his elbows on the table.

"I'm still thinking about that. I haven't forgiven you yet."

"Do I need to hit him? What did he do to you?" Archer asked.

"It's more like what he didn't do." My smile wavered.

I glanced at the ring on Michael's right hand. A large white opal sat at its centre with golden wings on either side. He wore light-blue denim jeans and a white button-up shirt. The ring should have looked out of place, but he pulled it off. I fiddled with my ring and wished for the millionth time the stone was still a sapphire.

"Onyx is pretty cool," Michael said.

"Not as cool as sapphire," I said.

Gracie, would you please find out why he's here, before I prise it out of him with a spoon? Archer thought.

He can hear you, you know.

Good. Archer glared at Michael.

Michael laughed. "Are you good with a spoon?"

Archer scowled. "Tell us, please, how can you possibly help? Grace isn't technically on your side anymore." The two guys stared at one another, testosterone bouncing back and forth between them.

"Nothing is ever as plain as black and white. The same goes for good and evil. Believe it or not, not everyone who's in Heaven's good graces actually wants to be there," Michael said.

That was something I could believe. There were a lot of things the Council did that I didn't agree with, but look where that had gotten me.

"I don't want you to get into trouble," I said. I didn't like the thought of Michael suffering the same fate as me. He was too important to consider throwing everything away. "Helping me will most definitely get you into the bad books. I'm not exactly popular at the moment. Ask Angelica."

"Yep, she's a whole different kind of trouble," Michael said.

"You're not wrong." Archer bit into his apple and chewed loudly.

I questioned Michael with my eyes but he wasn't giving anything away.

"Please don't worry about me, Grace. I can take care of myself."

"Are you going to tell me why you're here?" I asked.

"Let's just say I have a debt to collect." Michael got to his feet and shoved his hands into his jeans pockets.

"Is he always so cryptic?" Ryan asked.

"Only when he knows something and doesn't want to share." I leant forward onto the table and cupped my tea with my hands. The Styrofoam cup warmed my skin. "Technically, I'm still mad at him, so now is about the time I'm going to start ignoring him."

"Be careful, Grace. Please." Michael held my gaze with his deep brown eyes. His brow furrowed, and I wished he'd open up and let me in, but the wall in his mind was far too strong. "I wanted to warn you that you're heading into trouble."

"What kind?" I asked at the exact same time as Archer said, "What's new?"

Michael shook his head and pursed his lips. *I can't tell you. That would be sharing information with the enemy.*

Oh, I'm your enemy now?

In the Council's eyes you are. Michael turned away and headed towards the door.

"What? No goodbye?" Archer asked.

I like your brother. Michael's laughter rang through my head and he glanced over his shoulder as he walked through the car park. *I've always got your back, Grace. I know you, and I know you're where you are for a reason, but be careful. If you need me, call and I'll come.* Michael stared at me for a brief moment before stepping into his fancy car and closing the door.

Archer wiped the yoghurt off the table and threw the napkin, along with his apple core, into the empty tub before standing. "Why do I get the feeling that today is going to be one of those days?" He sipped his coffee.

Ryan cleared the table, putting our rubbish in the bin. "Come on, man. You should be used to it by now."

"He's right," I said, following both of them to the door. "Every day is one of those days."

12

JOSH

Lilith adjusted the curtains as the first morning rays hit the street outside. She stared at the folded fabric and wrung her hands. Lilith didn't usually do the nervous thing.

"Why are you so worried?" I sat in my wing chair and flicked the lamp on.

Lilith turned to me and pressed her lips together. "It might be safer if you don't know."

I stayed silent for a while, watching Lilith and trying to figure her out. Since I'd first met her she'd always been strong, and sassy, and acted as if she were indestructible. She didn't care who she killed or where we went, as long as we stayed away from the angels and hunters, and any vamp we met had this weird sort of respect for her—everything was good. But sitting there, staring at her worried eyes, everything changed.

I didn't know her.

I didn't know anyone, not even myself.

"Since you found me, all I have known is you, and what you've shown me," I said. "I'm living in a world where I know nothing about my past." I tried to keep my voice even, but by the time I'd finished my sentence I was yelling. "How can you say I'd be safer? I'm running from something I don't know anything about. Wouldn't it be better if I knew so I could stand up and fight?"

"You won't win," Lilith whispered. "Not against Lucas."

"Where did the Lilith who pulled me from a ditch go? Huh?" I shot up from my chair and ran at her, pushing her against the wall next to the front window. "I want her back. The Lilith in front of me is a spineless coward who can't even tell me the truth."

"The truth won't save you."

"Maybe not, but it might free me from this hell I'm living."

My fingers wrapped around Lilith's neck. I squeezed and she raised her chin. I loosened my grip and rubbed her lips with my thumb, pressing my hips to hers. She crushed her mouth over mine and slid her arms around my neck, showing me the Lilith I knew.

She pulled away and I dropped my hand to my side, stepping back. We'd reached the time of day when Lilith got to sleep and I had to suffer through the torturous daylight hours, alone with nothing but my thoughts.

Lilith tilted her head to one side. "Have you ever thought about why you can't sleep?"

"Not really," I said. "But I know that it sucks."

"You're the only vampire I know who can't sleep during the day. Except for Charlotte."

"Is she the one who's been following us? Who came here?"

Lilith nodded.

"So you do know her?" I asked.

Lilith looked away. Finally, I'd caught her out.

"It's complicated." She sauntered over to the base of the staircase and stopped, staring at me over her shoulder. "When I look at you sometimes I think you weren't meant to be a vampire. You've always been special, but I could never put my finger on how. It's like you have a conscience or something, or maybe your soul is different, I don't know." She pursed her lips. "Charlotte is like that. She can walk in the sun, and she doesn't sleep during the day, so maybe you can go outside, too."

"Are you crazy? I'd burn to death."

"For your own sake, I hope that's true."

Lilith put her foot on the first step. I wanted nothing more than to go upstairs and get into bed with her, but the moment she laid down, she'd be dead to the world. I didn't fancy cuddling up to someone who was pretty much a corpse.

"I'll see you at dusk." I returned to my chair.

"Maybe you should grow a pair and see if my theory is right."

I was still laughing when the bedroom door clicked closed. She wanted me to man up, I'd like to see her walk out into the sunlight. What a stupid idea. Still, I couldn't take my eyes off the window. Was I crazy for even entertaining the idea? For a couple of hours I sat in my chair, imagining what it would be like to have the warmth of the sun on my skin.

Anger welled inside me and I grabbed the lamp from the side table, hurling it across the room. It hit the wall and the antique glass shade shattered into tiny shards, raining onto the carpet in a glittery mass.

How had I gotten to where I was? I was tired of not knowing anything.

I settled back into the chair to wait for sunset. The curtains that covered the window usually changed in colour slightly as the sun rose and fell with the day, but this time they stayed the same for several hours due to the dull weather. By late afternoon I finally got up the nerve to walk to the window.

I hooked my finger into the edge of the soft velvet and pulled it back slightly. Moisture from the drizzling rain had turned the street black, and the leaves on the trees dripped water onto the footpath.

Everything I knew about vampires told me that if I walked outside, I'd die. There were times when I wished I had an easier existence, but I wasn't suicidal. As hard as my life was, I didn't want to stop being.

I let the curtain fall back into place and glanced at the clock on the mantle over the fireplace. Four pm, which meant I had a couple of hours at the most to wait before I could go outside and know for sure I wouldn't die. But instead of going back to the wing chair and taking up my trusty position, I went to the front door. I'd opened it before when the sun was up, so at least I knew I could let the fresh air in.

My chest tightened with anticipation when I rested my hand on the doorknob. The moment I opened it and the cool afternoon air hit my face, I felt better. I hated being holed up in a stuffy old house all day.

The sun hid behind grey rain clouds. I couldn't have chosen a better day to play with my existence. I stepped onto the veranda under the protection of the balcony above, and shoved my hands into my jeans pockets. Even if I didn't have the guts to walk completely outside, at least I could enjoy the fresh air.

"It's the direct sunlight that affects vampires."

I glanced down at the blonde girl. It unnerved me that I hadn't heard her approach. My senses were usually excellent; maybe I'd been too focused on thinking about the sun.

"You're back." I didn't know what else to say.

She came up the stairs and stood beside me on the doorstep. She was beautiful. More beautiful than anyone I remembered, and it was the first time I'd really had the chance to look at her. Her hair was like silk waving in a gentle breeze, its colour a lovely blonde tinged with red. She definitely wasn't human. Her eyes were as black as ebony, and I had no urge to rip her throat out.

"Can I come in?" she asked.

"Why have you been following me?" I wasn't sure if I should let her into the terrace. If Lilith had taught me one thing, it was to be wary of beautiful women. I didn't know how strong she was, if she were strong at all, but I didn't want to find out the hard way.

"There are things we need to talk about."

"Your name is Charlotte, right?"

The girl nodded. "Josh, please. I'm not going to hurt you."

Charlotte's hair glistened with droplets of mist, but the rain didn't seem to bother her. I stepped aside and let her into the hallway. She followed me to the living room and I settled into the wing chair. She went to the window and pulled the edge of the curtain aside, peering through the gap.

"I don't think anyone followed me."

"If you're talking about Lucas, he can't. The sun's still up," I said.

"I know." She let the curtain fall into place and sat on the couch. "But I have to watch my back."

"What are you?" I asked. Why not cut right to the chase? No one was being straight with me, and I wanted answers.

"You really don't remember?" Charlotte sat on the lounge, her back straight and her hands in her lap. The only people who could sit perfectly still like that, without even the hint of involuntary breathing, were vampires, but I still didn't believe she was one. She'd walked in off the street during the day. She couldn't possibly be like me.

I leant forward and rested my elbows on my knees. "I don't remember anything before Lilith."

"You obviously know you're a vampire, but there's a lot you don't know."

"Then please, enlighten me." I waved my hand, motioning her to speak, and sat back in the chair to wait.

"Show me your wrist." Charlotte's gaze flicked to my left hand. "You have a scar."

"How did you know that?" The long-sleeved shirt I wore covered the scar she was referring to. I'd never given it much thought; it had always been there. I rolled my sleeve up and rested my arm on my leg with the underside of my wrist facing up.

"The bite of our creator is the only scar that stays

behind once we're turned," Charlotte said. "Mine is on my shoulder." She pulled the neck of her top to the side and showed me a crescent-shaped scar. It looked out of place on her perfect skin.

"I don't understand," I said. "Lilith told me you're a vampire, but how can you be? You walked ..." I looked at the closed curtains.

Charlotte studied me. "I told you, there's a lot you don't know."

There were so many questions filling my head I thought it would explode. "How do you know Lilith? How do you know me? Do you know who my creator is?" When I returned my gaze to Charlotte, her brow furrowed and she bit her lip.

She tucked a strand of hair behind her ear and the action stirred something inside me. She froze, her eyes questioning.

"Your hair," I said. "When you did that it reminded me of something, but I don't know what. It's like I have these memories that want to come out, but something is holding them back."

"That's because something is. You have a mind block."

I stared at her. "You mean someone has done this to me? Why would anyone want to do that?"

"To cause trouble."

"And what did I do to deserve this? Who did I piss off this much?"

Charlotte shook her head. "It's not all about you."

"Then who is this about?" I ran a hand through my hair. "Okay, can we go back to the beginning for a minute? You still haven't told me how you can be a vampire and walk around getting a tan. Let's start with that."

Charlotte sighed and stood up. "Before I was a vampire, I was an angel."

The chair rocked from the force of me standing up. After everything Lilith had taught me, how could I let an angel into our house? I was across the room, ready to grab Charlotte and throw her against the wall, but when I reached her she'd gone. I spun around to find her sitting in the wing chair.

"How did you do that?"

"Josh, I'm not going to hurt you," Charlotte said.

I relaxed a little, but there was no way I was sitting down again. "Go on." I crossed my arms and waited.

"I can't explain everything to you, but you have to trust me."

I laughed. "I don't trust anyone."

"We were friends once. Good friends. We had each other's backs. You just don't remember. When you were human, you fell in love with an angel, and before you jump in, let me finish. You wanted to know the truth … so I'm giving it to you."

Charlotte stared at me, challenging me to interrupt.

"All right, keep going." I sat on the edge of the couch, ready if she tried any funny business.

"Grace is—*was* a Protection Angel and vampire hunter."

She wasn't making it easy to not interrupt her. How could I have been in love with not only an angel, but one who hunted my kind?

Charlotte continued talking, telling me how Grace had broken all the rules by wanting to be with me. Charlotte had come to our school to find Grace, and her brother, Archer, who also hunted vampires. I didn't like the sound of him.

"Where do you fit into all of this?" I asked.

"I was running from Lucas, but some of his vamps followed me. The short version is I wanted Grace and Archer's protection, and Grace fought hard for me, and you got caught in the crossfire. But I wasn't completely honest with her. When I told her the truth, all hell broke loose."

I shook my head and ran my hands through my hair. "I still don't know what the truth really is."

Charlotte's face was a blank, unreadable canvas. "I wasn't only an angel, Josh. I ..." Her gaze moved, staring at something behind me.

I sensed Lilith before she rested her hand on my shoulder. Her grip dug into my skin, and I prepared myself for the confrontation that would come.

13

GRACE
Late Saturday morning

By the time we got to the outskirts of the city, the sun was awake and the day well and truly started. Rain clouds hovered overhead, covering everything in a fine mist. Archer guided the car onto the bridge, slotting in with the traffic, and I sat back in my seat, staring at the little white peaks of the choppy water on the harbour.

Archer muttered some choice words under his breath when a taxi cut us off, exiting the bridge.

"Relax, Arch. Getting uptight will only make it worse," I said.

"I hate this." Archer scowled. "Everyone is in too much of a hurry. How are we supposed to get anywhere with all these cars?"

"When was the last time you came to Wide Island, Arch?" Ryan asked.

"Never."

Yep, Archer was a country boy, through and through. He was doing quite well for someone who had never driven in the city before. Since starting my assignment as a Tate twin all those years ago, I'd left Hopetown Valley once, and that hadn't turned out so well. The cities I remembered were out of date compared to Wide Island. All the buildings were so tall. Times had definitely changed.

Archer took the inner-city exit and I thumbed through the street directory to find the map we needed. The Defender didn't have satnav; we'd never needed it. After a few wrong turns, a heated argument, and getting stuck in traffic, it took us more than an hour to find where Josh should have been living, and then we had to drive around the block a few times until someone pulled away from the curb and we could nab their spot.

Archer parked the car on the tree-lined city street, a few spaces down from Charlotte's terrace. I jumped out and stuffed my hands into my jacket pockets, hunching against the chill. The terrace sat at the end of a row of identical houses. I looked along the row before staring at the door I'd stood in front of the last time I'd been to see Josh. It was still turquoise, and I still thought it an odd colour for a front door. The cast-iron fence and gate were a rusted mess. A screw had fallen out of the house number and it hung at a skewed angle. The place was a dump.

"Nice," Ryan said.

"Makes me glad I live in the country." Archer wrinkled his nose.

"It's just as I remember it. Come on." I opened the gate

and its hinges squealed.

"What are you going to say to him?" Archer said.

I hesitated. "I don't know. He might not even be here."

My hand shook as I raised it to knock. The last time I'd seen Josh, he'd been angry with me, which was the only reason I could think of why he hadn't returned my calls. Well, the only reason I wanted to think about.

The wood was rough beneath my knuckles, and more paint rained onto the front step. After my third knock I grabbed the doorknob and turned, but it was locked. Ryan pulled his wallet from his back pocket and flipped it open. He looked up and down the street before taking two paperclips out of the note compartment.

Archer raised his eyebrows. "You keep paperclips in your wallet?"

"You never know when you might need one." Ryan smiled, bending the ends of the clips.

"You can pick locks?" I asked. "I never knew ..."

"Even you don't know everything about everyone, Grace."

Ryan slipped the paperclips into the lock and jiggled them a few times, poking his tongue between his teeth. There was a click, and he turned the doorknob, pushing the door inwards to reveal the hallway. Darkness greeted us. The curtains were drawn, and no lights were on.

We made our way into the shadows of the house, the floor creaking beneath our feet. I glanced up the staircase and an uneasy feeling washed over me. A thin film of dust lay on the banister rail, untouched. I swiped my finger through it and rubbed the particles between my fingers.

When we reached the kitchen, I stopped and stared

at the mess, scanning the open room, which also housed the dining and living areas. The dining table had been split in two, chairs were upended, a scorch mark marred the middle of the kitchen floor, and some of the cupboard doors hung from their hinges. The living area was also a mess, the floor littered with pieces of foam from one of the destroyed couch cushions.

"What the hell happened?" Archer asked.

I couldn't answer. I was too stunned, staring at the wall behind the dining table.

"Why is that still there?" I finally said.

I wasn't expecting an answer. I'd never told the boys the full story about my one and only visit to the city. Josh and I had had a fight. The blood from the bottle he'd thrown at the wall was still there, but the rest of the mess had nothing to do with our argument. I wouldn't have busted his dining table, or exploded the couch.

Archer followed my gaze then went into the kitchen. He picked his way through the destruction to the wall, scratching the dark red stain with his fingernail.

"Is that blood?" He looked back at me.

"It's not what you think," I said. "He got mad, and threw a plastic drink bottle. It's pig's blood."

"You must have had one hell of a fight, Gracie."

"Why didn't he clean it up?" Ryan asked.

I shook my head. "The rest of it wasn't us."

Archer leant against the wall. "Someone came in here and there was a big kerfuffle, and now no more Josh?"

"Seems that way."

"Surely the police would have noticed this," Ryan said.

"Unless someone persuaded them not to." I shrugged.

"Glamour?" he asked.

"Or memory alteration," Archer said. "This reeks of Angelica."

"How can you be sure?" Ryan rested a hand on the kitchen bench.

Archer scanned the room. *We both knew what white-light burn marks looked like. They left a different kind of scorch than a fireball. Fireball marks were dark and hard-edged, whereas a white-light scorch had feathery, soft edges, as if it were attempting to apologise for its destruction.*

"I guess we can't be certain it was Angelica, but Angels of the Light have definitely been here."

"This is Charlotte's place, isn't it?" Ryan asked. I nodded. "Then why isn't she here?"

"Good thing she's not," Archer said. "Not really sure how that would go down."

"You'd take one look at her and melt into her arms." I smirked. Archer simply scowled.

Come on, you would, I thought.

And you wouldn't turn to a puddle of mush if Seth walked through the door? he shot back.

Probably, but I don't want to think about him right now.

Then stop making me think about Charlotte, Archer thought.

"You guys are doing it again." Ryan sighed.

"Sorry dude," Archer said.

We made our way back to the stairs. When we reached the landing, the second level was as gloomy as the first, and all the doors were closed.

Ryan opened a door at the end of the hall towards the front of the terrace, and it led to the master bedroom.

He pulled the floor length curtains aside and dull light filtered in, highlighting the dancing dust particles. I scanned the room and my heart saddened at what I saw: Charlotte's belongings strewn everywhere. Ripped clothing, sheets pulled from the bed ... As angry as I was with her, she didn't deserve someone to come into her home and destroy everything.

"This sucks," I said, picking up a black pair of jeans off the floor.

"Why do I get the feeling Josh isn't the only one we're going to be looking for?" Archer asked. He went to the door that led to a small balcony overlooking the street. "I don't like it here."

"I second that," Ryan said.

"This city scares me."

"There's nothing to be scared of, Arch," I said. "It's like home, but with more people and less trees. Have you forgotten what you're capable of? You can take on anyone with one hand tied behind your back."

He shook his head. "Maybe back home I can, but here ... the number of vamps scares me. Where there are more people, there are more vamps. How are we supposed to take them on?"

"Hopefully we won't have to," Ryan said. "When we find Josh, and sort him out, we can go home." He went to the dresser and picked up a TV remote, pointing it at the flat screen on the wall. It flicked on. "Well, I wasn't expecting that."

We didn't have a TV at home in the shed, but it wasn't something I missed. I went to the door and stared at the street below. Archer was right. Everything would be different in the city. We were going to have to be careful.

Archer joined Ryan, who was flicking through channels in front of the box. "Hey, go back. There was a news report."

"Um … Grace. You might want to see this," Ryan said.

The news showed an image of a pretty blonde girl, and I froze as I caught the end of the story.

"… found dead in a city laneway. Cause of death: trauma to the neck, resulting in heavy blood loss. At this stage police are treating it as a murder case, but they have no leads or suspects …"

"Turn it off." I didn't want or need to hear any more.

"You have to expect this sort of thing, right?" Ryan asked. "It's the city. It probably happens every night."

"But it shouldn't," I said. *What if it were Josh?* I stared at Archer, silently begging him to reassure me it wasn't.

You don't know that, Gracie. Just because he's dropped off the radar doesn't mean he's turned bad.

"I know you're doing your silent twin thing again," Ryan said. "If you want my opinion, I think we should go out there and find him. Now. Anything could have happened to him."

"We should arm up properly," I said.

Out in the hallway, all the doors were closed, like they'd been when we first came through. I moved to the top of the stairs, and Archer grabbed my arm.

Did you hear that?

I nodded, pointing to the door across from us.

There's someone in there, I thought.

Archer took a couple of slow steps towards the door.

"What's going—" I covered Ryan's mouth with my hand.

Vamps, I mouthed, then pressed a finger to my lips

and let him go.

I scolded myself for not sensing them when we'd first come in, but I was too busy thinking about Josh to pay proper attention.

Archer rested his hand on the doorknob and turned it. I held my breath, waiting for a vamp to jump us at any second. I may have been able to sense them, but it was difficult to pinpoint their exact location, since they didn't breathe. That's where fast reflexes came in handy.

The door opened into a bedroom. A lamp next to the bed cast a dull light onto the stack of phonebooks it sat on. I followed Archer to the middle of the room.

Stay alert, Gracie. They're in here somewhere, Archer thought.

"Up!" Ryan said.

I had enough time to tilt my head back before the vamp fell on me and we crashed to the floor. He was strong, but I was stronger. I drew my knees up and kicked him in the gut, throwing him across the room. He hit the wall with a crack. Plaster rained onto the carpet.

No sooner had I gained my feet than a door out in the hallway burst open and Ryan was knocked down. Archer hauled the female vamp off Ryan's back. Thankfully, she hadn't managed to bite him.

Archer threw her into the bedroom and she stumbled towards me. The guy picked himself up off the floor and locked his gaze with mine. They both launched another attack at the same time.

"Thanks, Arch," I said as I jumped and kicked the guy vamp in the chest.

Archer chuckled. "You can take them."

The girl crash-tackled me as I came out of my kick. The carpet broke my fall. It was a nice change to fighting in the forest and falling on sticks and rocks.

"Some help would be nice." I punched the girl in the face and her head snapped back, giving me the opportunity to get my knee up. I wedged my foot into her crotch and pushed. She fell onto the floor, but not before giving me a nice fingernail scratch down my cheek. I leapt to my feet, the wound on my face already healing.

"Who are you?" she asked, tilting her head to the side. "Since when does Wide Island have new hunters?"

"Who cares? Just kill them." The guy vamp headed my way again, and Archer grabbed him by the collar.

"If anyone does any killing today, it's going to be me." Archer shoved the guy against the wall next to the window. The heavy curtains swayed with the movement, and the vamp looked sideways. "That is, unless you tell me what I want to know." Archer tightened his hold around the vamp's neck.

Ryan moved into the bedroom, keeping an eye on all of us. He had a stake ready in his hand.

I raised my eyebrows.

"What?" He shrugged. "Figured I might be able to help."

The girl vamp turned towards Ryan and licked her lips.

I shook my head. "You'd be dust before you took one step."

She didn't listen.

I misted and landed in front of Ryan, taking a stake from my belt and driving it into the vamp's chest as she approached. Dust fell to the carpet in a heap.

Ryan looked over my shoulder from behind me. "That

won't be easy to get out."

"I did warn her." I sighed.

The guy vamp put his hands up, which made Archer tighten his hold again.

"You want to end up like her?" he asked. The vamp shook his head. "Then talk. Why are you here? And what happened downstairs?"

I went to the window and grasped the curtain. "We can do this the easy way if you like. But I have more fun with the hard way." I moved the curtains slightly and muted sunlight filtered through the crack in the middle.

"No, please. I'll tell you," the vamp said.

Archer pulled him away from the wall and threw him onto the bed. "Talk."

"We're lookouts. Waiting to see if they come back."

"Who?" I twirled my stake between my fingers.

"You probably don't know them," the vamp said.

"You'd be surprised who I know." I glared at him. "Do I need to convince you some more?" I ran the point of the stake down his cheek.

"Charlotte. Her name is Charlotte. She has another guy with her I've never met before."

"And why are you watching them?" Archer clenched his fists at his sides.

Good work at being intimidating, I teased him.

You're the one who ran a stake down his face.

"I don't know about the guy, but Lucas wants Charlotte," the vamp said. "Something about her blood."

"Lucas?" Archer glanced at me.

"Charlotte's creator," I said.

Charlotte had told me Lucas was her creator, and he'd

seduced her before he'd turned her. It was all lies. She'd asked him to turn her, but I didn't understand why.

"Great, here we go again." Ryan ran a hand over his face and sighed.

Charlotte had been an angel, and why she'd wanted to become a vampire was beyond my comprehension. I understood the fallen and the many reasons why an angel would choose to fall. But to become a monster ... I couldn't trust that what she'd shown me in the clearing after Seth had been taken was the truth. When it came to Charlotte, I had no idea what the truth was, or if her name and the word should ever be put into a sentence together.

"Didn't Lucas send that trio of vamps after Charlotte? Wasn't that why she came to you in the first place?" Ryan asked.

"I don't know her true intentions," I said. "There are a lot of things she held back."

"That's because you never gave her a chance to explain."

"Explain what?" Archer asked. "That she'd lied to us? Whose side are you on, Ryan?"

"I'm guessing you want to be on her side," the vamp said, pointing to me.

"All I'm saying ... we need to focus on the real enemy." Ryan ignored the vamp, frowning. "Yes, you're both angry at Charlotte. I get it. And I'm angry at Josh, too." I caught a glimpse of Ryan remembering his time in the forest with Josh. "They're our friends. We need to set things right. We could die any moment."

"Now you know how I feel," the vamp said.

"Shut up!" Archer and I said at the same time.

"You're not going to die, Ryan. I won't let you. And you didn't have to come," I said. "I wanted you at home, safe. But you insisted."

"Someone has to look out for you thrill seekers." Ryan smiled.

Archer and I laughed.

"You're all crazy," the vamp said.

Archer rocked back and forth on his feet. "You don't know the half of it."

I stifled another laugh when the vamp started wondering if he would be better off dead. I studied him for a moment, trying to see if I could hear anything useful, but there wasn't much going on. Either this one was too scared to think straight, or he wasn't the brightest candle on the cake.

I'm thinking we need to find Lucas, I thought to Archer.

And I think you're probably right.

Reckon this guy can help?

Do we have another option? Archer thought.

"Why are you staring at each other?" the vamp asked.

"They're probably deciding what to do with you," Ryan said.

The vamp scowled. "How do you know?"

"I don't, for sure." Ryan shrugged. "But they're talking to each other so whatever they're saying, it has something to do with you, and it probably isn't good."

Are you going to ask or shall I? Archer thought.

I smirked. *Oh, I think you should. It will sound better coming from you.*

Archer looked at the vamp and pursed his lips. The situation was not really a laughing matter, but I knew what was coming, and I really had to hold myself back.

"I can't believe I'm going to say this, but … take us to your leader," Archer said, spreading his arms wide.

Ryan snorted. "Dude, that's too funny."

14

JOSH

Saturday evening

I reached up and placed my hand over Lilith's to try and relieve the pressure of her grip.

"You're up early," I said, keeping my stare on Charlotte. "It's not quite dusk yet."

"Seems like I can't sleep properly today," Lilith said. "I sensed there was someone in the house—someone who doesn't belong."

Charlotte rose from the wing chair, her eyes filled with a fury that looked out of place on such a beautiful face.

"How do you know each other?" I asked.

"Lilith is the one who ruined my life," Charlotte said.

"I only did what's in my nature. You happened to get in the way."

"And look where it's gotten you." Charlotte took a step forward. "You've upset the balance."

"I don't need you to remind me how screwed up every-thing is," Lilith said.

I ran a hand through my hair. "What the hell are you talking about? Would one of you please give me an answer that doesn't involve a riddle? Assume I'm stupid and spell it out for me."

"I told you, the truth won't change anything," Lilith said.

Anger boiled inside me to the point where it exploded, and I launched off the couch into a backflip and landed behind Lilith. I locked my arm around her neck and pulled her against my chest.

"If you say that one more time, I will kill you."

"That wouldn't be the best idea," Charlotte said. "You'll make Lucas very angry."

"Big deal. He's already out to get me." I loosened my hold on Lilith. She pushed me away but didn't leave my side.

"Maybe we can talk him around," Lilith said.

Charlotte laughed. "You can't talk to Lucas. You can't trust him, either. No one knows him like I do. He has a plan, and it doesn't involve letting any of us go." She concentrated on Lilith, and her eyes narrowed. "Why do you want to protect Josh?" she asked. "You don't agree with what Lucas wants to do?"

"What exactly is Lucas planning?" I asked.

Lilith ignored me and went around the couch to face Charlotte. "No, I don't agree with it. But you already know that, what with your mind-reading skills."

"You can read minds?" I asked. "As if."

Lilith scowled before she continued. "I think Lucas has gone mad. I like this city the way it is. It was my city, until you came along and ruined everything. I was the one with the power. Those are my vamps he's leading down there, so no. I don't think what he's doing will benefit anyone except him."

Charlotte put her hands on her hips. "You don't want to walk in the sun? I find that hard to believe."

"Then look inside my head! You know it's true. It's not the way it's supposed to be," Lilith said.

"Most vampires would give anything to be able to walk around during the day."

"What are you talking about?" I said. "Would one of you look at me and tell me what's going on?"

Charlotte glanced from Lilith to me, and back again. "Have you told him nothing?"

"I'm trying to protect him." Lilith scowled.

"Using my blood, Lucas plans to build an army of vamps who can walk in the sun," Charlotte said. "And the only thing Lilith and I agree on is that it's a bad idea."

Lilith clenched her fists. "Walking in the sunlight would be wonderful, but not if every vampire in this city could do it. Imagine this place after a few years. There would be no humans left. If we could take them when we wanted, where we wanted, how long do you think it would be before our food supply dried up? Word would spread about Wide Island. No one new would come here, and we'd be out in the open, myth thrust harshly into the spotlight of reality. Then what? The city would be taken under siege. Humans would try to destroy Wide Island, and everything in it. We could leave, and take over other cities, but what good would that do? Imagine a world populated with nothing but vampires. We'd turn on each other because we'd be mad with thirst. We turn on each other enough as it is without making the problem worse."

I stared at the two most frightening women I'd ever met. They were both right. What vamp wouldn't want to go outside during the day? But Lilith seemed to have her head screwed on when it came to the future. No humans meant no food. A city populated entirely with vampires, going mad from starvation. I didn't particularly want to witness that, or be one of the starving.

"Lucas would say you think too much," Charlotte said.

I snorted. "Funny. Lilith tells me the same thing."

"You do think too much," Lilith said. "And Lucas doesn't think enough."

"Since when do you care about people?" I asked.

"I don't. I care about myself, and the survival of my kind. If Lucas gets hold of Charlotte, she can supply them with enough blood to dose up an army," Lilith said. "They'd string her up and bleed her continuously to maintain their power."

"The only problem is, if a vamp has too much of my blood, the effect can be permanent." Charlotte tilted her head slightly and stared through me.

The thought of anyone doing anything to harm her made my blood boil. I couldn't explain it. It was like a protective urge came over me at the mention of harming Charlotte.

"It's because we're connected," she said.

"I didn't say anything out loud."

"You didn't have to. She read your mind." Lilith moved to my side. "Once you know, you get used to it. I have lots of fun telling her where to go in my head."

I massaged my temples with my fingers. "You know

each other better than either of you led me to believe."

"We have history." Lilith smirked. "And most of it isn't very nice."

I looked from one girl to the other, then at my wrist. The crescent-shaped scar taunted me. Charlotte had told me she used to be an angel, or still was one, or something. She had to be part angel if she could go outside. But she hadn't answered my other questions. How did she know me, and did she know my creator?

My gaze rested on Charlotte.

"You have the urge to protect me for a reason," Charlotte said. "I wouldn't know where your scar was if I didn't know you."

"You're my creator?"

Charlotte nodded. "And Lilith is Lucas's. We're all one big happy family."

"Which leads us back to the real problem here," Lilith said. "As much as I hate you, I don't want Lucas to have you. He can't execute this plan. I won't let him take my city. Of course, I could try to kill you, but we both know I'd come off second best."

"Yes, you would. And no matter what happens, the hunters would keep it under control," Charlotte said.

Lilith's shrill laugh reverberated around the room. "Look what happened to the last hunters."

"Hunters?" I remembered what Charlotte had said about the girl called Grace, who I was apparently in love with. The girl whose name was engraved on the inside of the ring I wore on my right hand, and who had called me several times.

"Grace called you?" Charlotte asked. "And you didn't

talk to her?"

"Stop doing that, it's freaking me out. And no, I didn't talk to her. I don't remember her."

"Who is Grace?" Lilith asked, glaring at me.

"How many times did she call?" Charlotte asked, ignoring Lilith.

I shrugged. "I don't know, a few, maybe."

"Have you listened to those messages?" Charlotte asked.

"Why? What's the point?"

Charlotte stepped towards me. "Because even if you can't remember Grace, I can, and after the last time you two saw each other, there would have to be a very good reason for her to be calling you."

I fished my phone from the pocket of my jeans and swiped the screen. The tone rang through to my voicemail. "You have twenty-seven new messages."

Charlotte gave me a questioning look.

"My dad keeps calling me." I deleted the first lot of messages that were all from him then put the phone back to my ear. "At first I talked to him, then I ..."

I stopped at the sound of the voice that travelled through the phone. I remembered it from the first message I'd listened to. It was beautiful, and it stirred something in me, making me more and more frustrated with every word she said. I wanted to crush the phone in my hand and hurl it across the room. Why couldn't I remember? Surely if I were in love with someone who had the voice of an angel—who apparently *was* an angel—I'd remember.

Grace's last message said she was worried, she missed me and she was going to come and see me. I ended the call and looked at Charlotte.

"When was that call made?" she asked.

"Yesterday afternoon."

"Then she's probably already here. We need to find her."

"Why? What good will it do if I don't remember her?" I asked.

"It doesn't matter if you don't remember," Charlotte said. "What matters is that she's coming to look for you. She can help us fight Lucas."

"She's your ex, isn't she?" Lilith folded her arms over her ample chest, a look of pure hatred on her face.

"So what if she is? I don't remember her," I said.

"She better not get in my way."

Charlotte laughed. "It's you who'd better not get in her way. Grace is a very good hunter." She headed towards the front door and looked back over her shoulder.

"I know someone else who used to be a good hunter," Lilith said.

"What does that mean?" I asked.

Lilith stared at me but didn't answer.

I followed Charlotte. For a moment, I didn't care if Lilith wanted to come or not. She obviously wasn't who I'd thought she was, and I didn't know her well enough to trust her. Which made me ask myself, would there ever be a vampire I *could* trust?

I didn't think so.

There was so much I didn't know, and it seemed Charlotte had at least some of the answers, even if she wasn't being straight with me. Lucas wanted us to take her to him, and Charlotte seemed willing to try and stop him. It looked like we'd both get what we wanted. I wanted to be free of Lucas, but maybe Charlotte was right. Maybe even if I did what he asked, it wouldn't make a difference. All I cared about was remembering my past, and if that involved looking for some girl called Grace, then I'd do it. I was tired of walking around not knowing who I was.

"So you're coming with us?" Charlotte turned to Lilith.

"That depends," Lilith said. "What's in it for me?"

"I won't kill you."

Lilith scowled, and from the look in Charlotte's eyes, I didn't doubt for one second she'd kill whoever tried to get in her way.

15

GRACE
Saturday night

We needed the sun to be entirely down before heading out. I didn't want our informant bursting into flames the moment we walked out the door. He was no good to us dead. After manhandling the vamp downstairs and securing him to a chair with a heavy chain Archer had found in the garage, we cleaned the house up while we waited.

The dining table wasn't salvageable. We put it against the wall and stacked the chairs in front of it. I scrubbed the blood-stain on the wall to take my mind off Josh's room upstairs. I had memories of that room I'd rather forget, because as good as they were, everything that happened afterwards tainted them with sadness and regret. Giving myself to him had been amazing—at the time—but being with Josh sat at the top of the list of stupid things I'd done, right beside becoming a fallen angel.

"I don't think it's going to come off." Archer placed his hand over mine and gently pulled it away from the wall.

"I hate looking at it."

"What happened between you and Josh, Gracie?"

"I don't want to talk about it. And don't you dare force me to," I said.

I was good at blocking Archer from my thoughts. He hated that I did it sometimes, but there were some things I didn't want to share with him. Our link was supposed to help us in battle, not screen the soap opera of our lives.

"Should we make this our base?" Ryan asked. I loved how he knew when a change of subject was needed.

"We'll have to be careful," I said, glancing at the vamp chained to the chair. "They were guards. If they don't check in, more will come. I'll get our stuff."

I left Archer and Ryan to watch vamp boy and went out to the car. A yellow glow from the lampposts filled the street. The rain had stopped, but patchy clouds covered the dark sky.

When I reached into the back of the car to grab our bags, my necklace fell free from my top. The diamond tear swung like a pendulum, glinting under the street-lights. I grabbed it and tucked it away. Seth was the last person I wanted to think about. I needed to concentrate, but it was hard when the image of him standing on the forest path wouldn't leave me alone.

The hairs on my neck prickled, and I glanced down the street. A few cars went past, and people came and went on their way to wherever it was they were going. A figure stood at the mouth of the next lane that separated the blocks of terrace houses.

I froze.

Not again. I took a step around the car, trying to make out the person's face in the dark. When I reached the front of the Defender a group of people came out of the first terrace in the row. They passed the figure standing in the shadows, obscuring him from view. When they'd moved along enough for me to see, he was gone.

It couldn't be Seth. Angelica had him locked up.

I returned to the back of the car and fished Annie's ring from the velvet pouch in my pocket. Her soul moved around inside the tiger's eye, bouncing off the edges like a pinball. Usually she was a lot calmer.

"What's wrong?" Talking to the ring was something I did on occasion. I wasn't sure if Annie could hear me, but I guessed it didn't really matter. I cupped the ring in my palm and held it at chest height. "Do you know what's happening?" The light swirled around inside the stone. "Who am I kidding? You probably know everything that's happening. Why am I seeing Seth?"

"Talking to yourself again?" Archer stood in the doorway to the terrace.

I jumped and dropped the ring. It made a *clink* as it hit the ground, rolling behind the rear wheel of the car. I was grateful I hadn't parked next to a drain.

Archer chuckled. "Why so tetchy?"

I dropped to my hands and knees, the rough bitumen digging into my skin through my jeans, and retrieved Annie's ring. "I think I saw Seth again."

Archer stepped onto the footpath and glanced in both directions along the street. "Nope. No Seth."

"I'm not crazy."

"I know." Archer came to the car and shouldered one of the bags. "Were you asking Annie about Seth?"

I grabbed the suitcase and a backpack before slamming the back door of the Defender. "Maybe."

"And you think she can hear you?"

"I don't know." I shoved the backpack into his arms. "It's possible."

"What are you going to do with her?" Archer followed me into the house and along the hall.

"Set her free," I said. "Seth will know how."

We stopped in the kitchen and I let the suitcase drop to the floor. The mention of Seth again stirred all sorts of feelings inside me, and I looked at my hands. Ryan took the bags, and busied himself with sorting out the arsenal.

"What are we doing here, Gracie?" Archer asked.

"I don't know what you mean."

"You know exactly what I mean." Archer rested his hands on the bench. "You need to choose."

"I don't want to." I picked at my fingernails.

"I don't care if you don't want to. There are a lot of things we don't want to do. But this … this you have to do."

"How, Arch? I don't know how." A tear slipped from the corner of my eye and I swatted it away.

"That's something you need to work out. But you can't keep going on like this. You love both of them—I get it. But you can't have both. So what's it going to be? Are we on this search for Josh because we're taking him home, or are you going to break his heart again?"

I stared at my brother, overwhelmed by how much I could hate him and love him at the same time. He hated

Seth. Archer had seen how much hate I had directed at Seth over the years, and it had rubbed off on him. I had a very overprotective brother, and whether I liked it or not he was right. I did have to choose, but I wasn't going to do it standing in the kitchen of Charlotte's house with bloodstains on the walls, and a vamp in chains giving me the evil eye.

"Are we going any time soon?" the vamp asked. "These chains are really heavy."

"I will choose," I said to Archer, ignoring the vamp. "But you have to let me do it my own way."

Archer shook his head and pulled me into a tight hug. "What am I going to do with you, Gracie?"

I pressed my forehead to his chest and took a deep breath, squeezing my eyes closed to hold back the tears. Archer rubbed my back before letting go and inspecting the weapons Ryan had lined up on the marble bench top.

"Let's concentrate on getting both of them back first." Ryan handed me a dagger. "Then maybe it will be easier."

If only having them standing in front of me would make the situation easier. I was determined to find both my boys, but in my heart I'd already decided who I was fighting for—I just didn't want to admit it to myself, or anyone else.

The three of us took quick showers before arming up and preparing for a fight as we would any other time we went hunting. I strapped the dagger to my ankle before rolling my jeans over my boots. I ditched my red top for something a little more appropriate in order to conceal the stake belt strapped around my waist. Five stakes sat snugly in the loops. The loose-fitting, black off-the-shoulder top hid them nicely.

Archer and Ryan looked like regular street kids in jeans, T-shirts and hoodies; you'd never guess they had an arsenal hidden on them as well. I made sure Ryan was kitted out like us; even though he wasn't a fighter, he needed to be armed just in case.

What we didn't need we put back inside the bags and stowed them behind the couch.

"What do we do with him?" Archer nodded towards the vamp. "He'll try and run the moment we're out the door."

"I could probably persuade him to stay with us and not try any funny business." I stood in front of the vamp and stared him down, smirking.

"No, he's right. I'll probably run," the vamp said.

My smile widened. "Even if I told you this would be on your tail?" I opened my hand and conjured a fireball. It swirled above my skin, the flames curling around each other, and I flicked it into the air before catching it on my fingertips. The vamp flinched.

"Um … maybe I'll stay close."

"That's a good idea." I snuffed the flames out and unlocked the padlock on the chain. "If we're going to be working together, I should know your name."

The vampire snorted and stood up, the chains falling to the floor with a clink. "Let's get one thing straight. I don't work with hunters."

He ran towards the door, as I knew he would. I misted, landing in his path before he could make it outside, and punched him in the chest. He flew backwards along the hall and hit the kitchen counter, then landed in a heap, groaning.

"I told you not to run," I said. "Next time there will be fire behind that punch. Now let's go."

Archer picked the vamp off the floor and shoved him down the hall. "I'd advise you not to try that again. We know every move you plan to make before you decide to make it."

Maybe not *we*. *Me*. I'm the one who can read minds, but the way Archer said it made it sound so bad-arse.

"If you don't tell me your name, I'll call you stupid," I said. "Will you answer to that?"

Ryan closed the front door and locked it with a key labelled 'front' that he'd found in the kitchen drawer. Then we headed down the steps to the footpath.

The vamp growled. "It's Max, okay?"

"Well then," I said, stopping and facing him. "Please, Max, lead the way."

Max shouldered past me and led us down the tree-lined street towards the bridge in the distance. Archer and I flanked him, in case he decided to go back on his word. I made sure I was between Ryan and Max, since all he could think about was sinking his teeth into Ryan's neck. Max walked with his head down, and his shoulders hunched.

"Where are we going?" Archer asked as we rounded the corner at the end of the street.

"You'll see," Max said.

"He's taking us to the war memorial," I said. "It's in Dhye Park."

Max glared at me. "I don't like hunters; they think they're so smart."

I smirked. "I don't like vampires; especially the stupid ones."

16

JOSH

The moon peeked out from behind the clouds, and I was glad the rain had finally decided to let up. I didn't need the weather adding to my already glum mood.

We left after sundown, and Charlotte led us away from the city centre towards the outskirts of town. We walked for about twenty minutes at a human pace so as not to draw attention to ourselves. I had my head down, staring at my feet and trying to remember Grace, when Charlotte stopped in front of another terrace house with a weird-coloured door. It was the first in a long line of houses, and the one that looked the worst of the lot.

"Who lives here?" I asked.

"My terrace is much nicer," Lilith said, smirking.

"You used to live here with me," Charlotte said. "And this would be the first place Grace would look for you."

"What?" I stared at Charlotte. "I've never been here before."

Lilith glared at me. "You two lived together?"

"But we were never *together*," Charlotte said.

Well, that was a relief. I didn't like the thought of standing next to someone who I may or may not have been with. It was weird enough I couldn't remember Charlotte, let alone adding the complication of that kind of relationship.

"You better not have been." Lilith frowned. She was sexy when she was mad. "Who else knows this is your place?"

"Lucas," Charlotte said. "It was his at one stage, too."

"Of course. Which means every vamp in town probably knows as well."

"Why would Lucas have lived here?" I asked.

Charlotte ignored me. "My guess is Grace and Archer are here, since that's their car." She pointed to a black 4WD parked a few car spaces up the street.

"Why doesn't anyone ever answer my questions?" I looked at the balcony above, not expecting an answer to that question either.

So far nothing about the terrace had jogged my memory, but nothing ever did if I looked for it. The moments I'd had any inkling about something to do with my past, they crept up on me and took me by surprise.

"Come on," Charlotte said, approaching the door. "Welcome home, Josh." She put her hand into her pocket.

"Allow me." Lilith lifted her leg and kicked. Chips of paint and splinters of wood fell onto the step as the door swung open.

Charlotte sighed. "I have the keys." They clinked together when she held up her hand to show Lilith.

"Oh well, too late now."

"Whoever is in there definitely knows we're coming," I said.

"Hello," Charlotte called into the house. She took a slow step over the threshold. No answer. But really, who would answer if they were in someone else's house?

Once we were inside, Lilith closed the door. Charlotte got halfway down the hallway before she stopped and I bumped into her. Lilith shouldered past us and walked farther into the house.

"What happened here?" I stared at the smudge of blood on the wall.

The place was a mess, but at the same time it wasn't. All the furniture was broken, but it had been stacked or leant against the wall. The couch cushions had huge gashes in them, but they'd been put carefully back into place. The stuffing and foam were swept neatly into a corner. A huge scorch mark marred the floor, and another on the front of the kitchen bench.

"Grace has definitely been here," Charlotte said. "Who else would take the time to clean up my mess?" Her gaze settled on the blood-stained wall. "Actually, half of it was yours."

"What do you mean?" I asked.

"The blood stain ... you threw a bottle at the wall during a fight with Grace not long after we left Hopetown Valley. We never got a chance to clean it up," Charlotte said. "Angelica came for me. I think she came for both of us. We fought her off before we were separated. I didn't see you again until I tracked you down at Lilith's."

The scarred room and messed-up furniture teased me and I shook my head. "I don't remember."

"Some things aren't worth remembering." Charlotte pursed her lips.

I left Charlotte and Lilith in the living area and headed for the stairs. If I used to live in this house then surely there would be something I'd left behind, something that would give me a clue as to who I was.

At the end of the upstairs hall was an open door that led to the master bedroom. The things in that room seemed to belong to Charlotte. The bathroom door was open as well, the room empty, so I headed for the only closed door, which was at the other end of the top level. I took a deep breath I didn't need and turned the knob.

What greeted me was more than disappointing. It was downright depressing.

Someone had staked a vamp. A pile of dust sat on the floor in the middle of the room, and I made a mental note to tell Charlotte about it when I went back downstairs. The bed was made, but dirty clothes littered the floor. A bloodstained glass sat next to a lamp on a stack of phonebooks that made a bedside table. I went farther into the room. A small chest of drawers I hadn't seen from the doorway sat in the corner. Something stuck up from the top of it, and it took me a minute to realise it was a photo frame that had been laid flat.

When I picked it up and looked at the face trapped behind the glass, something in my mind flinched. I had that feeling again. There was a memory at the front of my thoughts, but something held it beyond my reach. The girl in the photo was beautiful, even more so than Charlotte and Lilith combined. I ran my fingers over the glass, wishing I could meet this angelic person.

I flipped the frame oven and opened the back, slipping the photograph out. A short message was written on the back in neat, pretty handwriting.

Dear Josh,
No words can fix what happened, but I needed to
say thank you. You gave me the most beautiful gift
when you gave me the ring, and I'm sad that I have
nothing to give in return. It's true, I never told you I
love you, but maybe one day I can.
Grace xxx

The glass in the frame cracked under the pressure of my fingers, and the wooden frame splintered in my hand. I shouldn't have been so angry. I didn't know this girl, or at least I couldn't remember her. So why did it hurt so much to find out she'd never told me she loved me? I'd obviously told her. I'd given her a ring, for God's sake. It probably had my name engraved on the inside like hers was on the one I wore. How cliché—we had matching rings.

The glass and wood fell to the carpet and I flipped the photo over to look at Grace. A red splotch appeared on her cheek and I wiped my thumb over it, unaware at first that it was blood from my tears.

"You okay?" Charlotte leant against the door.

"This is Grace?" I showed her the photo.

Charlotte nodded. "Yes, that's Grace."

"When I look at this photo, something … I think I'm about to remember her, but then it slips away." I folded the image in half and put it into the back pocket of my jeans. "It's very frustrating."

Charlotte sighed. "Things happened that messed us all up. I wish we could do it over, but we can't. I have regrets, but I can't change the past. What I can shape is the future. We can stop this army from happening, but we need each other. You have to trust me." She pursed her lips. "Do you trust me?"

I couldn't help laughing. How could she ask me that question? How was I supposed to trust her, when I couldn't even trust my own mind? "I want to, but all I know is Lilith. I have nothing before her."

Charlotte nodded. "I guess I'll have to live with that."

"If you can tell I've got a mind block, can you fix it?"

"That block was put there by an Angel of the Light, which means it can only be removed by the same angel," she said. "I have a pretty good idea who did it, but we won't know for sure until we find her."

"Great, someone else we *have* to find." I ran a hand through my hair and stared at Charlotte.

Her gaze moved to the pile of dust on the floor. "It looks like Grace is doing her job."

I shouldered past her to go downstairs and find Lilith. She hadn't moved from the kitchen. She hunched over the bench, inspecting some weapons.

"Found them in those bags." She pointed to a gym bag next to the couch.

Lilith picked up a miniature crossbow and pressed the button on the handle. The limbs flicked out and clicked into place, and the bow loaded a small arrow from a storage section in the handle. She aimed it at the wall and pulled the trigger.

The arrow embedded into the wall in the middle of

the bloodstain. Lilith smiled.

"Careful with that thing," I said. "You don't want to shoot someone you're not supposed to."

"Can I take it with us?"

"Why? You're a vampire; you have teeth to kill people."

"But I like having toys to play with." Lilith pouted, and for a moment I saw the Lilith I knew, the Lilith who'd pulled me out of a ditch and given me a home, oozing sex appeal with every move she made.

"I say we arm up," Charlotte said, following me into the room. "It won't hurt to have a little more punch on our side."

"Let's get one thing straight," I said. "We don't kill anyone we don't have to."

Charlotte smiled, but her eyes were sad. "I don't kill people full stop, Josh. I only kill vampires."

"Well, since I am one, that's nice to know."

"I won't hurt you."

"Yeah, because I won't let you." Lilith aimed the crossbow at Charlotte.

I moved in front of her. "Play nice, please."

Lilith lowered her arm and pouted again. She strapped the crossbow to her wrist and pushed the button to fold the outer limbs in. She hid the weapon under the sleeve of her black cardigan.

"We should decide on a plan." Charlotte leant against the bench.

"Well, we know Grace has been here, but we don't know where she's gone," I said.

"It will be easy enough to find her. Archer and Ryan have been here as well. If we lose Archer's scent, which is highly likely because he's a hunter, then we can probably keep on Ryan's."

Lilith lifted her nose and sniffed the air. I had to stop myself from laughing. She looked like a dog, and probably wouldn't be too pleased if I told her so. Charlotte was right though; I could smell one very distinct person, another not as strong, then a faint lingering smell, like fresh summer rain.

"That's Grace," Charlotte said. "You'll have no hope of following or finding her. She has the ability to switch it off. I'm guessing she's marked the terrace in the hope you'll know she's been here."

There was the dog analogy again, and the mind reading. I smiled.

"Can I ask one thing?" Lilith said. "Who's Ryan?"

Charlotte bit her lip and looked straight at me. "Ryan is Josh's best friend."

Great, just what I needed—more complications. Was there anyone who didn't know who I was? Because I didn't know any of them.

"Can we leave? If we're going to find all these people that I apparently know, shouldn't we have gone already?" I said.

"And the plan is?" Lilith asked.

"We find Grace," Charlotte said. "And we get her to help us fight Lucas. We all have our reasons why we want to stop this army, don't we?" Charlotte said.

"I want my city back," Lilith said.

I shrugged. "I don't know what I want."

"You will once you have your memory," Charlotte said. "We're not the only ones fighting this war. The other hunters and the city angels know what's going on. Everyone is looking for me for one reason or another, and none of them will stop."

Before Charlotte finished her little speech I knew what she was going to say, and I didn't need to be a mind reader to figure out the plan. Lucas wanted her, and it angered me more than I'd first realised, the thought of anyone hurting Charlotte. When the anger filled me up so much I thought I would burst, it surprised me. I cared about her on a level I didn't understand. She'd said we were connected, and I believed it was true.

"If Lucas wants me, he can have me. We'll attack from the inside. Since Grace and I aren't on the best of terms, she'll probably agree it's a good idea. Once we find her we can decide exactly what we're going to do." Charlotte slipped a stake into her back pocket. "Lilith, does Lucas still think you're loyal to him?"

"He doesn't think I'm not." She folded her arms.

"Then he won't know what's hit him."

I didn't want to hand Charlotte over to anyone.

"You don't need to worry about me," Charlotte said.

"You're sure about this?" I asked.

Charlotte nodded. "I might have a little something up my sleeve."

17

GRACE

Late Saturday night

Being a Saturday night, there were a lot of people out walking the streets. Every café and pub we passed was full to bursting. Music blared from the nightclubs as people lined up to wait to get in. Cars honked their horns, and sirens blared in the distance. I missed the relative quiet of the country, where it was just Archer and me arguing, and the sound of the birds in the trees.

When we reached the park, we ascended a large set of stone steps to the mouth of a tree-lined tunnel. Two rows of yellow lamps lit the way, casting an eerie but beautiful glow. Shadows danced through the trees as we walked, and I shivered at the sight of the majestic Moreton Bay Figs. The huge trees didn't have quite the same effect on me as they used to. It wasn't every day you got to see the gates of Hell, and since I'd discovered the reason behind my dislike for them, it had become easier to deal with.

"It's big," Archer said.

Big was an understatement.

I suppose if you looked at it from a country girl's point of view, it wasn't really big at all. The park could fit into the grounds of Hopetown Valley High fifty times over, but we were in the city. In a landscape of concrete and high-rises, green spaces like Dhye Park were huge.

The path Max led us along seemed to stretch on forever, and the noise of the city faded into the background. A few people milled about, walking in both directions. A young couple sat entwined on a park bench, oblivious to everyone around them. I smiled at their public display of happiness, but seriously, they needed to get a room.

Max drooled and a growl rose in his chest. He kept his eyes on the couple as we passed, and I gave him a good shove to keep him moving.

"Don't even think about it. You're not eating anyone on my watch," I said.

The end of the boulevard opened onto a large hexagonal area with a fountain at its centre. Rivers of water cascaded from the nostrils of two horses' heads, which flanked a man holding out his right arm.

"Ah! Apollo," Archer said.

"Huh?" I stared at him.

"Here we go," Ryan said. "He's about to launch into one of his geeky fits."

"The god of light and the sun, among other things." Archer walked slowly around the fountain. "And look, there's Diana, the goddess of purity, and there, the young god of the fields and pastures." Archer's eyes lit up. "Look, Grace,

Theseus. He's the one who vanquished the Minotaur. This fountain is the ultimate representation of good triumphing over evil." My dork of a brother stopped and leant on the fountain's stone lip, gazing into the dark water.

"Okay, thanks for the Greek history lesson." I laughed. "But I think we represent good triumphing over evil pretty damn well ourselves."

I took in the rest of our surroundings. The facade of a majestic gothic-style cathedral caught my attention, its spires reaching for the stars. The grand building looked out of place, like it had been left behind by some bygone era.

"How far is the memorial?" I asked Max.

"You won't be able to get inside," he said.

"That's not what I asked. And don't underestimate me."

Max smiled slyly. "You hunters are always so sure of yourselves. It's at the other end of the park. We have to cross the street into the next section."

"Let's go then." I grabbed his T-shirt and shoved him in the direction he'd indicated. "No rest for the wicked."

"Fingers crossed." Max laughed. *Once we get that bitch's blood, we won't need any rest.*

I stiffened, but pretended I didn't know what the thought was that had flashed through his mind. The moment Max had mentioned Lucas and Charlotte I'd been suspicious. It turned out Lucas still wanted Charlotte for the exact same reason he'd sent Mathew, Cain and Tyler to Hopetown Valley. So he could create an army of vamps that walked in the sun.

I relayed the information to Archer and he raised his eyebrows. "No surprise there."

"What?" Max asked.

"Nothing that concerns you, bad boy." Archer grinned, and led Max away a little.

He could probably hear me, but I needed to fill Ryan in. "Lucas is up to his old tricks," I whispered.

"Army?" Ryan asked.

"Yep." I linked my arm through his and we followed Archer and Max.

We left the fountain and the safety of the lighted area, entering another tree-lined pathway. There were less people in this section of the park, and I could see why. The moon had done a disappearing act again, and there were fewer lampposts to light our way. It was a good thing Archer and I had heightened eyesight. Ryan, though, wouldn't be able to see much until it was almost on top of him.

"Let's walk a little faster," Archer said. "I don't like it in here."

"No protest from me," Ryan said.

I fixed my stare on the street at the end of the long and gloomy tree-tunnel, the traffic noise a faraway hum. I caught up to Archer and Max and curled my fingers into the fabric of Max's T-shirt, in case he decided now would be a good time to attempt a getaway.

We were about half way from the fountain to the street when up ahead, two people stepped onto the path. The light from the lamps illuminated them from behind, and I couldn't see their faces. The way they stood made me stop, and I grabbed Archer's arm.

"This doesn't look good," I said.

"Muggers, do you think?" Archer asked.

The two figures took a few steps forward into a pool of

light created by one of the lampposts that lit the walk way.

No, I didn't think the man and woman were muggers.

The man looked directly into my eyes, and I was shocked at what I saw. We were up against another set of hunters. A smirk turned his lips up. He wore a long, black coat that stopped at his knees, and his feet were encased in combat boots. Black jeans hugged the girl's perfect legs. She also wore combat boots, and a black flying jacket. Her hair fell to her shoulders, the surrounding light shining off its glossy surface.

"Ryan, get behind us, please." He did as I said, and I tightened my grip on Max's T-shirt.

The couple walked towards us, and their rigid posture didn't make them look friendly.

The girl stopped and I stared into her eyes. "Why are you kicking around with a vamp?" she asked. "I guess it's not surprising, since you're fallen."

"What business is it of yours?" I asked.

She smiled and took a step forward. "You're on our turf."

"Are they about to do what I think they're about to do?" Archer said.

A second later the girl came at me. I shoved Ryan backwards as hard as I could, hoping my angel strength didn't hurt him too much.

Better hurt than dead.

The girl had a look of hate in her eyes. Max struggled free from my grip and I let him, preparing to take the girl out, but instead of continuing her charge, she took a sharp turn and went for Max. She jumped and grabbed the vamp, throwing him to the ground. He rolled onto his back, but before he had the chance to regain his feet, she brought her hand down towards his chest. He exploded into a cloud of dust.

"No!" I ran at the girl, tackling her to the paved pathway. We rolled a few times. She punched me in the jaw and I kicked her in the stomach. She flew off of me, landing heavily on the grass to the side of the path.

Archer came to help me, and the guy punched him. Archer hit him back. Ryan circled, looking for a way to stop them fighting. Blood dripped from Archer's mouth and a cut above his eye. That wasn't good. I'd lost my ability to heal others when I'd fallen. If he got hurt I wouldn't be able to help him.

Archer ducked another punch and headed for the girl.

"Arch." I grabbed his arm. "You don't want to pick a fight with her."

"Why?" He spun to face me, clenching his fists. "She dusted our informant."

"He was your informant?" The guy came and stood next to his sister. They had to be related, because they were hunters. Even though I'd never met another hunting team, one thing I was sure of was how they worked.

"You're fallen," the girl said, as if saying it out loud again would change it.

"And you're an arse," Archer said.

"Okay, everyone, stop." I turned to the girl. "I'm Grace. This is my annoying brother, Archer, and that's Ryan. You are ...?"

The girl eyed me, and I probed her mind for any information I could find. She had a pretty good wall in place and it made me smile. As soon as I'd realised they were hunters, I'd thrown up my own defences.

"I don't tell anyone who's fallen anything." The girl sneered.

"Not even your name?" Archer grinned. "Surely that can't hurt. And, trust me. Grace would have you on your arse in a second if you tried anything. She may be tiny, but she's mean."

I smirked. *Thanks Arch, you are officially an idiot.*

Yeah, but I'm your idiot.

"I won't tell you anything until you tell me why you're fallen." She stared at me, probing the wall I'd built in my mind.

"That's a really long story," Ryan said. "I'm thinking we don't have the next decade, and then some, to explain it."

"And you have a human with you," the guy said.

"Okay, can we maybe talk about the really important stuff like, I don't know, how we're trying to stop Lucas from creating a sun-walking army of vampires who want to take over Wide Island, and probably the world."

The girl raised her eyebrows. "You know about that?"

"I know a lot more than anyone ever gives me credit for."

"I'm Hope," she said. "This is my brother, Justice."

"Dude ..." Archer stared at Justice. "I'd say pleased to meet you, but you punched me, so ..." He shrugged.

"How do you know about Lucas and his plans?" Hope asked.

"We have insider information," I said. "And that vamp was going to lead us to him."

Hope laughed. "You mean the war memorial. You won't get in. If we haven't figured out how ... you won't."

"Maybe we could help each other," Ryan said.

"Not until I know why and how you know about what's

going on in my city."

Her city? Great, an angel on a power trip—just what I needed.

I stared at Archer. *What should we tell her?*

I don't know. I'm still getting over the fact her brother's name is Justice.

I've blocked her, I thought. *But she can probably hear you.*

Hope frowned. Archer raised his eyebrows and smiled at her. *Then if she knows Charlotte, and she knows about Lucas's plan, she'd probably know how he intends to execute it.*

Ryan sighed, looking between us. The silent talking was getting to him, but I wasn't about to force him to hear me. Being able to talk to someone in your head wasn't all it was cracked up to be.

"You know they're talking to each other?" Justice asked Ryan.

"Yeah, they do it all the time," he said.

"Not only are you fallen, but you've shared your secrets with a human?" Hope asked.

"Hey, don't judge me. You don't know what I've been through," I said.

Michael had told me if I needed him, to call. I didn't think he'd meant by phone. I glanced around, searching the shadows.

Now would be a really good time to show yourself, I thought.

"Okay, we aren't getting anywhere here," Archer said. "Can we walk towards the war memorial and maybe discuss this along the way?"

"No," Hope said. "We're not going anywhere until we find out what you're doing here."

"You can trust them." The voice came from behind me, and I'd have known it anywhere. If we'd been in Heaven, it would've followed exploding cloud dust. I turned around and stared into Michael's chocolate eyes.

"Hey, Grace," he said.

I smiled so wide my cheeks ached. I never thought I'd be so glad to see an angel who was technically my enemy.

18

JOSH

Charlotte stood on the steps of the terrace and turned her face into the night breeze. She stilled. Every muscle in her body went rigid. I did the same and attempted to tap into whatever it was she was looking for.

Lilith growled beside me, her gaze following a couple walking down the other side of the street. My nostrils flared and I clenched my fists. I hadn't fed for twenty-four hours, and as much as I hated feeding, my body screamed for it. I blocked the urge and concentrated on the faint scent of summer rain that lingered in the air.

"Do you think you can control your urges for one night?" Charlotte asked.

"I'm a vampire. I can't control anything," Lilith said.

"I'm a vampire, and I can."

"Lilith, we'll feed later," I said. "Can we concentrate on following Grace and the others?"

"This way." Charlotte stepped onto the footpath and headed towards the iron bridge in the distance.

Every human we walked past made Lilith's mouth water. I told her to keep thinking about what Wide Island would be like if the entire vampire population could walk around during the day. If her theory were correct, there would be no one left to salivate over in the first place.

There were a lot of people on the streets, making the most of the Saturday nightlife. I wondered how many of them wouldn't make it home tonight. Guilt filled my stomach with lead because it was the vampires—like me—who would stop some of them from going home to their loved ones. No matter what night it was, there was always someone who died in Wide Island. Only the ones who were found made the news.

We walked for a while until Charlotte stopped at the bottom of a set of stone steps. They led into a park, the walkway lined with lampposts that created shadows amongst the trees.

"I can't smell any of them," I said. "There's too much fresh blood around."

Lilith looked as if she were about to explode, and I admired her restraint. She'd never held out this long before. Usually she took what she wanted when the urge struck her.

"I've still got Ryan's trail." Charlotte climbed the steps. "Stay close. If we find them I'm not sure how Grace will react."

"What do you mean? I thought she was in love with me."

"She is, but I'm not her favourite person at the moment,

and we are consorting with a vampire."

Lilith snorted. "I'm *really* looking forward to meeting this girl."

All sorts of people milled around the park, from those crossing through to wherever they were going, to those who were homeless and had settled in for the night.

Charlotte led us past a huge, Greek god-inspired fountain, and into another tree-lined walkway. Cars sped past at the far end, the noise falling away into the trees, unable to penetrate the relative silence of the park. She stopped about half way from the fountain to the road, and cocked her head to one side.

"Something happened here." Charlotte turned in a slow circle. "They came through this way, but I'm not sure where they went."

"Have you lost the trail?" I asked.

Charlotte sniffed the air. "No, I don't think so."

Lilith scoffed, hands on her hips. "I can't smell any-thing other than dinner every time it walks past."

A guy ambled down the path. As he got closer he smiled at Lilith. She sneered and the smile fell from his face. He quickened his pace and didn't look back.

Charlotte sighed. "Hunters have been here, along with another angel."

"How can you tell?" I asked.

"Because I know the hunters of Wide Island. Trust me, they've been here." She walked a few steps and toed something on the ground. "See? Fresh ash."

I'd never get used to knowing that the little piles of dust we came across on a regular basis had once been people—or vampires. Some of them you could hardly regard as people.

"What now?" Lilith planted her hands on her hips. She was really putting out the attitude poses tonight.

Charlotte shrugged. "I don't know. Maybe we need to try and work out the reason Grace is here. We know she's looking for Josh because she called him, and she's been to the terrace, but we don't know *why* she's looking for him."

"It better not be to tell you she loves you." Lilith scowled. "If it is, I'll ..."

I stared at the girl who was all I'd known since she'd found me. Lilith may have been a vampire, but she was the one who had saved me. She could have left me where I was. Sure, I probably would have found my own way eventually, but as much as I hated the way we were, and what we had to do to survive, she was still my Lilith.

Slowly, I walked over to her and she turned her face away.

"Don't." I put my finger under her chin and made her look at me. "I don't remember this girl. How could I feel anything for her?"

"What if you do remember? What then?" Lilith wrapped her arms around herself.

"I won't let my past affect my future."

Lilith pressed her lips to mine and I pulled her close. I hoped what I'd told her was the truth. If Grace had never said she loved me after I'd apparently bared my soul to her, then she wasn't worth worrying about. I needed to worry about the present, and what I had right in front of me.

Charlotte cleared her throat, but we ignored her. It felt

139

like an eternity since Lilith had kissed me so passionately. It made me feel alive, even though I wasn't.

Light penetrated the darkness, and something whooshed past my ear. Before I had time to register what it was, and heed Charlotte's cry of "run," Lilith and I were weightless, flying through the air. With my arms wrapped tightly around her waist, we landed heavily on a park bench, splitting it in half and sending a loud crack through the park. I copped most of the brunt as Lilith came down on top of me, and I screamed in pain when a piece of wood pierced my left shoulder. Its tip poked through the skin next to my collarbone.

Lilith's eyes widened and she stared at the bloodied piece of wood sticking out of me.

"Missed my heart," I said, grimacing.

Lilith scrambled off me and helped me sit up. Blood stained the ends of her fingers when she touched the piece of wood. She went to stand but I grabbed her arm, mouthing *angels*. Lilith's eyes sparked with understanding and she held still.

"You have to pull this out of me." I pointed to the piece of wood. "I can't reach it."

"It's going to hurt," she said.

"Do it." I couldn't walk around like a shish kebab.

Lilith searched my face. "Ready?" She wrapped her hand around the section sticking out of my back.

I nodded and clenched my teeth.

White-hot pain seared through my shoulder as the wood ripped out of my flesh. It may not have been a death blow, but having something inside me that would have killed me if it landed in the right place didn't tickle.

140

Lilith pressed her hand to the hole in my back. "It should close over pretty quickly, but the less blood you lose the better." She glanced over her shoulder before staring back at me. "Angels," she whispered.

"We need to help Charlotte." I looked into Lilith's wild eyes. "We get up slowly, okay?"

Lilith wasn't used to being the one who was down. Without a word she nodded, then kissed me quickly before helping me to my feet. The pain shot from my shoulder and spread down my side in a steady pulse.

An angel I'd never seen before had Charlotte in a vice grip, and a wicked smile split her face. It looked out of place on someone who was supposed to represent the epitome of goodness, although maybe she saved her nice face for nice people. I'm pretty sure Lilith and I didn't fall into that category. Two more angels I'd had the unfortunate pleasure of meeting before flanked us.

"Are you love birds finished?"

I scowled. The angel who had mocked us was Zachary. We'd shared a couple of battles since I'd made a home in Wide Island, and his presence was beginning to feel like an eyelash sticking into my eye, very annoying. Charlotte grimaced as the angel holding her tightened her grip.

The hunters and angels always seemed to know our next move. If Charlotte was right and angels could read minds, then it explained a lot of things, but it also meant our only option was to face them.

Running would get us killed.

I turned my body towards Lilith, ready to protect her, and I wondered if it came down to it, whether she'd protect me as well. Would she die for me? I couldn't say yes for certain, but I hoped so.

"Hello Zachary," I said.

He flicked his head and his jet-coloured hair framed his perfect face.

Lilith stiffened beside me.

To anyone else Zachary would have looked normal in his faded and ripped Levis and white button-up shirt. Light or white clothing seemed to be their uniform, which made us a cliché when it came to good versus evil, since Lilith and I were dressed entirely in black. Charlotte also wore black, but I don't think it was because she wanted to fit with a particular side. She didn't seem to fit anywhere.

"It's nice to see you and Lilith haven't lost your chemistry." The other angel smirked, and laughter danced behind her jade-green eyes.

I'd first met Harmony when she'd tried to drive a stake through my heart not long after Lilith found me. She was a pretty thing, petite, with short spiky brown hair, a spray of freckles across her nose and that perfect angelic skin. I wanted nothing more than to rip the smirk right off her face.

"Now, Josh, that's not nice, is it?" Zachary said. His misty, grey eyes bore into me. He was all grunt and muscle, and made the girls look inadequate. I wasn't fooled, though; they could all pack just as much punch.

"I really hate it when you do that. Don't you have a privacy policy or something?" I said.

All three of them chuckled and it made my skin crawl.

I glanced around the park and weighed up our options. Three against three were good odds, but we were already at a disadvantage since the new girl wasn't letting go of

Charlotte any time soon. The angel had a small, blue ball of light on her fingertip, and she held it to Charlotte's cheek as if it were a knife.

Vampires are fast, but I hated to admit that angels were faster, what with the orbing thingy they could do. The way I saw it was we could run and potentially die, or we could fight and still potentially die.

I was always up for a good fight.

Inching closer to Lilith, I put my hand on the small of her back, and locked my gaze on the angel who held my creator at her mercy.

She was dressed differently to the others. My first thought was, *she's going to fight wearing that?* White linen was not practical. My second thought was a little less coherent. Her pale denim eyes drew me in, and her silky golden hair framed her perfectly proportioned face. Okay, she was the enemy, but I was still a man.

"Josh, how nice to see you," she said.

"Who are you?"

"I'm surprised you don't remember me." The angel smirked.

Lilith snorted under her breath. "Apparently you have met her."

I pinched her side and she flinched.

"Why is it that everyone knows who I am but me?" I was really getting tired of the entire situation.

"Amnesia." Lilith pulled away from me slightly.

"Really? That *is* convenient," the angel said.

"Exactly what I thought."

"Lilith, shut up," I said.

"I'm Angelica, and I can help you remember, Josh,

but somehow I don't think you'll like what you see."

I stared at the beautiful angel. "Show me? My past?"

"Don't believe her," Charlotte said. "She's the one who took your memory."

Angelica tightened her grip on Charlotte. She gritted her teeth, thrashing around in an attempt to free herself.

"Stay out of this," Angelica said.

"She might not show you the truth."

"I'll take my cha—"

Before I could finish, a sharp searing pain rushed through the side of my head and I doubled over. Lilith lurched as I pulled her with me, and she tried to steady us both. For a moment I couldn't see anything. Then all I could see was the face of my past. The face of someone who apparently loved me, but had never told me.

Grace.

She was pale and beautiful, with perfect sapphire eyes. Her short, wavy black hair framed her delicate features. Grace was heavenly, with a radiant smile. The photo in my back pocket did not do her justice.

The vision of Grace made the throbbing pain in my temples all worth it. Her smile filled me with happiness, which was something I didn't even realise I'd been missing, but through it all I remembered I didn't know this girl, not really. I couldn't remember anything about her. She was nothing but a beautiful image in my mind. There was nothing else inside me to connect us.

I fell to my knees, and Angelica assaulted me with another image, this one even more painful than the last. I grabbed my hair, twisting my fingers into the strands and yanking in an attempt to rip the memories out of my head.

"What are you doing to him?" Lilith shouted. She put her hands on my shoulders.

A series of images flashed through my mind. People I didn't remember. Charlotte was in the mix, and then the vision stopped and I saw only one person. I stared into my own eyes.

My chest tightened, the feeling of suffocation engulfing me, even though I couldn't die from asphyxiation. A scream ripped from my mouth and I dropped to the ground. My cheek hit the grass and a twig poked into my skin, breaking the surface, but the pain was nothing compared to what I felt in my mind. It was as if someone had poked the back of my eyes with burning sticks. All I could see was me, my face when I was human, my bronzed skin and blue eyes—eyes that reflected happiness.

The images flashed again, only this time every picture was of Grace and me. Together, we looked so happy, and it tore my lifeless heart to shreds. My chest ached for a girl I couldn't remember. I squeezed my eyes closed and tried to wipe the vision of Grace away, but it was no use. Open or closed, they saw the same painful picture.

Angelica laughed, and it stirred a hatred inside of me stronger than I'd ever felt before.

She laughed again. "No, Josh, there is someone you hate more than me."

At that moment, I doubted it.

"Why are you doing this to him?" Charlotte said. "You have me; leave him out of it. He never did anything to you."

"You sealed his fate when you made him like you," Angelica said. "Now you both have to die, but not before I have a little fun."

I didn't need to open my eyes to know Charlotte struggled in Angelica's grip.

"You have no idea what the word *goodness* means, do you?" Charlotte said.

Lilith tried to pull me off the ground, but I resisted her. Angelica held my mind captive with images of Grace, and movement made the pain more intense.

Then as quickly as the visions had been planted in my head, they were gone.

Air I didn't need rushed in and out of my lungs. Slowly, I got to my knees and raised my head, staring at the angel who I hated with every inch of my body.

"Like I said, Josh, there is someone else you hate more than me," Angelica said.

"Then it's a good thing I can't remember them, isn't it?"

I brushed the hair from my eyes and the dirt from my cheek, standing to face Angelica. Zachary and Harmony shifted position, moving closer with their fists clenched. It took all my self-control not to lunge at them and rip their throats out. It couldn't be done anyway. It didn't seem fair, really. Kill a vampire with a stake through the heart, or fire, or beheading, but an angel? We were yet to work out how to kill them. They had to have a weakness, but if they did they never showed it.

I wanted to fight them, but Angelica had Charlotte, and any move I made surely meant her loss. I'd seen angels disappear with people before. I didn't want Angelica taking Charlotte away from me.

"Why did you show me those things?" I asked, gritting my teeth. "Are they even real? They've told me nothing."

"They showed you what your life used to be like. You

can trust Grace. And more importantly, she trusts you." Angelica smiled. "The rest you'll remember when I let you, but first you have to do something for me."

"He'll never help you," Lilith said.

"If he wants Charlotte back, he's going to have to."

Charlotte struggled again but to no avail. Angelica ran her finger down Charlotte's cheek, and the little ball of light cut into her skin, drawing blood.

Charlotte screamed and her eyes rolled back in her head.

"What are you doing to her?" I stepped forward.

"Celestial fire has a better effect on vampires than real fire." Angelica pushed Charlotte to the ground and pulled her arms behind her back, binding them with a thin tendril of blue light. "Especially when the vampire is half angel."

Harmony stared at me. "You don't look surprised."

"She already told me."

"Now!" Angelica clapped her hands. Zachary pulled Charlotte to her feet and manhandled her so she stood behind Angelica. "This is what's going to happen. I'm taking Charlotte—"

"Over my dead body." I clenched my fists and growled. My fangs extended, and my gums ached.

"That won't achieve anything, Josh. You'll be dead, and you'll never know the truth. Don't you want to know why you're not with Grace anymore?"

I didn't know what I wanted.

"Even if I help you, you'll never let me live."

"What if I said I would?" Angelica asked.

"Don't, Josh." Charlotte's voice was weak, but I heard her.

147

"Grace has something of mine," Angelica said, ignoring Charlotte's plea. "And I have something of hers."

"So why don't you go and get it, and leave us out of it," I said.

"Because I think you can be more persuasive. Consider Charlotte your bond. You'll get her back when I get what I want."

"And what is that?" Lilith stepped forward, baring her fangs as well.

"That doesn't matter. All you have to do is give Grace a message for me. Tell her I have Charlotte, and if I don't get what I want, she'll die." Angelica smirked.

"Why would Grace care what happens to Charlotte?" Lilith asked.

"Because Charlotte is what got Grace into trouble in the first place. Her … and you." Angelica stared at me.

I wanted to ask what that meant, but I had a feeling I wouldn't get a straight answer. "We don't know where Grace is," I said.

"Then you'd better find out." Zachary tightened his grip on Charlotte and she whimpered. "She's already been through here. You'll run into each other at some point."

"How do we find you?" I asked Angelica.

"I'll find you when the time is right," she said.

"You can't take Charlotte." Lilith moved even closer to Angelica. She was braver than I was. The farther away I was from the psycho angel, the better. "We need her—"

"To save your own skin, yes, I know." Angelica regarded Lilith for a few moments. "I'm aware of the underground situation, Lilith. I know everything that's going on in this city."

Their gazes locked and Lilith lifted her chin, but she was the first to look away. There was no doubt Angelica had read her mind, which meant she knew more about what was going on than I did. It left an uneasy feeling in my stomach, but I had to try and trust Lilith. There was no one else.

The park filled with white light. It flashed out and the angels were gone.

"We are so dead," Lilith said.

I couldn't have agreed more.

19

GRACE

Early Sunday morning

Michael led us across the street and into the other side of the park. The trees lining the perimeter acted like a buffer, protecting the green oasis from most of the city noise. After passing through the hum of the traffic, the park was eerily quiet.

Archer hung back, grumbling under his breath at how much of a tool Michael was. Ryan walked next to me, his hands stuffed into the front pocket of his hoodie. Hope and Justice eyed me every now and then when they thought I wasn't looking.

"To what do we owe the pleasure, Michael?" Hope asked, her voice dripping with innuendo. I couldn't work out if it was sexual, or if she was proud she knew an archangel.

I knew him, too, and sometimes he wasn't that great.

"You don't come to the city very often," Justice said.

"Wait, you've come to the city before?" I asked, stopping. "You never came to Hopetown Valley."

Michael sighed but kept walking. "Yes I did, Grace. You just didn't know."

I quickened my pace to catch up with them. I wasn't about to let prissy little Hope mooch in on my archangel.

"When? And why didn't you tell me?"

Michael stopped and faced me. He stuffed his hands in the pockets of his jeans. "Because I was there for things that didn't concern you. Directly, anyway."

"What's that supposed to mean?" I asked.

"Why is everything to do with you angels so complicated?" Ryan shook his head and walked away a little. He stared at the war memorial. "We need a plan."

"You should listen to him." Michael broke eye contact with me and followed Ryan. "His head is in the game."

"And yours is up your arse," Archer said.

"Okay, stop." Hope put her hands on her hips. "Michael, why are you so friendly with a fallen angel? Grace, what the hell do you want? And Archer, what is with the smart mouth? The human is the most normal out of all of you."

Everyone started talking at once. Michael defended me, I mentioned Josh, and Archer grumbled something about how his attitude was fine. Ryan walked farther away.

"Wait, Josh who?" Justice asked.

"Joshua Chase. Tall, dark, handsome," I said. "Oh, and very much a vampire."

"Did he have a girlfriend called Charlotte by any chance?"

"She's not his girlfriend," Archer said.

Justice looked at Hope. "The ones we fought with

Angelica."

"Angelica!" I said. "Great, this is getting better and better."

Michael threw his hands in the air. "See? This is why I'm here."

"You mentioned Angelica when we saw you at the truck stop. What is she up to?" I asked. "So help me God, Michael, if you don't tell me I will—"

"What, Grace? What are you going to do to me? I have never done anything but help you. Everything I've ever done since you were created was to help you, even when you didn't want me to. You have to trust me. You have to trust that I can't tell you everything, or spell it out in black and white, because there is always someone watching. So, are you finished?"

Michael stared into my eyes. Anger flickered behind his, blue tendrils of heavenly fire pulsating behind his brown irises.

"I came here to find Josh, and somehow I'm being dragged into fighting a war that isn't mine," I said.

"Josh is at the centre of that war." Justice twirled his stake around his fingers. "I'd kill him myself, but something tells me I'd have you to answer to if I did."

"And this war became yours when you chose to take the fall for a vampire," Michael said.

"Charlotte is good!" I ran my hands through my hair.

"I know that, and you know that. But they—" Michael pointed to the sky "—do not believe it."

"Who the hell are you talking about?" Justice asked, clenching his jaw. "You fell for a vampire?"

"Don't you dare judge me," I said. "You don't know."

"That's right; you don't." Archer came to my side.

Michael took his hand from his pocket long enough to touch me on the arm. "After you left the last time you came to see Josh—"

"You knew about that?"

Of course he did. He knew everything. It was his job.

Michael pursed his lips and took a breath through his nose. "There was a battle at the terrace."

"We know. We saw the aftermath," Archer said.

Michael started walking towards the memorial again.

Justice shook his head. "I can't believe we're consorting with a fallen angel."

The next second, Justice's feet were off the ground and Michael held him around the throat. He'd orbed so quickly I'd almost missed it.

"If you want your city to survive, then you will do as I say, when I say." Michael's grip dug into the flesh on Justice's neck, making him gag. "Grace can be trusted. She is on your side, regardless of her status. Got it?"

Justice nodded as much as he could. Michael let go, and the hunter fell to the ground, gasping for air. He rubbed his throat and grimaced as he got to his feet, brushing the grass from his knees.

Michael resumed his path towards the war memorial and we followed. The night was relatively silent since it was past midnight.

I broke away from the group to get some space.

"Gracie, where are you going?" Archer asked.

I need some breathing room. I kept walking and didn't look at the others.

"Let her go," Michael said.

On my way across the open grassed area, I crossed paths with a homeless guy pushing his shopping trolley through the park. He stared at me with glazed eyes.

"You've lost your light," he said.

Apparently I needed to search for it in the darkest of places. His comment distracted me, and I was busy trying to figure out what he'd meant when someone spoke.

"Hi there," a vamp said from the shadows. "Looking for a good time tonight?"

I really needed to stay focused. I should have sensed him before he'd said anything.

"I'm always looking for a good time."

The vamp sauntered towards me, turning on his charm. It had no effect. I punched him in the face, breaking his grin, and then waited for him to get back on his feet.

My king hit had sent him sprawling, and he lay on his back in the shadow of a huge fig. His tight T-shirt accented the ripples of his muscular chest, and I cursed the fact that most vampires were good eye candy. Sometimes it was a shame to have to dust them. Angels were great to look at, too, but most of the ones I knew were either not on my side, or not very happy with me. This vamp had strong, brooding features, and dark spiky hair. My guess was he used an entire pot of hair gel, and spent at least an hour in front of the mirror to perfect his look.

Archer came over and leant against a tree, arms folded, with a smirk on his face. Once on his feet, the vamp took one more look at me and turned to run.

"Whoa, not so fast, fang boy." Archer lunged and grabbed him, pushing him in my direction. Since he was a bit taller than me, I jumped and threw my arm out, clotheslining him, putting him flat on his back again. Then I sat on him. He struggled beneath me and I pinned his shoulders to the ground, kneeling on his arms.

"You're new. Where's Hope?" He stared up at me.

"Something tells me you're not in the best position to be asking questions," Archer said.

I raised my eyebrows, stared down at the incredibly handsome vampire, and smiled. He struggled again, but I pushed harder on his shoulders and he stopped.

"You're strong for someone so tiny," he said.

"This is nothing," I said. "You should see me on a good day. Now tell me: Joshua Chase, do you know him?" The vamp stared at me with a vacant expression, and after I tried to listen in on his thoughts I came up with nothing. "What about Lucas? What can you tell me about him?"

The vampire's face darkened and he squirmed beneath me. "Lucas owns this city. You don't want to cross him."

Now we were getting somewhere.

"We can tell you about Lucas," Justice said. He stood off to the side with Hope next to him.

"Oh, hey guys," the vamp said. "Don't suppose you could help me?"

"Nope," Hope said.

I glanced over my shoulder to see Ryan and Michael standing where I'd left them.

"You really shouldn't play with them so much," Archer said. "Put him out of his misery."

"All right then." I released one of the vamp's arms and reached behind my back to pull a stake from my belt.

"Hey! What are you going to do with that?" The vamp tried to snatch the stake from my grasp.

"Um, I'm thinking I'll stake you with it."

"Won't you at least let me plead my case?"

"What case?" Archer scoffed. "You're a vampire."

"Would you believe me if I told you I was nice?" he asked. "And I'll tell you everything you want to know."

"No." I brought the stake down into his chest. My butt hit the ground and sent dust pluming into the air. I waved it away with my hand and coughed as I got to my feet.

Are you finished? Michael asked in my mind.

Hey, a dead vampire is a good one. Just doing my job.

We headed back towards Michael and Ryan. Michael walked to the end of the Pool of Reflection, and I stood at his side, knowing he had something to say. The others stayed silent, watching the city lights dance across the glassy surface of the pool.

"Angelica wants Charlotte," Michael said. "She still won't let what happened in Hopetown Valley rest."

"I knew she wouldn't," I said. "She's demented."

"She's only doing what she's told. Unlike some."

"Don't throw that in my face," I said.

"Grace, I agree with what you did, remember? She came to me afterwards, asking what she should do. She also wants Annie back, and on that part I have to agree with her."

"She can have her. All she has to do is ask."

"Again, not that simple." Michael sighed. "She needs to get Seth to unlock Annie."

"That shouldn't be too hard. She took Seth," I said, my voice so low I wasn't sure he heard.

Michael reached over and took my hand. "I know. And everything is way more complicated than it should be."

"I still haven't forgiven you."

"You will." Michael turned to look at me. "Angelica has taken Josh's memory."

"What? Why?"

"To hurt you. To take away from you the one thing she has always wanted. Love."

I didn't understand. Every single angel in Heaven loved Angelica. It was like a prerequisite for being an angel. Love was what angels were all about.

"Why does she hate me so much?"

"I think Seth has something to do with that," Michael said.

Was he serious? What did he have to do with it? Angelica and Seth had never seen eye-to-eye, even before his fall.

"She's jealous?" I asked. Michael raised his eyebrows and I groaned. "You have got to be kidding me."

"She has watched him follow you from the very beginning, and when the opportunity came for someone to go to earth to right a wrong that a particular angel refused to, she jumped at the chance."

"She's doing all of this because she's jealous?" I couldn't believe it.

"If it's any consolation, she's got nothing on you." Michael turned to face me and his smile warmed my heart. "You're pretty much perfect. I get what Seth sees in you."

"You forget that I'm fallen."

"For a good reason."

Being an angel didn't make me completely perfect, especially since I'd spent so much time on earth. Falling in love was one of the things that had gotten me into trouble in the first place. That, and my loyalty to people I'd thought were my friends. I had my beliefs, and I stuck to them. But it seemed I wasn't the only angel who wanted happiness with someone else. The thought of Angelica and Seth together made me want to laugh hysterically. He would never love Angelica that way. He'd barely tolerated her when we were in Heaven.

I'd learned a lot of things the hard way, and I couldn't wait for Angelica to learn them the hard way, too.

"Are any of you angels actually good?" Archer asked. "Or do you all go around doing whatever the hell you like for your own selfish reasons?"

"Just because we're angels doesn't mean we can't have a bit of fun," Michael said.

"Yeah, this is a real party." Archer rolled his eyes.

Justice grabbed my arm. "Um, hey—"

"So much fun, in fact," Archer said, "that I can't wait to see what happens in the next episode of—"

"Archer! Would you stop and look around."

I pulled free of Justice's grip and followed his line of sight. Ryan stood on the grass to the left of the Pool of Reflection, away from the rest of our small group. The trees cast his face half in shadow. Hope was in front of him. A vampire launched at her and she staked it in the chest. The ash fell at her feet. Ryan slowly backed towards us until he stood next to Justice. I'd given Michael my undivided attention, but I should have known that where there was one vampire, there were usually many more.

Archer was right: I was lost in my own dramas for my own selfish reasons.

Vampires surrounded us.

"Great hunters we are," I said, scolding myself as well as the others. "Where did they come from?"

"We're on top of the biggest vampire lair in Wide Island." Justice pulled two stakes from his belt. "It was only a matter of time before they showed up. But this is nothing we can't handle."

There were more than thirty vamps closing in on us, and probably a lot more on their way. Archer and I could take five between us easily, but even at that ratio our group was outnumbered. Still, it would be good to get some dust on my boots.

"I guess we're fighting." Archer pulled out his own stake.

"Ryan," I said.

"I know, Grace. Stay out of trouble."

I looked at Michael. "You ready to get your hands dirty?"

"Sorry, Grace. This is all you. I'll be back when you need me later."

My mouth hung open, but there was no time to protest. Michael orbed before I could give him a mouthful. He was going to cop it big time when I saw him next.

Justice ran towards the wall of vampires lined up on the war memorial steps. The vamps filed down the stairs and onto the grass. Hope, Archer, and I followed Justice's example, and in a few minutes we'd downed one vamp apiece. Ryan got into the fray as well. He kept behind us and finished off anyone we didn't dust on the first attempt. I admired his bravery—but so much for staying out of trouble. From the moment he'd found out about my world, I knew he'd be able to handle it.

"Grace, duck," Archer yelled. His stake flew over my head and impaled a vamp in the chest. The creature fell backwards over the Pool of Reflection, but exploded into a cloud of dust before he hit the water.

I sprang back to my full height and fought hand to hand with a blonde vampire chick. She was pretty scary in the looks department, all mean and tough. Good thing I didn't scare easily. I floored her with a low kick and she landed on her back. She opened her mouth, but I didn't give her the chance to speak before I put my stake in her chest. I wouldn't lose any sleep over wondering what she'd had to say.

Hope orbed past me and took out another vamp headed my way. With our combined efforts we'd reduced the field to half in less than five minutes.

"Bravo!" A voice carried over the pool from the war memorial steps. "You lot put on a pretty good show."

The vamps that were left fell back and disappeared into the shadows.

Archer came to my side. "Who's he?"

"That's Lucas," Hope said. "He doesn't come out in the open much. This must be a special occasion."

Lucas made it to the bottom of the steps before he stopped clapping. He stood at the head of the pool as if he had all the time in the world. Technically he did, since he was immortal, but I was hoping to end that pretty soon.

I walked towards Lucas and the few vampires who had assembled behind him. He locked his gaze on mine, and a smile crept slowly onto his face.

"Ah, new hunters," he said. "To what do we owe the pleasure?"

"Just passing by," Archer said. "Thought we'd dust a few vamps along the way."

"They're the ones I told you about," a vampire said from behind Lucas.

I knew the voice, and before I could place it, Cain stepped out and stood next to his leader.

"Hello Cain," I said. "I was wondering how you've been."

He scowled. "You ruined everything, and I'm going to make you pay."

"Seriously, is this guy for real?" Archer said. "If I remember correctly, we wiped out about twenty of your mates last time we met. And now we've downed about twenty more. What makes you think that's going to change?"

Lucas stepped forward. "You don't want to fight me."

"Actually, I do." I tightened my grip on the stake in my hand.

Arch, Hope; keep the other vermin off me.

When I hit Lucas, the other hunters scattered in all directions. I couldn't be sure if they killed any of the remaining vamps, but the sounds of hand-to-hand combat surrounded me.

Lucas was stronger than I'd expected, and he hit me like a battering ram. I hadn't met a vampire I couldn't overpower, yet he gained the upper hand, grabbing my shoulders and hurling me up the sandstone steps. I landed with a heavy thud, and something cracked. The edge of a step cut into my side, and when I tried to move it felt like someone had dropped a lump of concrete on my ribs. It made it hard to breathe.

"I'm not going to let you ruin everything," Lucas said.

Justice took a swing at Lucas's back, a stake firmly

in his grip, but he missed his mark, stabbing Lucas in the shoulder instead.

Justice crashed to the ground with Cain on top of him. Lucas fell to his knees in agony, screaming for his troops to fall back. Cain grabbed his leader and hauled him to his feet. They disappeared from sight and I wondered why no one was chasing them.

I pushed myself up on my elbows, grimacing through the pain in my ribs. "You won't win. We won't stop until you're dead."

Then I looked at my friends.

Ryan lay sprawled on the ground, one leg dangling into the pool. Archer was by his side, blood dripping from a cut over his eye. Justice was still beside me, and Hope pressed her hands to his chest, and the cuts and scrapes on his arms and face disappeared as her light flowed into him.

Hope came to my side and I pushed her away. "Ryan and Archer." She tended to the boys while I got to my feet. We stood in a tight circle at the bottom of the steps, surrounded by bloodstains and piles of ash.

"Lucas is waiting for Josh and Charlotte to show up," I said.

"Yeah, I got that much from him, too," Hope said.

"What now?" Ryan rubbed the back of his head and winced.

I laughed, but the sound was empty and humourless. "Now we fight a war I didn't want to fight. But we need rest, first. You guys copped a hiding."

"I'll be fine," Ryan said, but he couldn't hide the pain behind his eyes.

Lightning flashed and lit up the sky in the distance. More rain clouds rolled in. I led the way along the path beside the pool.

"We can orb and mist back to the terrace once we reach the shadows," I said.

"Can't we go now?" Archer asked.

"Shadows are best," Hope said.

"But there's no one to see us."

"Walk, Arch." I grabbed his arm.

When we neared the exit to Dhye Park, my skin prickled and I stopped. The last time I'd felt that way, Josh and I were … no, I didn't want to remember, but I could sense him. I spun around and searched the shadows, the feeling getting stronger the more steps I took towards the street.

Then I saw him, and everything else fell away.

My feet took on a mind of their own, and I ran towards the one person I'd been waiting to see since Mr Chase had dropped the bundle of flyers at my feet.

Josh was alive, and I'd found him.

20

JOSH

Lilith wrung her hands and searched the darkness amongst the trees. I'd seen her more nervous in the past twenty-four hours than I'd ever seen her before.

"What do we do now?" she asked. "If Charlotte doesn't get to Lucas, we're dead."

"We're as good as dead anyway."

I picked up the faint scent trail of the human we'd been following before Angelica so rudely interrupted us, but without Charlotte I couldn't get a hold on Grace, or the hunters. They had a knack for being able to go around undetected, and I wondered how Charlotte had been able to smell them in the first place.

"Why do you think Angelica wants this Grace girl?" Lilith asked.

"Beats me. I can't remember anything to do with either of them. She said Grace has something she wants."

"Well, now Angelica has something we want."

"I think we should go and tell Lucas what's happened," I said.

Lilith stared at me, her mouth gaping. "You do have a death wish."

"Like I said, already dead."

"We can't turn up without Charlotte."

"Do you have a better idea?" I asked.

"No." Lilith pouted. She pressed herself against me and ran a long finger up my chest. "But I can think of other things we can do."

I sighed and pushed her off me. "Now is not the time."

"Let's go and feed then. I'm starving." Lilith licked her lips.

A couple of cars buzzed along the quiet street as we emerged onto the footpath to cross into the other side of the park. The hour was late, and I didn't like our chances of finding someone to eat. We'd have to hope someone was passing through.

When we reached the top of the steps we fell back into the shadows, away from the light of the park's many lampposts. Lilith led me to the edge of the grass lawn that lay in front of the war memorial.

"What the hell happened here?" she asked.

The scene before us was nothing short of a massacre.

To a normal person nothing would look out of the ordinary, but to a vampire … we were looking at piles of our own dead.

A group headed in our direction, and I immediately recognised Wide Island's hunting, duo, Hope and Justice. I'd come across the hunters a few times. They were not the people to mess with in this city, so I'd made sure I stayed away as much as I could.

The girl at the head of the group caught my eye, and I moved from the edge of the shadows into the glow of the lamp. She turned towards us, and the sight of her face pierced my heart. I took a few steps forward, and Lilith grabbed my arm to hold me back, but I shook her free.

The girl on the grass ran towards me, closing the distance between us quicker than I could have. She disappeared for a second in a cloud of black mist, reappearing a few metres away. She stopped and stared.

I could have stared at her for an eternity.

Grace looked even more beautiful in real life. She was angelic. I had no words to describe her beauty.

And I couldn't remember anything about her.

She broke the spell and moved towards me again. Lilith launched past and tackled Grace to the ground before she could get any closer. A guttural growl tore from Lilith's throat.

"Don't touch him," Lilith said, as they rolled along the grass.

Grace came out on top and punched Lilith in the face. Her head snapped sideways and blood sprayed from her mouth.

"Who the hell are you?" Grace punched her again.

Lilith returned the blow, but she missed and caught Grace on the shoulder. "I'm his girlfriend."

Grace stopped and jumped up, letting Lilith go. She scrambled to her feet and the girls faced each other.

"What did you say?"

Lilith smirked. "That's right. I'm his girlfriend. You've

been replaced." She pulled up her sleeve. The limbs of the crossbow clicked into position, and the arrow automatically loaded. She aimed it at Grace.

Grace frowned and kicked Lilith in the gut. Lilith flew backwards and slammed into a tree before falling to the ground. She fired the crossbow, but Grace turned to mist and the arrow passed through her.

She came back behind me. "You're dating a vampire?"

Lilith growled again, and I stared at the girl who I had a more memorable history with than anyone else I knew.

"You shouldn't have done that." I turned to Grace. "Now you've made her mad."

Lilith was up and on Grace again, the two of them punching and kicking each other anywhere they could.

A guy ran across the grass, followed by Hope and Justice. "Josh!" He stared at me, his mouth hanging open.

Someone else who knew who I was. But I didn't know him.

Lilith cried out when Grace stomped on her leg, cracking the bone. Lilith fell to her knees and Grace wrapped her arm around her neck from behind. She held a stake over Lilith's heart.

I ran at the girls and grabbed the arm Grace had around Lilith's neck, freeing her and yanking Grace to the ground. She held onto me and we rolled, before stopping with her on top.

She smiled. "Hi, Josh."

"You try to kill my girlfriend and all you have to say is hi?"

She frowned and I immediately wanted to take my words back. How could I say something to make her look so sad?

What was I talking about? I didn't even know her.

"You do know me," she said. "Angelica took your memory."

"Because I knew you in my past doesn't change the fact I don't know you now."

"Josh." Grace said my name on the end of a long breath. As if it hurt for her to say it.

I squeezed her shoulders. Her palms lay flat on my chest, her touch spreading warmth into me. Feelings I never knew I could feel bubbled to the surface. Some of them were so unfamiliar I didn't have names for them.

Grace smiled.

And I smiled back.

"Oh my God, you are making me gag," Lilith said. She got up and rubbed the leg Grace had broken. The bone would have already healed.

I ignored her and went back to staring at Grace. Her lips were a rosy pink, and all I wanted to do was kiss them until they bled.

Grace cleared her throat. "Um … there are at least two people here who can hear every thought you're thinking. Me included."

"Would you get off the ground?" Lilith said.

"Hey, Grace has been waiting a long time for this. Let her have her moment," the guy I didn't know said.

Grace laughed and it sounded like music drifting on a light breeze. "You're not going to kiss me then?"

"I don't know you," I said. "I think I should get to know you first."

She leant down and pressed her lips to mine in a chaste kiss. Lilith had never kissed me like that, and it was better than any kiss I could remember.

"I know you," Grace said. "So I think it's okay."

She rolled off me and pulled me to my feet. Her strength surprised me, for someone so small. When she let go of my hand, reality came crashing down around me. It was as if she took the happiness away with her touch. I wanted to touch her again to see if the feeling would come back. Without her hand in mine, all I felt was emptiness.

I looked at Lilith, and reality slapped me again. How could I kiss another girl in front of her?

The smile fell from Grace's face. "Josh?" She took a step towards me.

"No. Don't touch me." *Even though I want it so badly.*

"What's wrong?"

I clenched my fists in an attempt not to lose my temper, but it was no use.

"I don't know you!"

Grace flinched. "You do, Josh … Try to remember."

"I can't, okay?" I ran a hand through my hair and grabbed a chunk of it in my fist. "She took everything. I don't remember you. I don't love you. So you need to go."

"That's not true. I know it's not. You can ask Archer and Ryan. They all know you love me."

"What does it matter?" I walked right up to Grace and towered over her, our noses only centimetres apart. "You never told me you loved me back."

A tear slipped down Grace's cheek, but she didn't deny what I'd said.

"Please," she said. "Fight it. Try to remember."

"I have!" I yelled in her face.

"You need to fight harder."

Apart from what I'd been told, and what Angelica had planted in my head, I knew nothing about my history with Grace. Something bad must have happened between us, or we'd be together and not standing in a park arguing. Did I want to remember? Did I want to put myself through pain unnecessarily?

Like all my memories, Grace stood beyond my reach.

"Why should I fight? Give me one good reason," I said.

Grace faltered. Her mouth opened, but no words came out and she closed it again.

"See?" I said. "You can't even tell me if we have anything worth saving. How can I fight for you when I don't know what I'm fighting for?"

21

GRACE

Josh and I stared at each other while everyone else stared at us. I wanted them all to go away so we could talk alone. With so much negative energy bouncing around it was hard to find the happy in amongst the pain.

Hope and Justice were strung out, studying the movement of every shadow. Ryan sat on the grass, leaning against a tree. He needed rest badly. And Archer was like the ever-faithful puppy, not far from my side. It was nice some things hadn't changed. At least I could rely on him to always be who he was.

The vampire chick launched at me for the second time. I heard her coming, but I didn't have the emotional capacity to care. The others would never let her get the upper hand. I was surprised she tried to attack me with so many hunters around. She grabbed my shoulders and threw me to the ground. Archer ran and jumped, kicking her in the back, and she stumbled until she fell next to me.

I couldn't believe Josh was dating a vampire, especially one so stupidly jealous.

"Give me one good reason why I shouldn't put a stake in you right now," I said, getting to my feet.

"You touch her, and I'll hurt you," Josh said.

Archer laughed. "I'd like to see you try. You really have lost your memory."

"Why are you dating a vampire, Josh?" I got up, and dirt rained onto the ground as I dusted myself off. "You hate vampires."

"Or at least you did when you were human," Ryan said. He sat with his knees up, chin resting on them.

Josh ran a hand down his face. "Lilith has helped me. Leave her alone."

The only way I'd be leaving her alone was if she became a vegetarian. I couldn't see that happening any time soon. The only vamps I knew who didn't eat people were Charlotte and Josh. Even Josh's eating habits had become questionable. If he'd lost his memory, he could also have forgotten he didn't eat humans.

"I don't like her." I stared at Lilith, who had taken up a position beside Josh.

"You don't have to like her," Josh said. "It's not up to you who I date. I don't even know you. I don't know any of you. Well, except for Hope and Justice, but it's not like we're friends or anything."

"Well, I know *you*," I said. "And you would never be with someone like her."

"What? I'd be with someone like you?" Josh pulled a piece of paper from his back pocket and unfolded it. "You even admitted you couldn't say it back." He thrust the photo in my face. Then he tore it in half and let it flutter to the ground. "Something was wrong then, and I think it's still wrong now."

My cheeks flamed, and I looked away. What could I say to convince him, when I couldn't convince myself?

"This is getting us nowhere," Archer said. "We've found him, Gracie. Now what?"

Everyone looked at me.

I shifted my weight from one foot to the other and fidgeted with the hem of my top. "We take him home."

Josh turned his back on me and walked away. "I'm not going anywhere with you."

"Don't you want to know why I came looking for you?" I said.

Lilith stopped and faced me. "That would be nice, actually. Since you don't really love him."

"What?" I glared at her. "I—"

"No, you don't. If you did, you would have told him by now." She smirked. "You had the opportunity right before the 'I don't know what I'm fighting for' speech."

Being able to read minds was hard. You'd think I'd be able to find out everything I needed to know by looking in everyone's heads, but it wasn't always that simple. I could only read immediate thoughts, not memories, and right then Lilith was focused on two things: hating Lucas, and hating me. The hatred was so strong it overpowered everything else, and I couldn't see past its fog. I wondered what had happened to make her so bitter. Then again, I'd never met a happy vampire.

"Your dad is worried about you," I said, ignoring Lilith.

"He's got the police involved."

Josh doubled back towards us. His eyes darkened as his brow knitted together into a frown. "They won't find me."

"I know. But when he said you'd stopped calling, I had to come and see if you were okay."

Josh laughed, and the sound echoed around the empty park. Dawn wasn't far off, the city slept as much as a city could. Lilith looked around, her eyes darting to the horizon. She was nervous about the rising sun—as I would be if I were her.

Josh stopped and fixed his gaze on mine. "I am the furthest thing from okay that you could possibly get."

"Then let me help you," I said.

"The last person who tried to help got taken away."

Josh's thoughts filled with images of Charlotte.

"You've seen Charlotte?" I asked.

He frowned.

"Where is she?" Archer asked, too enthusiastically.

Lilith smirked, and I was getting sick of it. I had to stop myself from punching her.

"You won't find her," she said. "At least, not until Angelica wants you to."

Oh, crap.

"Angelica has Charlotte?" Archer asked.

"Yes, and she said to give you a message," Lilith said. "You have something she wants. If you don't give it to her, Charlotte is dead."

It seemed the battle against the vampire army was not the only war we were fighting. What I wouldn't give for Angelica to leave me, and everyone I knew, alone. She wanted Annie's ring. All she had to do was ask and I'd give it to her but Angelica, being the power-hungry bitch that she was, had to play dirty instead.

Josh grabbed Lilith's hand and pulled her away. She winked at me before taking the lead, and they disappeared into the trees.

I wanted to go after them, but all I took was one step before Archer grabbed my arm. "Let them go. We have other problems."

"Like psycho angels with hidden agendas," I said. Then something occurred to me and I turned to Hope. "If Charlotte is from here, and this is your city, why didn't you kill her?"

"She left." Hope shrugged. "Out of our jurisdiction."

She made it sound like something from a crime TV show.

"Come on. We need time for everyone to heal fully," I said. "There's no point following Josh. He won't listen to me right now."

"Grace has a point," Hope said. "Some of us need sleep. The vamps won't be out again until dark, so we should be safe."

I snorted and shook my head. "You have no idea what you're up against, do you?"

"I'm up against this sort of thing every day." Hope put her hands on her hips. "They will still be there tonight. And now they can't get Charlotte because Angelica has her, so no blood, no army of sun-walking vamps."

"Should you tell her, or should I?" Archer asked.

I put my hands on my hips, too. "Charlotte is Josh's creator."

"Ah, damn." Archer slapped his leg. "I wanted to tell her."

It took a moment for realisation to dawn on Hope and Justice's faces, and when it did their expressions went from shocked to angry in a few seconds.

"His blood is the same as hers?" Justice asked.

Archer clapped him on the shoulder. "As far as we know, Josh can walk around in the sun."

"Crap." Justice pinched the bridge of his nose. "Does Lucas know?"

"Let's hope the answer to that is no," I said.

Justice rubbed his face. "This keeps getting worse with every passing minute."

I couldn't have agreed more.

22

JOSH

L ilith led me through the train station and into the subway tunnel. We managed to avoid sunrise by about ten minutes. We'd never cut it that fine before, and it was the first time we hadn't made it back to the terrace to wait out the day.

In a way I was glad not to be sitting in my wing chair with hours of waiting ahead of me, but I was also nervous about being away from the safety of the terrace while the sun was up.

Lilith stopped in the doorway that went into the cavity behind the tunnel.

"I don't think we should go back in there," I said.

"We have to fight Lucas."

"Why?" I stared at Lilith. "Let's get out of here. We can leave the city and never look back."

I wasn't sure if I believed the words that came out of

my mouth. A beautiful girl stood in front of me, one who had been there for me when no one else had, and all I could think about was Grace. If I ran away with Lilith, would I ever stop thinking about the fallen angel from my past? I didn't remember her, and I hated it, but I also didn't know if I wanted to remember.

"If we run, he will hunt us down … He'll never stop," Lilith said.

"We can't attack them ourselves. We need Charlotte."

Lilith hesitated. She didn't usually hesitate. "We'll think of something."

Lilith disappeared into the wall and I had no option but to follow. This time, I paid more attention to where we were going. I pushed Grace out of my mind and focused on Lilith in front of me, because I wanted to be able to get out again if I had to. The rock walls were cold beneath my fingertips as I trailed my hands along them, cataloguing every turn we made until we reached the small stone room.

I stopped in the doorway, all sorts of thoughts racing through my head.

"What's wrong?" Lilith faced me, the light from the naked bulb dancing in her eyes.

"Can I trust you?" I searched her face for anything that would tell me no.

"Josh, baby. Of course." Lilith stroked my chest in the dim light.

I pushed her hand away. "I mean it. When the shit hits everything, can I trust you?"

Everyone had been telling me for the past few days that I had to trust them. Well, now was the time I really needed to know.

"I will do whatever it takes to get my city back," Lilith said. "They're my vamps in that lair, not Lucas's. I created him; I should be leading him. Not the other way around."

"But will you have my back?"

"Will you have mine?" she asked. "If it's anyone who should be sceptical, it's me. You're the one with the hunter for an ex."

"I guess we'll have to agree to disagree," I said.

Lilith pressed her foot to the stone on the floor and the door grinded as it slid open. We entered the passage that led to the platform overlooking the cavern. Lilith was about to walk onto the metal when I heard someone say her name. I grabbed her arm and held her back, pressing her against the wall. Footsteps clanged on the metal stairs.

"He told me he was going to kill her," Cain said.

"Who, Lucas? He wouldn't ... She made him."

"Doesn't matter ... She wants the city."

"How do you know?"

"Wouldn't you?" Cain said. "I'm not stupid ... Something's going to go down when she turns up."

I tugged Lilith down the passage back towards the stone room.

"We need to get out of here," I whispered in Lilith's ear.

Lucas couldn't be trusted. None of them could.

She jammed her foot down on the stone that opened the door from the passage, and it slid open. The sound seemed so much louder than it had when we'd come in.

"Where do you think you're going?" Lucas stood in the doorway.

Lilith turned around to go back towards the platform,

but Cain and another vamp were headed our way. Lilith backed away from them until she bumped into me. There was no room in the passage for us to get past anyone in either direction.

"Charlotte isn't with you?" Lucas asked. "That's a shame."

"We had a little trouble," Lilith said. "Angelica got to her."

Lucas raised his eyebrows. His lips curled back from his teeth and he snarled. "How could you let that happen? You're useless."

I stood between Lucas and Lilith, acting braver than I felt. "She is stronger than us. It couldn't be helped."

"It looks like I'll need you then." Lucas took a step towards me, but he stumbled and fell at my feet.

Charlotte stared at me from the doorway to the stone room.

"Don't stand there," she said. "Run!"

I leapt over Lucas before he could get up, glancing over my shoulder to see if Lilith was coming, but Cain had her in a headlock.

"Come and get her." He bared his teeth, saliva dripping from the ends of his fangs. It made me ashamed to be like him.

Lilith's eyes widened and I wanted to get to her, but Charlotte shoved me into the room and stood in the doorway, holding me back.

"Don't be stupid, Josh. She isn't worth dying for."

"How did you get free?" I asked.

"Angelica isn't as powerful as she thinks she is."

Lucas faced Charlotte. "Looks like I didn't need these two to bring you here. You were *smart* enough to do that yourself."

"And now I'm here, you can let Josh go," Charlotte said.

I tried to push around her, but she stood as firm as a brick wall.

"I guess that's a fair trade." Lucas grinned.

There was no way this would be over. He may be allowing me to go, but some time, some other way, he'd get to me.

"Go find Grace," Charlotte said, not turning to look at me. "She'll be home."

How was I supposed to do that? The sun was up. I wasn't convinced I could wander through the city in broad daylight. The tunnels would only get me so far. And where the hell was home?

"Trust me, Josh. Remember what I told you." Charlotte pushed me into the room. "You'll be fine."

This time she did turn to quickly look at me, and there was something in her eyes that made me believe her. She stamped her foot on the floor and the door closed, blocking me off from her and Lilith.

I never got the chance to find out the details of how Charlotte got away from Angelica. I'd have to ask later when there was more time. I pounded the rock with my fist and contemplated opening the door again to go back in. The hot-headed side of me wanted to, but the rational side knew I needed to get out of there.

Find Grace.

That was the last thing I wanted to do. I had so many mixed emotions when it came to her. I couldn't remember her, but she stirred something inside me I couldn't explain, and I didn't like it. I hated not knowing the truth.

I retraced my steps through the tunnels, but I got lost

and ended up wandering back and forth in the dark for I don't know how long. My laughter bounced off the walls around me. Since I couldn't die from anything other than a stake, beheading, or fire, I could spend an eternity trying to find my way out.

When I'd almost given up, I found the door back into the subway tunnel. I'd never been so happy to see light penetrate the darkness. I waited for a passing train before I made my way along the tunnel to the platform. There weren't many people around to notice me. They'd either boarded the train, or were headed up the stairs and out of the station. Those who did spot me climbing up from the tracks turned the other way. That's how everyone was in the city. Mind your own business, or you could get into trouble.

I stared at the train guard at the ticket gates to the station, using my glamour. He let me through, no questions asked. When I reached the end of the pedestrian tunnel, I stopped at the bottom of the stairs. Sunlight shone halfway down the steps, the stairway roof creating a shadow. People jostled around me, coming and going from the busy station.

Could I really cross the line into the light without burning to death?

What a spectacle that would be—bursting into flames in front of all those people.

I stuck to the left wall and took a few steps up, towards the light. Maybe I could stick my hand into it to test it. I stopped one stair below the line of muted sunlight, gathering the courage I needed to take the final step.

I flexed my fingers at my sides, trying to imagine how

much it would hurt when my skin caught on fire. Slowly, I put my hand out, watching the line of light come closer to my fingers as I stretched them forward.

A wave of people came up the stairs behind me, pushing me across the line. In a flash, everything became brighter. My skin prickled and I cried out, falling to my knees. I twisted against the wall, covering my face with my hands, waiting to die.

"Watch it," an angry voice said.

"Move out of the way," someone else said as they tripped over my foot.

I held my hands out in front of me and watched the sunlight dance across my skin. It made it glow, as if it had a small amount of light below the surface, bursting to get out.

My body sat half in and half out of the sun's rays. From the waist down I was in shadow, but it was only my arms and face that felt the slight tingly prickle.

Charlotte hadn't lied.

She was my creator, and I had her blood running through my veins.

The tunnel had cleared of people, and I got to my feet, standing completely in the light. I turned my face up to the sky. Patches of grey-blue peeked through the heavy winter clouds. I climbed the stairs to the street, surrounded by the hustle and bustle of the city noise. My ears were in surround sound. I was so used to only being out at night, when there were less people and less cars; everything during the day was so much louder.

I passed through Dhye Park, away from the station and the war memorial, concentrating on walking at a human pace. I didn't want to draw unnecessary attention to myself. I couldn't quite believe I was able to walk around during the day.

All sorts of different emotions coursed through me as I walked. Why didn't Charlotte make more of an effort to tell me I was like her? Why didn't Lilith want me to know she had a history with Charlotte? And Grace … In one moment I hated her, and then I loved her. Why was she really here? Did she care enough to come and find me, but not enough to try harder? Was I expecting too much from someone I didn't remember?

Charlotte had said Grace would be at home, and she was counting on me to know where she meant. I had two choices when it came to a place to call home in this city—Lilith's place, or my original terrace with Charlotte.

I was betting on Charlotte's, and I hoped Grace was there when I arrived.

We had some things to talk about.

23

GRACE
Sunday afternoon

We misted and orbed back to Charlotte's terrace to find the door kicked in. Archer secured it enough so we could get some rest, but I was on edge. It had probably been Lilith and Josh. She'd been wearing my crossbow, and an arrow was embedded into the bloodstain on the wall. I'd also found the empty photo frame in Josh's room, the glass broken. He could've already had the photo on him, but if someone was after Charlotte again, vamps may have stopped by for a visit.

Archer took the first watch, and with the five of us, we each managed to get a few hours rest.

The contents of the fridge were next to nothing, unless you counted the bottles of blood, so Justice took a quick trip up the road to the nearest service station for some food.

"Some weapons are missing," Archer said. Our bags

sat in the middle of the floor. He put them back behind the couch.

"The mini crossbow. Lilith had it," I said, biting into my sandwich. "Don't stress, we have a room full of weapons at home."

Archer threw me some stakes to replace the missing ones from my belt, and he restocked his own.

Hope stood at the glass doors, staring into the small courtyard. She'd been quiet since we'd left the park. Justice sat on the couch, picking at the edge of the slash in the cushion. His eyes had that vacant look achieved when someone was lost in their own thoughts.

I wasn't sure if I completely trusted them yet. Everything I'd been taught told me I could. They were hunters, the same as Archer and me. But I'd never come across another hunting team before, and the last angels that came to earth didn't particularly like me, even when I was technically on their side.

Hope reminds me of you, Archer thought.

She's nothing like me. I straightened and laid my sandwich on the bench.

Archer smirked, but didn't say anything. He polished the blade of his dagger with a tea towel he'd found in the bottom drawer.

Someone knocked on the door.

"Who would that be?" Justice said, pushing up off the couch.

"Beats me." I grabbed one of the crossbows from the suitcase and loaded it with a wooden arrow.

"Grace, it's the middle of the afternoon. What do you need that for?" Ryan scratched his head.

"There's a psycho vampire out there on a mission to create an army of sun-walking vamps." I clutched the weapon, my finger on the trigger.

"She has a point," Justice said.

I motioned for him to get the door. Archer stood next to me, at the ready with a stake in his hand.

The knock sounded again, then a voice, "Josh. Are you home?"

Archer sighed, and his shoulders drooped. "More trouble."

I lowered the crossbow. "Let her in, Justice. We know her."

He hesitated before opening the door.

Abby had her hand up, ready to knock a third time.

"What are you doing here?" Archer asked.

Abby gave Justice a once-over before sidling past him into the hallway. "Nice to see you, too, Archer." She stopped when she saw what I had in my hands. "Were you expecting someone else?"

"Abby ..." I shook my head, and pinched the bridge of my nose. This was one headache I didn't need. "How do you know Josh lives here?"

She frowned. "He told me his address after he left."

It seemed Josh hadn't cut all his ties to home, and for some reason it bugged me that he'd stayed in touch with Abby.

"He won't return my calls. Did you find him? Where is he? Why isn't he here? And who are they?" Abby turned up her nose.

Hope mimicked Abby's expression. She took a few steps away from the glass doors, and Abby stepped into the kitchen from the hallway. Hope went to the sink, never taking her eyes off Abby, and poured herself a glass of water.

"Who's this?" Hope turned to me.

"Josh's ex-girlfriend."

"I thought you were his ex."

I pursed my lips. "I am."

Hope scoffed, and Justice groaned, running a hand down his face.

"Let's get one thing clear," Justice said. "We're not here to sort out your relationship problems."

"I never asked for your help," I said, "with anything."

"It's true; she didn't." Archer leant against the counter and smirked.

"We have bigger problems," Hope said.

I gritted my teeth. "Don't you think I know that?"

"Why does everyone always have to argue?" Ryan threw his hands up and walked down the hall towards the door. "I'm going to get some fresh air."

Abby stared at the stake in Archer's hand and shook her head. She reached out and picked up a stake, inspecting the pointy end. "I've been thinking about what I saw the other night."

Hope's eyes widened. "How many humans have you told?"

"It's not like we told her on purpose," I said. "She got mixed up in a fight." Hope was getting under my skin. I wished she would leave. I didn't need her, and I made sure she could hear it in my head.

"You do need me," she said. "I know this city better than anyone."

I laughed. "It doesn't matter how well you know this city. All that matters is how well you know how to fight a vamp on a power trip, while fighting an angel on a power trip at the same time."

"Josh really doesn't have cancer." Abby stood in the middle of the kitchen, staring at Archer.

Everyone looked at her. I was at a loss for words.

"Josh is a vampire, Abby," Archer said. "Would you for once, try not to act so … stupid?"

The front door flew open and Ryan skidded along the hallway floor on his back. Josh stepped into the doorway, his eyes dark with anger. He ran at me, grabbed my shoulders and pushed me across the room until the glass doors to the courtyard stopped me. The back of my head hit the glass and it cracked. The crossbow slipped from my hand and clattered to the tiled floor.

Abby screamed.

"Why didn't you tell me?" Josh shook my shoulders.

I put my hand to my head and winced at the lump that had formed. It started going down as quickly as it appeared.

"Tell you what?" I asked.

Ryan got to his feet, wincing. "Get off her."

"Josh, what are you doing?" Abby asked.

"I have her blood! I can walk in the sun." Josh shook me again. "Why didn't you tell me?"

Anger boiled inside me, and I looked Josh straight in the eyes. I'd come to the city to find him, and make sure he was okay. Well, I'd found him, but he was far from okay. The guy standing in front of me was someone I didn't know. The Josh who had loved me was gone, and there was no trace of him behind those eyes. That Josh would never have treated me this way.

I raised my arms and pushed him off me, then kicked him in the stomach. He stumbled back and bumped into the kitchen bench. Archer grabbed him by the neck and slammed his head onto the marble bench top. His lip split, spraying blood across the surface. Josh grimaced and squeezed his eyes shut.

"No one treats my sister like that." Archer slammed Josh's head down again.

Abby sobbed, tears streaming down her face.

"Arch, stop." I put my hand on his arm.

"If I had my way, I'd put a stake in you." Archer shoved Josh. "You're nothing but a—"

"Don't," I said. "You can't blame him. None of this is his fault."

I turned to Josh, wishing I could change the anger in his eyes to what it used to be. There was a time when I loved the way he looked at me. He'd been so nice and pure hearted. But all that had changed. The memory loss had changed him. The city had changed him. I wanted to hunt Angelica down and make her pay for what she'd done.

I took a deep breath. "I can't help you if you attack me."

"Why do we even want to help him in the first place?" Justice asked.

"Shut up, dude," Ryan said. He stood beside Abby and put an arm around her shoulders.

Josh ran a hand through his hair in that way I remembered he used to when he was human. "They have Lilith."

I clenched my teeth. "And?"

"We have to get her out of there. Lucas will kill her."

"She's killed him before," Hope said. "I'm sure she can do it again."

"I'm sorry, Josh, but Lilith isn't our priority."

Josh growled and his fangs extended. I knew how he felt. I knew what it was like to want to fight for someone so badly that you lost your judgement when it came to everything else. It hurt that Lilith was that person for him. *It should have been me.*

"What's the one thing we all want?" Josh asked.

I looked at the others in turn. Justice spun a stake between his fingers.

"Lucas dead," I said after no one answered.

"They have Charlotte, too. We can save both of them and get Lucas." Josh wiped the blood from his mouth with the back of his hand. Archer had given him a beating, but he didn't seem too put out by it.

Hope pursed her lips and stepped towards Josh. "Let's get one thing clear. I don't like you. I will not protect you, or any other vampire, no matter who they are." She looked at Justice and he stopped spinning the stake.

He nodded, and they both headed for the door.

"Where are you going?" I asked. They must have spoken to each other silently.

"To fight." Hope glanced over her shoulder. "One way or another, Lucas has to be stopped."

At least there was one thing we could agree on.

24

JOSH

Grace didn't move when Hope and Justice headed towards the door.

"We'll catch up," she said.

The blonde girl with the tears streaming down her face stared at me. She wasn't familiar, but then, none of these people were. I only felt like I knew Grace a little because of Angelica and her mind invasion.

"What happened to you?" the girl whispered.

"You shouldn't have come, Abby," Grace said.

"I … I had to know."

"I don't know you," I said. "I don't remember you."

Abby flinched. Her brow furrowed and she formed an O with her lips. "Three years meant nothing to you?"

Three years? Was she an ex-girlfriend as well? If the circumstances were better I'd be big-noting myself. She seemed to be on okay terms with Grace, too, which was weird for an ex. Lilith would have torn both of them to shreds by now if she could.

"What are we supposed to do with her?" Archer said.

Ryan turned to Abby and she covered her face with her hands.

"You need to go home," he said.

Abby nodded. She came over to me and stared into my face. "You may not love me anymore, but I care about you, and I want to help. Tell me how I can help."

Archer coughed behind his hand.

Abby stood close enough to me that I could take her and sink my teeth into her neck before anyone had the chance to move. I balled my hands into fists and fought the burn in my throat.

"No one can help me," I said.

The air beside me shimmered, and a ball of light materialised. Blue tendrils swirled around the edges of the orb. More spinning lights broke away, spreading to create the shape of a person, and Angelica appeared. I pushed Abby out of the way. She crashed into Grace, who managed to keep both of them on their feet.

"I'm pretty sure I can help you," Angelica said.

She reached out to grab me and I ran. Something curled around my ankle and I fell to the hallway floor. Blue fire extended from her hand and bit into my skin. She dragged me along on my stomach, and pain shot up my leg. I gritted my teeth so I wouldn't cry out.

When I reached her feet she shot another tendril of blue from her fingers and it wrapped around my body. She pulled me up.

Grace lunged at Angelica, but the kitchen of the terrace

disappeared, replaced by darkness. It was so thick even my vampire eyes couldn't penetrate it. Then it began to recede, and a sky filled with tiny lights came into focus. They couldn't have been stars because they moved through the blackness without any clear purpose. Last time I checked, stars didn't bounce around all over the place.

When I looked down, the dizziness washed over me again. My feet were on a solid surface, but it was as black as the sky. It gave me the unsettling feeling that I wasn't standing on anything.

Laugher penetrated the darkness, and a space to my left lit up enough for me to see someone sitting on the non-floor. Blue light pulsed through the restraints that bound his wrists and ankles. His shoulders shook as the laughter bubbled out of his throat, but the-should-be-happy sound didn't reach his eyes. They were dark and filled with hatred.

Great, someone else who hated me and I didn't even know who he was.

"What's he doing here?" the guy asked.

Angelica stepped out of the dark and stood beyond my reach. The blue fire binding my wrists and ankles burned me.

"You two need to learn to get along," she said. "It's time for you to help me get what I want."

The guy on the floor laughed again. "You won't get away with this. Someone will notice you've brought a vampire to the In-Between."

"Who? This is my place. I'm the Guardian ... the one responsible for the fallen. No Angel of the Light would have the guts to come here."

"You'll never win," the guy said. "Grace is far more powerful than you'll ever be. She has something you don't."

Angelica's jaw clenched. For a being that was supposed to be full of goodness, she was scary.

"If Grace had done what she was supposed to do and killed Charlotte, we wouldn't be here, would we?"

"If you want Charlotte dead, why did you let her go?" I asked.

Angelica frowned, her forehead creasing between her eyes. "Charlotte is like a nail in the bottom of my foot."

"You didn't answer the question."

"That's because she didn't *let* her go, did you?" the guy asked.

"Everything will work out in the end." Angelica smiled, but it was too wide and toothy to be genuine. "You'll see."

I struggled against my restraints. They dug deeper into my flesh and I winced.

"Don't move too much." The guy sat with his knees up and his arms resting on top of them. The blue around his wrists flickered in the darkness, bathing his face in a soft wash of colour. "It only makes it worse."

"Who are you?" I asked.

His shoulders shook again. This guy did a lot of laughing, which in itself seemed funny because he didn't come across as being an overly happy person.

"Looks like you did a good job." He glanced at Angelica.

She shrugged.

Angelica's eyes locked on mine, and a sharp pain seared through my head. I fell to my knees, my bound hands stopping my complete fall. The blackness beneath me was replaced by more images Angelica fed into my brain. No matter how many times I blinked I couldn't get rid of them, and the pain exploded behind my eyes like a series of fireworks.

Noise filled my ears—people talking and laughing. Flames flickered across the scene and two people came into focus through the fire. It was Grace and the guy next to me, staring into each other's eyes, like lovers who hadn't seen one another for years. I wanted to gouge my eyes out and I didn't know why. What I saw ripped me in two. My heart swelled with hatred for him. Someone I couldn't even remember. He reached up and caressed Grace's face and she closed her eyes; then the vision was gone.

My chest heaved involuntarily. The same man from the vision sat across from me. My body shook with hatred so powerful I wanted to rip his throat out, and I couldn't remember his name. When I raised my head, he stared at me with a snarl on his face.

"The feeling's mutual," he said.

"Don't tell me you can read minds, too," I said.

He smirked. "It's an angel thing. But don't worry. Once we're out of here, I won't be able to hear you."

"It's how the In-Between works," Angelica said. "If you're an angel, you can hear everyone, which means all these souls can hear your thoughts." She gestured to the lights. "But you're a vampire, you can't read minds."

"It gets a little noisy for us," the guy said.

Angelica clapped her hands and smiled. "Right, I'm going to let you get reacquainted."

She disappeared in her balls of light, and when she'd gone the blue fire that had bound me fell away. I got to my feet, rubbing my wrists. The guy stayed where he was, also free to move as he wanted, but he didn't.

I took one step towards him then stopped. I wasn't sure why. Every fibre of my being wanted to attack him and pound him into the blackness.

"She only gave you one side of the story," he said. "You can't trust her."

"I can't trust anyone."

He regarded me, his head cocked slightly to one side. The silence was like a weight bearing down on us, squashing us into the darkness. The lights continued to float around in the oblivion.

"I'm Seth," he finally said.

"I don't care."

"We both love her," he said, ignoring my retort.

"If you're referring to Grace, I don't remember loving her."

"All the better for me, then."

"I don't like you much, do I?" I asked.

"Like I said … feeling's mutual."

Seth got to his feet and squared his shoulders. He didn't have a shirt on, and the muscles in his arms flexed intimidatingly. He was bigger than me—slightly taller. If I'd still been human I wouldn't stand a chance against him. But I wasn't human anymore, so I clenched my fists and waited for him to come at me.

"I'm not going to fight you," Seth said.

I lowered my hands. "That's disappointing. If we hate each other, it seems like a good thing to do."

"Grace wouldn't want it." He stuffed his hands into the pockets of his black jeans. The darkness made his blond hair appear grey. "And Angelica is expecting it."

"Then where does that leave us?"

"My entire existence has been a fight." Seth shrugged. "I've done things ... some I'm not proud of ... some I wish I could undo."

What was he getting at? I didn't know this guy, or I didn't remember him. Actually, I didn't really feel anything for him now Angelica wasn't there. When she'd been standing next to me, I'd been filled with so much hatred for Seth I thought I'd explode.

"Angelica has that effect on people," he said.

I ran a hand through my hair and looked out into the blackness. The lights floated around in every direction with no set pattern. They bobbed along in the void, sometimes bouncing off each other.

"Where are we?" I asked.

Seth stood beside me and we watched the floating lights together.

"The In-Between ... The place where the fallen are sent."

"Those lights are fallen angels?"

"Their souls, yes."

"And they can hear me?" I glanced at Seth from the corner of my eye.

"Yep. And I won't be able to hear you once we leave, because Angelica has my ring."

"You're one of them?"

He folded his arms and didn't answer.

There were more questions forming in my head than I knew how to ask. Sometimes it felt easier not to want to ask them, because every question led to more questions, and no answers. But I did wonder why Seth was there and not floating around with all the other souls, and what he'd done to make Angelica tie him up.

I looked at the angel I'd known in a past life and waited. If he could read minds, he'd answer me eventually.

Finally, he said, "It all comes back to Grace."

25

SETH

The In-Between

Angelica really did a great job on Josh. His head was so mixed up I didn't know which thought to listen to first. I couldn't blame him. Everything was complicated, and trying to explain it made it even more so.

I blocked Josh's thoughts, and those of the fallen drifting through the abyss. I wasn't looking forward to losing my powers when Angelica decided it was time to resurface, but for the time being the noise was too much. We stared at the floating souls, standing side by side in silence. I could get used to Josh with no memory. It would make my life a hell of a lot easier. Still, I wasn't sure if Grace already knew, and if she did, it would tear her up.

She cared too much sometimes, but that's what I loved about her.

I'd seen Grace only twice since that night in the clearing,

and both times were under the control of Angelica.

Angelica, playing her stupid games—I was tired of them. They'd almost broken me, and I hoped the next time I saw Grace would be the time I got to stay.

Seeing her and not being able to talk to her or touch her, made me realise nothing else in my world mattered apart from Grace. I'd changed, and I needed to make her see that. I'd spent so many years convincing her to listen to me, and now that she had, I would spend the rest of my life making up for what I did.

"What's Angelica going to do to us?" Josh asked, breaking my reverie.

I laughed. "She won't be able to do much. She can't get rid of me until she gets what she wants from Grace. And she won't get that if you're dead."

"What does she want?"

I scoffed, shaking my head. "What she *thinks* she wants is a ring. What she *really* wants is revenge."

"Don't we all … You seem pretty relaxed about being a prisoner."

"I've known Angelica a long time," I said. "She's not as tough as she makes out to be." *But I also wasn't as relaxed as he thought.*

"No one ever is."

I let Josh's words hang in the air for a while before I responded. "I've spent a lot of time being angry. If I've learnt something, it's that angry gets you nowhere."

"Angry is all I've ever known," Josh said.

There was a time when I'd felt the same way, but it didn't matter anymore. There was only one thing that mattered to me.

Grace.

Josh watched me from the corner of his eye, and I pretended not to notice. I concentrated on the millions of fallen souls floating around us. I wasn't sure if the In-Between was worse than Hell. I'd done one, but never stepped through the gates of the other. Actually, a life without Grace would be worse.

I couldn't be sure how long we stood like that. Time was different in the In-Between. An hour could be minutes, or vice versa. Angelica would return eventually, and when she did I'd be ready to fight as hard as I could. But first, I had to get to Grace.

"You have to be ready," I said.

Josh turned to face me. "For what?"

"Anything."

Words hung on the edge of Josh's lips as orbs of light split the darkness, and Angelica appeared, along with two more angels.

"Tie them up," she said.

The girl angel shot blue celestial fire from her fingertips, and it coiled around my wrists and ankles. I didn't fight it. There was no point. The guy flicked his fingers and bound Josh in the same way.

Angelica smirked. "Come on, boys; it's show time."

26

GRACE

Late Sunday night

Ten minutes after Angelica had taken Josh, she came back. You'd think we would have been ready for her, but I wasn't expecting to see her again so soon. She didn't hang around for long, only enough time to tell us to be at Dhye Park before dawn, or Josh was dead. I left another fireball scorch mark on the wall. Unfortunately it passed through her as she orbed.

Archer, Ryan and I spent some time getting our weapons ready, but no amount of stakes or crossbows could defeat Angelica. The only way to stop her would be to knock her out and strip her wings—something that wasn't easily done to an angel. Then there was the dilemma in that she was technically the good guy, and I didn't actually want to kill her. I wanted her to leave me, and my friends, alone.

After a few hours rest, we made Abby promise not to

leave the terrace. At first she argued that Ryan got to go, so why couldn't she? The simple answer was that Ryan could fight. Abby wouldn't be strong enough to protect herself, and I couldn't guarantee her safety. In the end she agreed to stay put. Although, her head was so full of confusing thoughts I couldn't lock on to what she was planning to do. I had to be satisfied with her word.

"You have my number?" I asked.

Abby nodded, and snuggled down into the couch. Her eyes drooped, and I hoped she'd be able to sleep some more.

"Time to go," Archer said. "Only an hour or so before dawn."

After making sure the door was secure, we decided to mist to the park, even though Ryan hated it so much. I didn't want to waste any time traversing the city again. We went upstairs to Josh's room and stood in a loose circle. Archer and Ryan grabbed my arms and a few seconds later we were in the park. We hung back in the shadows, the lights from the war memorial reflecting off the pool in front of it. Ryan breathed loudly in my ear and I glanced at him.

"Don't freak out on me now," I said.

"I'm cool." He tightened his grip on the stake in his hand.

"That won't be any good against Angelica. You know that, right?"

Ryan shrugged. "Gives me something to hang on to."

Archer put a finger to his lips and pointed to the lawn in front of the Pool of Reflection. Balls of pure white light spun in circles until they meshed together to form a person.

Angelica stood with her hands clasped in front of her.

Her linen pants flapped gently in the light breeze. I wished the clouds would all band together and dump a storm on top of her.

That's not very nice, she thought, and it echoed in my head.

I stepped out from behind the tree that hid us and moved to the edge of the shadows. *I'm not in a very nice mood.*

"Come on, Grace." Angelica's voice travelled across the clearing. "We've got a lot to talk about."

"She's not wrong there," Archer said, under his breath.

The three of us stayed close together and walked towards Angelica.

I wanted to know what she had planned, but her block was strong. I checked my own defences, putting up a brick wall in my mind to make sure she couldn't get in.

We stopped about ten metres away.

"You have something I want," Angelica said.

I laughed. "You have a few things of mine, too."

"First, you give me Annie's ring."

Archer snickered. "You must think we're stupid."

When we'd arrived in the park I'd had a good look around. There was no sign of Josh. She was hiding him somewhere; I had to figure out where. For a moment I allowed myself to hope I had a chance of finding Seth, too. Maybe I could get something out of Angelica that would tell me where he was, but I didn't like my chances.

My gaze travelled around the park one more time, searching the shadows for any sign of the people Angelica was using as pawns in her silly games.

"They're not here—yet," Angelica said.

"You don't get anything from me until I see Josh." I

dug into my pocket and pulled out the little red velvet pouch. "You hand him over, and it's yours."

Light filled in the shadows on the left side of the park, and an angel appeared. He shoved Josh, making him fall to his knees. Josh's hands and ankles were bound with celestial fire. It pulsed blue, reflecting off his angry face.

"Don't do anything to help that bitch." Josh spat a wad of blood onto the grass.

"Let him go," I said.

Angelica smiled her fake smile, the one that said 'I've got something else to show you'.

Archer came closer and put his hand in the small of my back. He didn't try to speak to me, but I'd spent so many years fighting by his side I could take an excellent guess as to what he wanted to do.

I weighed up my options. Misting to Josh would take only a second, but that left Archer and Ryan with Angelica, and I didn't trust she'd uphold her 'protect the innocent' policy with Ryan. She'd already shown us her true colours once when it came to getting what she wanted.

"Bring him closer, then I'll hand you the ring," I said.

Angelica laughed as more light lit up the darkness in the trees. This time it was to our right. Another angel appeared with someone in her clutches. The feisty brunette manhandled her prisoner, who was also bound by the wrists and ankles. She threw him in front of her, and he burst from the shadows onto the grass. The light from the lamps in the park turned his blond hair white.

"Now things are going to get interesting," Angelica said.

The man on the ground raised his head, and I froze.

A sob ripped itself from my chest and fell into the

night. It had felt like an eternity since I'd looked into Seth's eyes.

Angelica laughed her sickeningly sweet laugh. "We do have a bit of a dilemma now, don't we? Which one?"

Archer moved towards Angelica. "You bitch!"

I grabbed his arm and held him back.

"Who's it going to be, Grace?" Angelica said. "The one you gave up everything for, or the one who sacrificed everything for you?"

27

GRACE
Monday morning

Seth got onto his hands and knees and stared at me. Every cell in my body ached to touch him. I thought I'd missed him, but seeing him again made me realise it was more than that. I didn't just miss him; I yearned for him, and everything about him.

The brunette angel clutched a rope made from blue celestial fire. She tugged on it, and Seth clenched his jaw.

Angelica had me at a stalemate. If I did go to Seth, Josh would die. The angel holding him hostage pressed a stake to his back, ready to strike. But if I went to Josh, would I get to him in time? I couldn't risk losing either of them. That had happened too many times already.

"Who's it going to be, Grace?" Angelica smirked.

Grace, a voice spoke in my head. But it wasn't any old voice; it was Michael. *Act as if you can't hear me, and listen carefully.*

Can Angelica hear you?"

No. Michael scoffed. *I'm an archangel. She thinks she has power, but she has no idea. Now listen. Angelica is in big trouble. The Council wants her to go home, but she's refused. She thinks she has a job to finish, but it's gotten out of hand.*

I stopped myself from laughing. *That's an understatement.* I looked from Seth to Josh, and back again, trying to make it appear as if I were deciding what to do.

We need to sort this out, once and for all, Michael thought. *It's gone on long enough.*

I'm the first person to agree with you. What do you want me to do?

You need to go to Josh.

My gaze rested on Seth again. He devoured me with his eyes, and the thought of running away from him hurt more than I'd expected. I'd wanted this moment to come every second since he had been ripped away from me. How could I turn from him now?

I can't, I thought.

Grace, Michael thought in his stern brother voice. *You need to trust me. Seth can take care of himself, and he isn't in danger. Angelica needs him. You need to protect the weakest link first.*

I covered my face with my hands.

"Too much for you, is it?" Angelica laughed.

Seth, I thought, raising my head, making sure my block against Angelica was still in place.

He can't hear you, Michael thought. *Angelica has his ring, but she won't hurt him. She needs him to unlock Annie.*

The red pouch in my hand all of a sudden felt heavy.

What do I do? I thought. *And what about Archer and Ryan? She hurt Ryan the last time she wanted to get to me.*

Once Angelica sees me, she won't hurt them. When the star explodes, go to Josh. And don't let Angelica into your head.

Angelica was the last person I wanted in my mind, after everything she'd done. I may have been the one who fell, but she didn't deserve her wings. She'd fought for the wrong reasons, and bad luck to anyone who stood in her way.

Seth hadn't taken his eyes off me. I couldn't speak to him, so I couldn't ask him if he was in on this supposed rescue mission. From the look he gave me, I thought it could be a possibility, but he hated Michael. The idea of them working together on anything didn't seem to fit.

"Gracie, what's going on?" Archer said in my ear. "Now would be a good time for some sort of decision."

I glowered at my brother. "You're good at stating the obvious."

His mouth opened, but he snapped it shut again.

The angel holding Josh captive smiled and pressed the stake harder into his back. Josh's face twisted in agony when the angel pulled on the rope of celestial fire wrapped around his wrists. Seth was bound in the same way, but when I looked at him, his face gave nothing away. Michael was right. Save the weakest link first.

I turned my head in Josh's direction, and something white flickered near his head. A butterfly flew around him in a dizzying haphazard way before landing on his shoulder. Josh looked sideways at the butterfly. I blinked away the tears that threatened to pour out.

Emma?

The butterfly left Josh and fluttered across the grass towards me. I held out my hand and it came to rest on my palm. Its wings beat slowly up and down.

Archer rested a hand on my shoulder and Ryan came closer.

"Is that …?" Ryan trailed off. "Like the one at Emma's funeral?"

"I think so," I whispered.

The butterfly left my hand and flew up into the night air. The clouds had parted, and the butterfly's white wings glowed against the inky sky. It continued its path towards Seth, coming to rest on the grass in front of him. Seth stared at it for a few moments before raising his head and locking his gaze on me. A small smile played at his lips.

What was Emma trying to tell me?

I tore my gaze away from Seth and looked Angelica straight in the eyes.

"You're going to wish you'd never messed with me." I turned my back on her, facing away from the war memorial.

There were no stars visible through the glow of the city lights, but they were there, and I waited for Michael's signal.

Ryan fidgeted with the sleeve of his hoodie, and glanced at everyone positioned around the park before finally stopping at me.

"Arch is right," he said. "It's decision time, Grace."

"We have a mess to clean up first."

The sky lit up with a white flash, and a small ball of light streaked between the clouds.

"What was that?" Ryan craned his neck to follow the path of the star.

"Get ready for everything to explode." I misted and landed in front of Josh.

Michael landed behind the angel holding Josh hostage. He formed a ball of light in his palm and hurled it at the angel's back. It exploded on impact, sending out a wave of light, and the angel collapsed on top of Josh.

Michael placed his hand on the angel, transforming him into a mass of tiny balls of light, orbing him away from us. Archangels had the power to orb people or objects and not themselves, but because I couldn't do it, I'd never seen it done before.

Josh sat back on his haunches, still bound by the celestial fire. I gripped his upper arms and helped him to his feet. His muscles flexed under my fingers, and the familiar spark I felt when I touched him coursed into my hands. Warmth followed it, and it brought back memories I couldn't deal with.

"Why did you choose me?" The surprise in Josh's eyes shocked me. "That's what this is all about, isn't it? Making your choice?"

He moved close enough so the tip of his nose tickled my cheek. He pressed his forehead to mine and I responded, tilting my head back. Everything about Josh was so familiar, and his words gave me hope that maybe he'd remembered something about us.

Josh moved closer still, his bound hands between us, his lips about to touch mine, but I looked down at the last second. He brushed my forehead with a kiss. I had to explain that I'd come to him because I'd followed Michael's instructions. Before I could, Angelica's scream of rage echoed around us.

My explanations would have to wait.

Michael smiled, and winked at me. "I think she's angry."

I spun around to face the war memorial. Hope and Justice stood in front of Archer and Ryan, protecting them. Hope deflected one of Angelica's light balls, aimed at Archer, with one of her own. Their collision exploded light through the park.

Angelica's lips pulled back into a snarl, an expression that looked completely wrong on the face of an angel. Angry was an understatement. The brunette angel orbed with Seth to where Angelica stood in front of the Pool of Reflection. Angelica snatched the rope of celestial fire, and pulled. When her gaze locked with mine she tugged Seth's restraints again. His jaw tightened, but his eyes gave nothing away.

"Looks like you've made your decision," Angelica said, her voice travelling across the grass.

"I haven't decided anything yet." I didn't know if I was trying to convince her, or myself.

Michael unbound Josh and the three of us walked across the grass towards the others. Archer and Ryan hadn't moved. They stood close to Hope and Justice, Archer's expression telling me everything I needed to know.

He was ready to fight.

Josh hung back and I ran to stand with Archer and the others.

Michael moved to the space between Angelica and the

rest of us, as if he were waiting to referee a boxing match.

Angelica pulled on the rope of celestial fire she held in her hand. The blue light coiled around Seth's wrists, cutting into his skin. Until now he'd been strong, but this time his expression betrayed him with grimaces of pain. At least he didn't cry out.

"Annie's ring." Angelica held out her hand.

"Let him go first," I said.

She laughed, and pulled the rope of fire again. Seth clenched his jaw.

Michael stood with his feet apart and folded his arms. "Angelica, let him go."

"I'm curious," Justice said. "Why are we making her free a fallen angel? Isn't she on our side?"

"Dude, shut up," Archer said.

Angelica cocked her head to one side, regarding Michael for a moment. "Justice asked a pretty good question. Why are you letting him go? He belongs to me."

"Not anymore," Michael said, rocking on his heels. He held out his hand. "I presume you have Seth's ring?"

Angelica's mouth opened and closed a few times. "Why do you want it?"

"Insurance."

"For what?" Angelica asked. "He belongs—"

"Where I say he belongs." Michael took a step towards Angelica. "Have you forgotten who you're talking to? You don't question your arch. My business with Seth is no concern of yours." Michael waited with his hand outstretched for Angelica to hand him Seth's ring.

Angelica clenched her fists and pressed her lips together. I didn't take my gaze from the hand that held Seth's ring.

When she uncurled her fingers and placed the ring on Michael's palm, I let out a long, controlled breath.

"Your turn," she said.

"I don't like this," Hope said. "Whose side are we on, anyway?"

"You're on my side," Michael said. "You do what I say."

Hope stared at him, her mouth open.

"I wouldn't argue if I were you," Archer said in her ear. "I don't like the guy, but apparently he's bad-arse."

Hope rolled her eyes.

"It's true." Michael smirked. "I am. Like he said."

I pulled the drawstring open on the velvet pouch and tipped the ring onto my palm. Annie hadn't betrayed me, but she had lied to protect me. She'd watched over me since my first incarnation on earth, and I'd never known. Handing her back to Angelica was the right thing to do. Annie shouldn't have had her wings stripped. Seth should never have taken them, but he'd done it for me, to protect me.

When I looked up, Seth stared at me. He hadn't taken his eyes off me for longer than a few seconds since he'd arrived in the park. He nodded, and I dropped the ring into Angelica's outstretched palm.

Seth shifted on his knees and brought his hands up. "You can untie me now."

Angelica laughed.

She had to untie him. Until he freed Annie, he was safe. She couldn't hurt him if she wanted Annie back, but once she was free, who knew what Angelica would do?

I looked at Michael. His jaw clenched and he frowned. He raised his hand and a ball of light shot from his finger, colliding with the rope of celestial fire in Angelica's hand.

The fire flicked up her arm, and she cried out, dropping the rope. It fell to the grass and disappeared, along with the restraints around Seth's ankles.

Seth rubbed his wrists and stood up, moving slowly to my side. I had to resist the urge to throw myself into his arms.

He looked down at me and smiled. "Hey." His arm brushed my shoulder, and he curled his little finger into mine.

"Hey yourself," I said, gripping his finger so tightly I thought I might break it. He didn't seem to mind.

"Gracie," Archer said. "Check this out."

When I turned towards him, the white butterfly flitted past and circled the air in front of Ryan's face. His eyes were sad, and a small smile touched the corners of his mouth. When he reached up, the butterfly landed on the tip of his finger. His smile widened, and it flew off again, this time heading back towards me. It didn't stop though; instead, the butterfly flew circles around Seth and I, leaving a faint trail of light in its wake.

Josh stood quietly watching everything, and when our eyes met, he scowled. I let go of Seth's hand and moved towards Josh. The butterfly stopped in my path, and my heart lurched.

"Emma?" I took another step, but it didn't move out of the way.

"Who's Emma?" Josh asked.

Angelica chuckled. "I should do something about that memory of yours."

"She's my best friend," I said.

Josh raised his eyebrows. "That's a butterfly."

Emma's butterfly still blocked my path, so I held up my hand and it landed on my knuckles.

What are you trying to tell me? I asked it.

The butterfly took off and flew to Seth. It hovered in front of his face, and then brushed his cheek as if it were giving him a kiss, before flying away and landing on a branch in a nearby tree.

"You've broken the rules by allowing the butterfly, Michael," Angelica said. "What would the Council say?"

"It's nothing compared to what you will have to answer for."

Angelica clenched her jaw. "We better get on with this then."

Michael sighed. "Seth. Get this over with, please."

Seth stepped forward and went to take Annie's ring from Angelica.

She shook her head. "I'll hold it. All you need to do is put your blood on the stone."

Since I'd laid eyes on Seth, he'd said one word, and that word had been directed at me. I wanted so badly to hear the sound of his voice, but he didn't say anything. He didn't protest, and did what Angelica asked him to do.

Seth bent down and took the dagger from my ankle strap. His fingers brushed my leg as he rolled my jeans up, and heat shot through me. He used the dagger to cut the end of his finger. Blood welled onto the tip.

Angelica held the ring out, and Seth smeared his blood onto the stone. The stone absorbed it. The white mist inside swirled beneath the surface of the tiger's eye before exploding outwards, filling the park with rays of divine light.

28

JOSH

The force of the light shooting from the ring in Angelica's hand threw me backwards, and I skidded along the grass. Everyone had been knocked over, and they all grumbled as they got to their feet.

Another angel stood beside Angelica and helped her up. She was also divinely beautiful, with her hair pulled back sharply from her face.

"You got what you wanted. Now leave," Grace said.

I hoped Angelica wouldn't listen.

I wanted my memory back.

"Really, Josh?" Angelica looked at me. "If I were you, I'd walk the other way and never look back. Grace has caused you nothing but pain, and you want to remember it all?"

"I'm sure he can decide for himself," Grace said, planting her hands on her hips.

Archer sighed and ran a hand down his face.

"I think she's right," Seth said. He glanced at me over his shoulder. "Let Josh decide what he wants to do."

Anyone with half a brain could see Grace had chosen Seth over me. It stung when I'd tried to kiss her, and she'd turned her head away. I wasn't sure why it bothered me so much, because I didn't remember anything about our relationship. At some point I'd loved her, but that was obviously over. Maybe Angelica was right. Maybe I didn't want to know.

"If you don't do it, I will," Michael said.

Angelica tilted her head to the side. "You can't. Only I can fully restore his memories. And I'm beginning to wonder whose side you're on."

"I'm not on anyone's side," Michael said, his nostrils flaring. "Somehow, I've become a mediator in your childish game. You've got a lot to answer for."

Annie stepped forward and stood between Angelica and Michael. "What happened while I was gone?"

"Where do we start?" Archer said.

"Angelica decided to take things into her own hands," Grace said.

"And look where that got her." Archer shifted on his feet, shaking his head.

Why was I standing there? These people had me caught up in something I didn't want to be involved in. All I wanted was to find Lilith and get back to the terrace, which was not going to be an easy thing to do once the sun came up. I may have been able to walk around during the day, but she couldn't.

The sun rose far quicker than I thought it would. My arms dropped to my sides and I watched in awe as light seeped into the day. I didn't recall ever seeing the sun move into the sky while I was standing in the open. That it wouldn't burn me made me happier than I'd been in a long time.

Blue streaked past the corners of my vision. Michael shot blue fire from the ends of his hands, and the thin tendrils wrapped around Angelica's wrists. He did the same to Annie, binding her tightly.

Then a blinding pain seared through my head, and I fell to my knees.

Grace was at my side in an instant, holding my arm. "What are you doing to him?"

"You wanted me to give his memory back." Angelica smiled. "You never said I couldn't make it hurt."

"Not like this, it's cruel." Grace tightened her grip on me.

An image of a dark room formed in my mind. Beams of sunlight shone through the slits of windows in the walls. Dust danced in the light. The memory was different this time, like it wasn't really mine. It was as if I were an observer, watching someone else, only that someone was me.

Charlotte sat on the floor, my head cradled in her lap. Streaks of red lined her face. She looked at Grace, who sat with her back against the wall, her knees drawn to her chest, sobbing. Charlotte bit into my wrist. Then with one sharp fang she slit her own wrist, and pressed it to my lips. The pain became so intense I thought I would vomit, even though my stomach held nothing.

In the vision, Grace got to her feet and left the stone room. She walked away and didn't look back, leaving me to lie motionless on the hard floor. Something in my head snapped, and I realised that was the moment I'd really lost her.

From that point on, everything had changed.

The rest of my memories came flooding back in a wave so intense I thought it would reduce me to dust. A lifetime of visions stormed into my head, pushing down on me. Once it passed, I remembered everything, and the myriad of emotions rising inside me caught me off guard. Intense love for Grace, a love I didn't want to feel, and a hatred for Seth that was so strong, the first thing I wanted to do was rip his throat out. It was even stronger than the way I'd felt when Angelica had taken me to the In-Between.

When I opened my eyes, my face lay pressed into the grass. Grace shook my shoulders. She knelt beside me, crying, and pleading with Angelica to stop. I shook her off and flew to my feet. Grace tumbled backwards onto the grass.

"Don't touch me."

"Josh, what did she do to you?" Grace asked as Seth helped her up.

A laugh bubbled from Angelica's mouth. She winced as she struggled against the rope around her wrists.

"Michael, what are you doing? Let us go," Annie said.

He shook his head. "Afraid I can't do that. Angelica needs to go home."

"Like hell I do," she said. "I have unfinished business. Charlotte is still out there."

"I'll handle Charlotte," Michael said. "You're on probation. The Council is not happy."

"I was acting on orders."

"As much as I dislike the Council, I'm pretty sure they wouldn't have ordered you to put innocent people in danger," Grace said.

"Well." Angelica smirked. "At least now he remembers everything." She nodded towards Josh.

"How do I know you haven't planted something false in his head?" Grace asked.

"You can read minds. You'll know if something isn't true."

"Yes, but will he?" Grace clenched her fists. "Can you get her out of my sight please, Michael?"

I admired Grace's strength and spark, and searched my mind for a good memory, one we shared that would calm the anger rising inside me. Our eyes met, and I remembered when she'd come to the city not long after I'd left Hopetown Valley—the argument, the pain, the most amazing night of my life, followed by more pain.

The good memories hurt more than the bad ones.

She chose Seth.

No amount of happy memories would make up for losing her.

Grace bit her lip, and tears formed at the corners of her eyes. She stepped towards me, and I wished she wouldn't. She would only make it harder. The best thing I could do was to forget about her, and get on with my sorry existence.

She reached up and placed her hand on my cheek. "I'm sorry for everything."

I wanted to yell at her, to scream that it wasn't fair, but what good would that do? It was already hard enough. What had Seth told me? Angry gets you nowhere.

"You told me to fight, but if I'm fighting for you, I'm

fighting a losing battle." I looked over the top of her head at Seth. He clenched his jaw and fixed me with a mean stare.

"I won't lose you completely," Grace said.

"It's already too late." I pulled away and stepped back.

The park filled with early morning sunlight, and I turned my face to the sky. At least one good thing to come of all this was that I didn't have to hide during the day anymore. I hated being confined to the terrace. Getting out would make things easier.

I was about to turn away and never look back when Justice spoke.

"We have a bit of a problem."

Everyone looked towards the steps of the war memorial. A group of vampires had assembled under the portico. Cain stood at the head with Lilith in his clutches.

29

GRACE

Josh's jaw clenched and I followed his line of sight to where Lilith stood with Cain and the other vampires. Josh wanted Lucas's blood, and I didn't blame him. I wanted it, too. But Lucas was nowhere in sight.

Angelica struggled with her bonds. "Untie me, Michael. Annie and I can help."

"I don't want her helping us. We can't trust her," I said.

Michael nodded. "Sorry, Angelica. You've got the Council to answer to. We can handle this."

Her eyes grew wide as Michael placed his hand on her shoulder. She disappeared like the other angel had, in swirling balls of light. "Try to keep her in line up there." Michael sent Annie next, before she had the chance to protest.

I could imagine how annoyed Annie was, after being locked up for so long, and getting thrown into the middle of everyone else's problems. Still, I had more important things to worry about.

With a hard shove, Cain pushed Lilith into the early morning sunlight, making sure he and the rest of the vamps were protected by the shadows. Josh cried out, but when she didn't burn he snarled. Soft beams filtered through the trees in the park, casting dappled patches of light onto Lilith's skin. She shrieked, her eyes widening, and her hands shaking at her sides.

"She's the test," Hope said.

Justice flexed his fingers around his stake. "Looks like it worked."

"We need to get Charlotte out of there." Archer said.

I couldn't have agreed more.

The vampires behind Lilith stepped into the sunlight.

Seth cleared his throat. "Something you want to give me, Michael?"

Michael flicked Seth's ring into the air, and Seth caught it in his right hand. His eyes never left mine as he slipped it onto his finger. Instantly, his mind opened up to me and let me in, and it felt like coming home.

Seth itched to unfurl his wings, but we were out in public. Several people had come into the park, probably cutting through on their way to work. The number one priority was to stop the vampires before any of them attacked someone innocent, or got away. Going for a fly would have to wait.

"No human casualties," Michael said. "I'll worry about clean-up. Get them down as fast as you can. And don't forget to protect each other." He looked at each of us in turn. "Even Josh."

Michael's willingness to bend rules made me smile. For an archangel he was pretty cool, but something told me I'd have plenty to answer for once all of this was over.

We formed a tight group and made our way towards the vamps.

"If we want to end this, we need to get inside," I said.

"How do we do that?" Hope asked. "The entrances are pretty well guarded."

"Kill everyone but Cain," I said. "He'll take us in."

Josh growled. "If any of you kill Lilith—"

"We won't." I pursed my lips. "For now."

The vamps circled around the edge of the park, cutting across the grass to meet us in the middle. All of us were completely exposed. Cain thought it was a good plan, and I resisted the urge to laugh when I heard the thought in his head. He was under the impression that we would hold back with plenty of witnesses around. But Michael had said he would worry about cleaning up. I imagined 'cleaning up' involved altering the memory of anyone who happened to see something they shouldn't.

"This is going to be fun," Cain said when he reached us.

"I don't doubt it," I said. "Last time we met was a ton of laughs."

"If I remember correctly, I got away."

"I won't make the same mistake twice," I said.

A vamp in the back of Cain's group stepped out where I could see him. "Are we going to fight, or play chit-chat all day?"

"Fighting sounds good to me," Archer said.

"You okay?" Josh asked Lilith.

She turned her face upwards and closed her eyes. The

sunlight made her skin glow, probably an effect of drinking Charlotte's blood.

"Never better." She opened her eyes and smiled.

"Be careful, Josh. She isn't like you," I said.

Then it was on.

A passer-by walking her dog screamed when Michael staked a female vampire who had chosen to attack him. The vamp fell to a heap of dust at his feet and he went into damage control mode. An orb flew from his finger and hit the lady in the chest. She kept walking with a dazed smile on her face. Then Michael turned his palm upwards and light streamed out of it. It jettisoned into the air, falling down around us and enclosing us in a dome. When the light hit the ground it spread out through the park like a shockwave, washing over everyone within range.

"We're good now. Don't hold back," Michael said.

Cain launched at me, his arms outstretched. I braced myself for the impact, ready to fend him off, but he knocked me off my feet. My back hit the grass as his weight came down on top of me with surprising strength. Last time we'd fought I'd gotten it over him easily. This time it was harder. I was in the process of flipping him onto his back when Seth grabbed him and tossed him off. Cain landed on his stomach, the side of his leg touching the wall of Michael's barrier. On impact it burnt through his clothing, singeing his skin. He cried out, and Seth planted his foot into Cain's back.

Seth adjusted his grip on the stake I'd given him earlier, and I misted to his side, grabbing his arm. "Don't stake him. We need him to get inside the lair."

Lilith turned and faced the vamps, protecting Josh.

She planted a kick into the chest of one of them. Her willingness to attack her own surprised me, and I hated the fact I was grateful to her for looking out for Josh.

Archer loved getting his hands dirty as much as I did. The look of excitement on his face said everything as he dusted two vamps. It reduced the enemy and levelled the playing field. Justice and Hope got one apiece, giving us the advantage. I admired their fighting style. Still, their teamwork wasn't as refined as ours.

"I heard that," Hope said, smiling in my direction.

I laughed.

Seth pinned Cain to the ground, and I dusted a vamp mid-air as he launched at Seth's back. Ash covered him and he shook it from his hair. Josh and Lilith hung back and circled the group, their hands linked together. I didn't doubt that if given the opportunity they would run. And I didn't understand why Josh wanted to protect her now he had his memory back. I didn't think he would ever want to protect a vampire, even though he was one. Then again, I'd thought the same thing about myself, and look where that had gotten me when I'd vowed to protect Charlotte.

Within the next few minutes, the rest of the vamps were dust. Josh, Lilith and Cain were the only ones left.

"Get up." Seth kicked Cain, and he rocked onto his knees. When he stood, Seth pulled back his arm and punched Cain in the mouth. "That's for touching Grace."

I sighed. He hadn't changed.

I have. Seth smiled crookedly at me. *But not when it comes to you.*

I planted my feet firmly in front of Cain. "You're going

to take us to Lucas.”

“No way in hell am I ever helping you.” Cain wiped blood from his lip with the back of his hand.

“Where’s Charlotte?” I asked.

Cain laughed. “You’ll never find her.”

I wasn’t so sure about that. “You shouldn’t underestimate me. Last time you did that it caused all sorts of trouble.”

Ryan sat on the grass, out of breath, his arms resting on his knees. Josh and Lilith stood huddled together. Hope and Justice wanted me to kill Cain, but we needed him.

Hope, Michael, Seth. I have an idea. The three of them looked at me and waited.

So, spill, Hope thought.

We need to get Cain to think about where Lucas is, and where they’re keeping Charlotte. I pressed my lips into a thin line.

Ryan flopped back onto the grass and sighed. “When you’re finished, fill the rest of us in.”

We can all orb or mist. If we can see the place in his head, we should be able to lock onto the location enough to get there.

You’re a genius, Gracie, Archer thought. He couldn’t hear the others, but he could hear me.

Why didn’t you think of that? Justice frowned at Hope.

She shrugged.

Seth smiled, and turned to Cain. He folded his arms over his bare chest and studied the vampire. “I’ll bet you have Charlotte locked up pretty tight.”

“She’s probably guarded well, too,” Hope said.

“I don’t think she would be,” Michael said. “Lucas isn’t that smart.”

Cain furrowed his brow and snarled. *Our plan was working.* He had formed a pretty clear image in his head of Charlotte. Her wrists hung from chains bolted to a stone wall. A film of moisture covered the rock, and a naked bulb lit the cramped space. The images in Cain's thoughts were enough for me to get a good lock on Charlotte's location.

What about Lucas? Hope thought. *Can we get anything out of Cain on his whereabouts?*

"Lucas sent you out here as test dummies, didn't he?" I asked.

"And Lucas is in his lair, all nice and cosy," Seth said, "while you're out here doing his dirty work."

Cain's mind filled with thoughts of Lucas. He didn't particularly like him, but Cain and Lucas had one thing in common—their hunger for power. Without knowing, Cain showed us exactly where Lucas was, sitting on his throne, waiting for his small test army to return. Lucas was about to get more than a bunch of idiot vamps coming back. He would get us.

"I'm not telling you anything," Cain said.

Seth laughed, and the sound made my heart swell.

Grace and Seth, you take Archer, Ryan, and Lilith, Michael thought. *I'll take the others. I want to split Josh and Lilith up. I don't trust her, and you can use her since she knows the lair.*

Lucas or Charlotte? I stared at Michael.

Who do you want?

Charlotte. I reached out and squeezed Archer's hand.

I wasn't the only one fighting for the people I loved.

30

JOSH

We stood in a loose circle. Grace, and the other angels, stared at each other, not talking. At least, not out loud. When Angelica shoved my memories back inside my head, I remembered all the mind-reading stuff.

While they had their silent pow-wow, I glanced around the park at the people walking by. Most of them were dressed in suits, but some jogged past in their gym gear. None of them noticed us trapped inside the bubble Michael had created.

"What are they doing?" Lilith whispered.

"Deciding our next move," I said.

I was glad Lilith couldn't read my mind. Now that I remembered everything, there were a lot of things I was unsure about. *Lilith, Grace, Seth…* I looked at Ryan sitting on the grass, and guilt punched me in the gut.

He had been my best friend, and I'd tried to eat him.

I walked over to Ryan, Lilith in tow, as she wouldn't let go of my hand. He turned his head slightly when I stopped near him, looking at me with that expression I knew so well. The one that said it doesn't matter what's happened; it only matters what we do next.

"I'll have your back from now on," I said.

"I never doubted you wouldn't." Ryan crossed his legs, picking at the grass.

Lilith's hand tightened around mine.

Ryan laughed, a short, sharp, sound. "Your girlfriend looks like she wants to eat me."

Lilith growled, but she let go of my hand and went to the far side of the dome, as far away from Ryan as she could.

"She can't help it," I said.

"I know." Ryan smiled. "I don't blame her. And I don't blame you."

Ryan was far too forgiving. He forgave me.

I wouldn't forgive me.

Ryan stood and we watched the others. Grace looked at me over her shoulder a few times, and each time she did it made my insides feel like someone was stirring them with a hot knife.

I wanted to wash my hands of her, but something inside me also wanted the opposite. The more I tried to ignore it, the more it tormented me. I wanted to convince myself I hated her, but it wasn't working very well. The memory of being with her was the most tormenting. How she'd felt in my arms, her soft skin.

Seth glared at me, his body tensing. A smile crept onto my face. He'd seen my thoughts. Grace furrowed her brow and avoided my gaze. She'd seen what I was thinking, too.

Seth slipped his hand onto Grace's back, and she leant towards him, like a magnet. I may have been with her in a way he never had, but she'd chosen him. Seeing him touch her angered me. I clenched my fists, using all my willpower to keep them at my sides.

"You seem to be taking this pretty well," Ryan said.

If only he knew.

"What choice do I have? She's made her decision." But at least Seth had another reason to hate me. Grace's first would always be me.

"Time to go," Michael said.

"I'm not taking you anywhere." Cain backed away a few steps.

"Michael's wall is still up," Grace said. "I wouldn't try to run unless you want to be a fried vamp."

Grace, Archer, and Seth made their way over to Lilith.

"Ryan, you're with us," Grace said.

Ryan gave me a nod and joined the group, standing with Grace between him and Lilith.

Michael, Hope, and Justice moved with Cain towards me. "Is someone going to let me in on the plan?" I asked.

"Hang on, and get ready to fight," Michael said.

Grace's group joined hands, except for Lilith. "I'm not going anywhere without Josh."

"You know the inside of Lucas's lair?" Grace asked. Lilith nodded. "Then unless you want me to stake you right now, you're coming with us."

I wanted to protest, but I didn't. Trying to convince everyone I cared about Lilith wouldn't change the fact that she was a vampire, and it wouldn't make me love her more than I loved Grace. It seemed that loving both of them was impossible, but so was loving neither of them.

"You'll never get in," Cain said.

"And you need to stop underestimating us." Grace smiled. She grabbed Lilith's arm and the five of them disappeared in a cloud of black mist. Cain growled.

"Our turn." Michael clapped his hands together.

"Will they kill Lilith?" I asked.

"What are you going to do if they do?" Justice asked. "She's a vampire. In case you haven't noticed, most of the people here kill them for a living."

There was no doubt Lilith was bad, but there was a part of me that wanted to believe she wasn't. She'd been there for me when no one else had. I owed her.

"You owe her nothing," Michael said. "And if you want to get out of this alive, you'll forget about her."

"I don't like you," I said.

"Not many do. And you need to remember the only reason I haven't put a stake in your sorry arse is because of Grace and Charlotte. Now shut up, and hold my hand."

Michael held his left hand out. I hesitated, but eventually took it. With his other hand he grabbed the scruff of Cain's shirt and shoved him into the centre of the group.

"Why are we taking him with us?" Hope grimaced.

"He knows his way around the lair. Now come on," Michael said.

Hope slipped her hand into my free one, a look of disgust on her face, and Justice gripped Cain's shoulder, completing our circle.

"What do we do once we're inside?" I asked.

Hope raised her eyebrows. "You're seriously asking that?"

"Dust the vamps … find Lucas and kill him," Michael said. "I don't care which order we do it in. Just do it. Grace and the others will get Charlotte out. Once she's safe, and Lucas is dead, this will be over and I can go back to my peaceful cloud field."

"I'm guessing we need to be ready for anything," Hope said, "since we'll be landing in the middle of the lair."

"Yep," Michael said. "Be ready to fight as soon as we land."

Cain laughed. "This should be interesting."

"We can handle them," Hope said. "If they're as dumb as you, it should be easy."

Michael stared straight at me, his fist tight in Cain's clothes as he struggled. I didn't like Michael, but I liked Charlotte, and I wanted to get her out as much as he, and Grace, did. She'd also helped me when I'd needed it. When Grace and the others had turned their backs on me, Charlotte had been there. At first I didn't want to know, but she'd brought me around, and taught me a few things. I owed her as well.

Travelling with Michael was similar to travelling with Grace, but now that I was a vampire it didn't upset my stomach quite like it had the first time. The memory of when she'd showed me her wings hurt. She was so beautiful, even the sight of her in my mind hurt my eyes.

When we landed, thoughts of Grace raced through my head, and she was the first person I looked for. But she was nowhere to be seen amongst the crowd of vampires that gathered in the cavern. There were hundreds of them, leaning against the walls and gathered in small groups.

Too many to fight and survive.

Lucas lounged on his throne at the head of the huge room. He jumped to his feet when he saw us, a smile creeping onto his face.

"It looks like we've landed in the thick of things." Hope stood with her back to Justice, adjusting the grip on her stake.

Cain struggled in Michael's grasp, and it surprised me when Michael let him go. The vampire streaked across the room and stopped beside his leader.

"We can't fight all of them," I said.

Michael held his arms out from his sides. "Have a little faith, Josh. We only need to fight one."

Balls of pure white light formed in his hands. He brought them above his head in an arc, and then with a forceful downward swing, threw them at the rock floor. A wave of light, similar to the one he'd let off in the park, rippled out from his feet. The wave swept through the room, knocking everyone outside our group to the floor.

The only one left standing was Lucas.

31

GRACE

Our group landed in the room I'd seen in Cain's mind. Two vamps leant against the wall next to an open arched doorway. Their eyes widened, and it took them a few seconds to react to our arrival before they lunged at us. Everyone scattered. I stepped forward with my stake raised, dusting the closest vamp. The second one stopped her charge, backing away towards to the door. Archer crash tackled her and they fell against the wall. He grunted when he hit the rock, ash raining onto his feet.

"Is that the best they've got?" I asked.

Archer and Ryan went straight to Charlotte and lifted her up to take the weight off the shackles that held her to the wall.

Lilith moved into a corner. I blocked her thoughts. She was thinking too much about Josh, and the images in her head were personal ones I didn't want to see. I

didn't think true vampires could have feelings, or heart, but it seemed they could. I'd always thought they were nothing but killing machines, bent on destroying life, and eating their way through whomever they could.

Maybe I was wrong.

I don't think you are, Seth said in my mind. *And it sucks, seeing private things you never wanted to know.*

I locked my gaze onto his. *I'm sorry … I …*

Grace, you don't have to explain.

I nodded and pursed my lips. Of all people, I should have learned that every action had a consequence, but I insisted on doing everything the hard way. I never thought about Seth finding out I'd been with Josh. It's not that I wasn't ever going to tell him, but I wished I could on my own terms.

Now is not the time to worry about the past, Seth thought. *We can talk about it later … and you could never do anything to make me stop loving you.* He touched my cheek with his fingertips.

Lilith seems to really care about Josh, I thought.

You can't trust her.

There was a time when I didn't trust you.

Seth smiled with closed lips.

"A little help here," Archer said.

We turned our attention to Archer. Blood dripped from Charlotte's wrists, and trailed along her bare arms. Her head hung to the side, her eyes closed. When Archer held her face in his hands, I saw tears form at the corners of his eye. He blinked them away, and gently shook her.

She didn't respond.

Tubes ran from both of her arms into collection bags

that hung on the wall beside her. Lucas had strung her up to bleed her dry. Bite marks covered her arms, and her clothing was ripped in places, revealing more bites.

"Charlotte," Archer said, tapping her cheek with his hand. "No, no." He shook his head. "Wake up!" He slapped her hard enough to knock her head to the other side.

"Go easy on her, dude," Ryan said.

Archer was about to lose it. His head was a jumble of mixed-up thoughts. What he wanted to do to Lucas, how he hated himself for having been so angry with Charlotte. I agreed with him on that one. I was guilty as well. If we hadn't turned her away, we wouldn't be in this mess.

We'd probably be in a *mess,* Seth thought. *Just not this one.*

I smiled weakly. I'd forgotten what it was like to have him so close, looking in on my thoughts.

Archer yanked the tubes from Charlotte's arms and threw them to the floor. Her eyes fluttered, and she opened them slowly, blinking through the blood that had collected on her eyelashes like little beads. Archer held her up to take the weight off her wrists.

"We need to get her off the wall," Archer said.

I looked around for something to prise the shackles open, but there was nothing in the room apart from us, and the bags of Charlotte's blood.

Lilith stood near the arched doorway. It was the only way in and out of the room. "If the others are in, then it won't be long until Lucas finds us." She looked out and around to the left, then stepped into the passageway.

A siren blared, and a red light on the ceiling in the corner of the room flashed.

"What did you do?" Ryan asked.

Lilith looked both ways before coming back into the chamber. "There must have been a trip wire or something to set off an alarm."

"Come on, we can't do anything about it now." Archer lifted Charlotte into his arms, and the pull of her wrists against the shackles made her sob. "She's so weak."

"I have an idea." I went to Charlotte and inspected the metal that encased her wrists.

I held my forefinger in front of me and conjured a ball of fire on its tip. It hovered above my nail, twisting and turning, the fire writhing over itself. Surely I could generate enough heat to melt through the metal.

"What are you going to do with that?" Ryan asked, looking over my shoulder.

"Hold her still, Arch."

I drew a line, crossways along the shackle on her left hand. The metal glowed bright orange and I hoped I wouldn't hurt Charlotte too much.

"Don't burn her," Archer said.

Shut up! I yelled at him in my head.

Charlotte cried out, but I didn't stop. She blinked a few times before closing her eyes and burrowing her face into Archer's chest.

The shackle broke and Charlotte's arm dropped away, dangling at her side. The shackle clinked against the stone wall.

"Hurry," Lilith said. "They're coming."

"Keep them away." I glanced at Seth as I went to work on Charlotte's other wrist.

What about her? Seth nodded towards Lilith.

Fight with her, but not for her. I don't trust her, but she seems to want to stop Lucas as much as we do.

Seth stepped out into the gloomy passage, back to back with Lilith. He held his stake at the ready. He looked right at home with a vampire fighting by his side. But then again, Seth looked happy fighting anywhere. All those years of pent-up anger—I guess he had to release it somehow.

The second shackle bounced against the wall and Archer dropped to the ground as soon as Charlotte was free. He laid her down, cradling her head in his lap, muttering to her to wake up.

Charlotte tried to talk, her lips moving, but not much sound coming out.

Blood, I heard in my mind.

"Grace," Seth said. "A little help?"

The blaring siren stopped. A rumble coursed along the passageway, and small pieces of debris fell from the gaps in the stone blocks that made up the walls.

"Charlotte," I said. "You have to wake up."

Blood. I need blood.

"Whose blood?"

"Who are you talking to?" Archer asked.

Then I realised what had happened.

"Charlotte spoke in my head," I said.

"How is that possible?" Archer's eyes widened.

"She used to be an angel, you idiots," Lilith said from the passageway.

I stared at Charlotte. *We have a lot to talk about when this is over.*

If you want to stop Lucas, feed me my blood, Charlotte thought.

My nose wrinkled in disgust. Not much freaked me out these days when it came to the gory details. I was used to seeing vampires feed, but drinking your own blood? Yuck!

"Gracie! We have to do something." Archer glowered at me.

I jumped up and ripped the blood bags off their hooks on the walls. When I pulled the tube out of the bottom, blood poured out, leaving a trail across the floor and up Charlotte's arm to her open mouth.

Grace, I need you! Seth's voice exploded in my head.

I shoved the blood into Archer's hand. "All of it," I said. "She needs her strength back, now."

Vampires filled the passageway in both directions, but it was only narrow enough to fit one, maybe two people side by side. Dust littered the ground at Seth and Lilith's feet, and for the first time I noticed Lilith had a stake in her hand. She also had the small crossbow strapped to her wrist.

"Not sure I can help much," I said. "There's no room."

"You hold them off here," Seth said. Then he finished his thought in my head. *I'll mist behind them. Take them by surprise.*

They'll be coming at you from both directions, I thought.

Seth kicked the next vamp in the stomach, causing him to fall back onto the vamps in the line, creating a mild domino effect. It gave Seth enough time to grab me and pull me close.

I'll be fine.

Then he kissed me hard, leaving behind an ache in my mouth as well as my heart.

32

JOSH

Lucas stared at us from his position on the raised platform, Cain in a heap at his feet. His face darkened, and his lips curled into a snarl. I knew how he felt. So many things had happened in the past few months that had pissed me off as well.

Justice laughed and looked at Michael. "Why the hell do we need hunters like me, when the world's got you?"

"They're not dead," Michael said. "The only way to kill a vamp is by stake, fire, or beheading. They'll wake up."

"How soon?" I asked.

As if in answer to my question, a few vamps stirred. They writhed on the ground in a drunken stupor, trying to get to their feet. One after another, the rest of them started to come around.

"Sooner than I'd thought." Michael made his way through the sea of vamps, across the floor of the cavern,

243

and the rest of us followed. "They must be high on Charlotte's blood. Am I wrong?" He stared at Lucas.

Lucas sniggered. "You angels think you're so smart. And you." Lucas glared at me when we reached the base of the platform. "You're going to wish you never crossed me."

I scoffed. "Next time, send someone who can actually fight."

"What do they say?" Michael asked, laughing. "If you want something done right, do it yourself."

Before Lucas could reply, a deafening siren sounded through the chamber. Hope clamped her hands over her ears, looking around frantically for the source of the sound.

Lucas's face split into a wide grin, and he bent forward, a laugh pouring from his mouth. It was a horrible sound—the mirth of a madman.

"Your friends won't get out," Lucas said. "There are too many of us." He kicked Cain, who groaned and clambered onto his knees. "You're an idiot for leading them to us. Which part of *kill them* did you not understand?"

Cain scowled but kept his mouth shut.

Michael sighed. "When will you get that you can never win this war? Angels, fallen or otherwise, can't be killed by the likes of you. But vampires—all you need is a splinter through your heart ..."

Vampires all around us got slowly to their feet. Hope and Justice stood back to back, as I'd seen Grace and Archer do so many times before. I hoped Grace was okay—I had to trust that she could look after herself.

"Um ... you might not be able to die, Michael, but I can." I backed away a few steps from a vamp that looked ready to rip my head off. "I hope you've got more magic light stashed away somewhere."

"I've probably already attracted unwanted attention from above," he said. "We'll have to do things the old-fashioned way."

"Fine by me," Justice said.

The siren stopped and the ground shook. Lucas laughed again and I wondered what was so funny. Nothing about anything that had happened over the past few days was even remotely humorous.

"The others are after them," Lucas said. "If they don't kill them, they'll bring them back here."

"There are more of you?" Hope asked, looking around the chamber filled with vampires.

"There are more of us than you can possibly imagine," Lucas said. "And most of them have had at least one dose of the miracle blood."

The vamp that had been eyeing me off launched at me, and that was the cue for everyone to start fighting. I stayed as close as I could to Michael. I was strong enough to fight, but not ten to one. Automatically, I reached behind me for a stake from the belt Grace had given me, but it wasn't there. I was in a room full of vampires, fighting for my life, and I didn't have a stake.

"Josh," Hope yelled from across the room. The fray had driven us apart. "Here!"

She threw a stake to me and I caught it, swinging it down into the chest of the vampire in front of me. She disintegrated onto my feet, and I shook the dust off. I remembered how much Grace loved getting dust on her boots. I couldn't understand why. It was horrible.

"Head in the game, Josh," Michael said. He orbed away

and landed in the middle of a group of vamps.

"Josh, duck!" Justice yelled.

A stake flew over my head as I crouched, embedding itself into a vampire behind me. He exploded, adding to the already dust-littered floor.

Hope and Justice carved their way through the field of vampires. They took down four vamps to every one of mine. There were so many of them. We needed Grace and Archer, and Charlotte.

It was then that I wished I were an angel, or someone who couldn't die so easily. I didn't want to die. Not yet. Not until I could tell Grace how much I loved her. Not until I had another chance to fight for her.

As much as I wanted to hate her, I couldn't. I loved her more than anything, and it took facing death for me to realise it. With every vamp I dusted, it brought me closer to being able to see her again. And as I staked each one, I counted the seconds until I could stop fighting and go and find her.

33

GRACE

Lilith's back brushed mine while we fought the vampires in the dim passageway. I wanted to turn around and stake her, like I'd staked the vamps that lay in piles of dust on the floor at my feet, but the thought of Josh held me back. He was all Lilith could think about, and I didn't want to be the reason for more anger in his eyes. I'd already hurt him too much.

I blocked Lilith's thoughts because she was driving me crazy.

Ryan stood back from the doorway, waiting for the right time to talk to me. His head was filled with thoughts about Josh, and Charlotte, and the mess we were in. I concentrated on him, sifting through the clutter, but I couldn't come up with anything clear. I was surprised he hadn't gone completely mad.

"Ryan, what's wrong?" I said. "You're standing there

waiting to ask me something."

"I want to fight."

"There's not enough room out here."

"Well, make room. We have to get out of here."

"I'm working on it," I said.

I pulled my arm back to stab a vamp in the chest, but he disintegrated in front of me before I had the chance. My arm came down and drove the stake into someone's chest, but it wasn't a vamp.

Seth cried out and doubled forward.

"Oh my ... I'm so sorry." I ripped the stake out and put my hand over the hole in his chest. The muscles flexed beneath my fingers, blood running between them and making them sticky.

Seth clenched his teeth. "That hurt."

"Well, toughen up, princess. We've got a crazy vamp to kill." Archer stood next to Ryan, Charlotte leaning against his side.

"How about I stab you with a stake ... See how tough you are." Seth grimaced.

Archer glared.

Charlotte wasn't her former self, but the bite marks on her arms were healing, and she had her eyes open, so I guessed that was something.

I wiped my hand on my jeans, leaving a smear of Seth's blood behind, and then retrieved my stake from the floor where it had fallen amongst the ash. We'd killed all the vamps who'd come at us, but more could turn up at any moment.

"Where's Lilith?" Archer looked into the passage.

I sighed, turning to face the only way she could have

run. I squeezed my eyes closed and pinched the bridge of my nose.

"You lost her?" Archer said.

"Please, don't start." I dropped my hand to my side.

"Are you serious, Gracie? You didn't know she'd taken off?"

I turned on my brother. "I was busy fighting—"

"And staking me," Seth said.

"You should've been paying more attention," Archer said.

He backed away when I came towards him, anger rising in my chest. "While you were in here playing doctor, I was paying attention … to all the vamps that are now dust. Do you see any left?"

Archer frowned. "You should have been able to predict her escape."

"I blocked her out."

"You what?"

"All she was thinking about was Josh," I said.

"Come on, stop arguing," Seth said. "We should try and find the others."

Archer looked at Seth as if he'd grown another head. One that played nice. "And how are we supposed to do that without Lilith?"

"We came here based on what you saw in Cain's head," Ryan said. "Can we get to the others the same way? Did you see where they were going?"

"Not enough to get a good lock on their location. I'd been concentrating on Charlotte."

"I know the way." Charlotte stepped around us and out the door. "It's not far."

Ryan was the first to follow. "Beats staying here."

Seth motioned for Archer and me to follow. The wound on his chest had almost healed, with only a small patch of dry blood left around the edges.

We walked in silence for a few minutes. The siren had stopped, but the red lights along the passage pulsed in a steady rhythm. I hoped Charlotte knew where she was going.

The passage came to a dead end, and I was about to point it out when Charlotte pressed her ear to the wall. I strained my ears, sifting through what I could hear in my head, and attempting to determine what were thoughts and what were real sounds.

Charlotte pulled back and searched the floor. When she'd found what she'd been looking for, a smile crept onto her face. It had been a while since I'd seen it. Charlotte's smile made her beautiful, like it wasn't just her lips moving, but her entire body swelling with happiness. It was kind of infectious.

She stomped on the floor and what looked like a plain old rock disappeared into the stone. The wall in front of us slid open, revealing a room lit with another bulb hanging from the ceiling. It blinked off, fizzed with a static noise, and then came on again.

"Bad connection," Archer said.

"The wiring is old." Charlotte shrugged. "Not much of it works ... only the bits that need to."

On the other side of the room was another door. It was well hidden in the wall, but the rock key sat on the floor next to it. It looked the same as the one Charlotte had stomped on.

"Where does that go?" I asked.

"Into the main chamber," Charlotte said. "I told you it wasn't far."

"Are you okay?" Archer put his hand in the small of her back.

Charlotte nodded and faced the door. "I have to be. We've got a vampire to kill."

34

JOSH

Vamp dust billowed around me, and I spun, ready to drive my stake into the chest of the next one coming. No sooner had I dusted one than another took their place.

I concentrated on reaching Lucas, who stood with Cain near the throne, arms crossed, surveying the battlefield before him. It was impossible to get close enough to kill him.

Michael fought the mass of vamps protecting Lucas. Hope orbed to his side to help, and together they thinned the army lined up in front of the platform.

"All of them need to die," Michael said, his voice travelling across the open room. He drove his stake into another vamp, and for a moment the way to Lucas cleared, until another vamp closed the gap.

"Are you nuts? We can't possibly kill them *all*," I said.

"Killing vamps is what hunters do."

I didn't think it was a good time to remind him I wasn't a hunter.

The sound of rock grinding on rock entered the cavern, and I turned towards the noise. A fist connected with my cheek, sending me reeling backwards. I stumbled, and fell onto my back. The vamp that had punched me jumped on top of me. She was quick, and all arms and legs. She flew into a psycho rage, growling and gnashing her teeth. I put my arms up to fight her off. For such a small creature she had surprising strength.

Lucas's laugher bounced off the rock walls. From the corner of my eye I saw him and Cain standing on the stage, watching the battle on the cavern floor.

I tried to roll out from under the girl vampire, but she clamped her knees around my waist. Her fingers tore at my clothes, her nails drawing blood as they scratched my chest. I managed to get a punch in, but the angle was wrong, and it had no effect.

Then she exploded into dust and it rained down on top of me, falling into my mouth and eyes.

Lilith reached out and I grabbed her hand, pulling myself up. The sight of her made my chest tighten. I didn't want to admit I'd been worried about her, but I also didn't want to admit I was more worried about Grace.

"Thanks," I said, not really able to manage anything else.

How had a smaller vamp gotten the better me? I should have outmatched her in size and strength. It should have been my stake through her heart, not Lilith's.

Several vamps scurried for an exit. Hope and Justice mowed down all those that crossed their path, but a few disappeared into crevices, and down passageways off the main cavern. There were so many ways in and out of the room it was hard to tell how many had fled the fight scene.

Michael appeared at my side, his mouth pressed into a thin line, and his forehead creased. "Where are Grace and the others?"

Lilith took a step back and narrowed her eyes at Michael. "No doubt they're coming."

"You deserted them."

"I came for Josh."

"Well, isn't that touching," Michael said. "Make yourself useful and talk some sense into Lucas."

Lilith gave me a look that said we needed to talk. I couldn't have agreed more. Whether we would get the chance was another thing all together.

"What makes you think Lilith can do that?" I said. "None of us can."

Michael clenched his fists and scowled. "Because Lilith created him. She can be the most compelling."

"Lucas won't listen to me," she said.

Michael grabbed Lilith around the neck and pushed her up against a rock column. "Make. Him. Listen."

I grabbed Michael's shoulders and yanked him away from Lilith. He turned on me. I'd never seen an angel so angry before. It didn't look quite right on his face.

The grating rock sounded again, and this time I was able to see where it came from. Charlotte, Grace, and the others filed into the room through the door to the right of Lucas's throne. They spread out on the platform, surrounding Lucas and Cain. Lucas's smile dropped away as he turned to see who it was. He wasn't quick enough.

Within half a second, Grace had him on the floor. She pressed her foot hard into his throat, a stake in her hand, poised to strike. Charlotte stood beside her.

Archer king-hit Cain and he hit the floor with a thud before scrambling backwards to the wall. Seth scanned the cavern, his gaze stopping when he reached me.

"Looks like Grace is here to save the day," I said.

She raised her head and stared straight into my eyes.

I was angry with her about so many things, and I was tired of swimming in my massive ocean of emotions. Neither of the girls I thought I loved were any good for me. Grace would never choose me while Seth was around, and because of that I wished I'd died that night when Charlotte had turned me.

Grace could hear every thought that passed through my mind. For once, I was okay with the mind-reading. I wanted her to know how she affected me, and how much I loved her, even though right then, loving her was the one thing I really didn't want to do.

Seth smiled and I clenched my fists at my sides. I flexed my fingers to relax them, thinking how great it would be to rip the smile off his face.

Dust littered the cavern floor, and the last few vamps standing clambered for the nearest way out. I glanced around at those I'd been fighting with. I would never be one of them—part of Grace's circle. Maybe I had been once, but not now.

My clock was ticking, and the only thing keeping me alive was Grace. I had a feeling that even Charlotte's days were numbered. Michael didn't seem the type to let any vampire live. He didn't come across as very forgiving.

All eyes were on Grace and Charlotte. Grace adjusted the grip on her stake and raised her hand above her head. Charlotte grabbed her wrist on the downward swing, stopping the kill shot. The girls stared at each other for a moment, and Grace took her foot off Lucas's neck, kicking him. He rolled onto his back and stared up at them, a silly grin plastered on his face. Charlotte pressed her lips together.

"Hello, sister," Lucas said, laughing. "So nice to see you again."

35

GRACE

Maybe I'd taken a knock to the head, because I wasn't sure I'd heard Lucas correctly.

"What did he say?" Archer asked, coming to stand beside Charlotte.

Charlotte stepped back and let Lucas get to his feet. He straightened out to his full height, towering over me. Good thing I wasn't easily intimidated.

Cain pushed himself up against the wall, eyeing us warily. I hadn't forgotten about him, but he would have to wait.

Charlotte stood still, a statuesque pose I'd come to know so well.

"Haven't you told them?" Lucas asked. "I feel … hurt." He mockingly placed his hand over where his heart should have been.

Archer slipped his hand into Charlotte's. I loved how

my brother had a way of knowing when someone needed something. Even though that someone had lied to him, to all of us, he still wanted to help her.

"Arch, this is Lucas," Charlotte said. "My brother."

Archer's gaze moved from Charlotte to Lucas and back again. "How is that even possible?"

Lucas sniggered, and I turned to Charlotte to try and read the expression on her face. She had a pretty strong wall in her head. It had always been there, right from the beginning, and I hadn't paid too much attention to it. She'd come to me looking for protection, and I'd given it to her, no questions asked. When we'd had our show-down in the clearing back home, she'd opened her mind to me. What she'd shown me then was bad enough. What she showed me now was even worse.

"You still kept secrets," I said. So many lies covered up, and I finally understood why. "You were hunters ..."

Lucas's shoulders shook with laughter.

"What?" Archer asked. "Like us? You're joking, right?" He stared at me. "Okay ... not joking."

Charlotte nodded. "I was a Protection Angel, like Grace and Hope, and Wide Island was our city. When Lilith turned Lucas after a big battle, I thought I could save him. I thought if I was like him, things could go on the way they were. I let him turn me, and I've regretted it ever since."

Archer took a deep breath. I didn't stop what he was about to do. I didn't want to. He flexed his fingers then curled them into a fist, and put everything he had behind the punch he planted on Lucas's jaw.

Lucas's head snapped back, and he stumbled into his

throne, falling on it hard before ending up on the ground again. Archer had put so much behind that punch that his feet had left the ground.

"I hate you … for everything you've done to her." Archer shook his hand, and drops of blood flicked into the air.

Lucas growled, and Cain stepped forward, baring his fangs. Seth misted, reappearing with his hand around Cain's neck, and threw him on the ground next to Lucas.

"What now?" Josh stood in the middle of the cavern with Lilith at his side.

For the first time since we'd burst into the big space, I actually took in the scene before me. Piles of ash littered the floor. Hope, Justice, Michael, Josh, Ryan, and even Lilith held stakes or weapons in their hands. Dirt and blood covered our clothing and skin.

Lilith seethed at Josh's side. The hatred she felt for me rolled off her in waves. She needn't have worried. The feeling was mutual, but I realised I'd have to deal with her later. I'd already spared her too many times for Josh's sake.

Michael circled the room, inspecting the crevices and tunnel entrances. Archer stood over Lucas, who hadn't gotten up after he'd hit him. Hope and Justice moved over to the edge of the raised platform. Ryan sat propped against one of the pillars, his hair full of ash, and his face streaked with dirt. But it was Josh I was most concerned about. He knew I could hear him, and he wasn't holding back with his thoughts.

Michael jumped up onto the platform. "Grace, we have more pressing issues. Why is there no stake in Lucas's chest? Or Cain's, for that matter?" He stared at Archer.

"I thought I'd give Grace the honours." Archer smiled.

"He's Charlotte's brother," I said. "I … can't."

"Yes … I know that." Michael gritted his teeth. "But he is evil, and needs to be taken care of. Now."

How could I say the words I was thinking, and not have everyone think I was crazy? He was her brother. I finally understood why Charlotte had kept her secrets. I probably would have done the same thing—maybe.

"Exactly why are you here, Michael?" I asked. "You were never clear about that."

"I had business to attend to."

"Angelica? Well she's gone, so feel free to leave any time."

He seemed to have forgotten I was mad at him. Just because he'd helped us in this fight didn't mean I was happy to forgive and forget.

"Not just Angelica, and you need to let the anger go eventually," Michael said.

Seth walked slowly over to Michael and stood so close to him their noses almost touched. "Leave her alone." Seth turned his back on Michael and waited.

Charlotte fidgeted with the stake in her hand. She'd gone from the-fires-of-hell angry to plain sad in a few minutes.

"I thought I could save you." Charlotte's voice was no more than a whisper, but it was loud enough to bounce off the walls of the cavern. "I gave up everything for you, and it didn't make a difference."

"Seems to be a lot of that going around," Seth said.

"I left," Charlotte said. She tightened her grip on the stake, her fingernails picking at the splinters on the handle stub. "But you couldn't leave it alone … once you knew. Your greed got the better of you."

Lucas sat up and draped his arms over his knees. "You should have killed me when you had the chance, Charlotte. Before you made me do what I did to you."

"Don't worry. I'm planning on killing you now."

"And …" Justice motioned in the air with his hand. "Wondering why someone hasn't yet. This chit-chat has been nice, and I don't know about you guys, but I could use a bit of fresh air."

"Get up." Charlotte stood over Lucas, waiting.

"You don't have to." I put a hand on Charlotte's arm.

She shook her head. "Yes, I do. I should have done it a long time ago, and after everything he's put me through, I need to."

Lucas got to his feet. "You and me. One on one. Everyone else off the stage."

Archer manhandled Cain to the edge of the platform and shoved him off. The rest of us followed, leaving Charlotte and Lucas facing each other, the throne between them. If she wanted a showdown with her brother, we'd let her have it.

Ryan got to his feet to join the group. He ran a hand down his face as he spoke. "I feel like we're behind the hall at school, waiting for Ivan or Blake to knock the teeth out of someone's head." Dark patches circled his eyes. He needed sleep.

"Hang on, there's something I need to do first," I said.

Charlotte and Lucas looked at me, confusion clouding their faces.

I twisted on the spot, and brought my arm around in an arc. The point of my stake embedded into Cain's chest and he exploded. His ash covered Archer's shins and feet as it fell to the floor.

"I told him he shouldn't underestimate me," I said. "See what you get for not paying attention?" I glanced at Lilith, and she shrunk back behind Josh.

"Thanks, Gracie," Archer said. "Now I'm covered in bits of Cain."

"Should we maybe concentrate on what's important here?" Justice said.

Up on the platform Lucas and Charlotte were fighting, and they were not holding back. They went punch for punch and kick for kick, and it didn't look like either of them would slow down.

"This could go on forever," Seth said. "Should we help her?"

"No!" Charlotte said. She ducked a punch and landed one in Lucas's ribs.

"Come on, Charlotte. You can do better than that." Lucas swung at her again, but she leant to the side and his fist glanced off her shoulder.

Lucas stopped and clenched his fists at his sides. Charlotte sidestepped around him until she stood in the middle of the platform. Lucas started moving again, only not towards Charlotte. He went behind the throne, putting his hand on the top of the arch, caressing it gently.

Lucas smirked and laughed. It started at his shoulders and rippled down through his body. He puckered his lips and let out a loud whistle.

"Um, Grace?" Archer said. "This doesn't look too good."

I glanced around the cavern at the various passage entranceways, where several vampires emerged from the shadows. They came out of the tunnels in a deafening roar, streaking past us and heading towards Charlotte. I guessed there were at least forty of them, if not more. They all had black soulless eyes, and hungry, sneering expressions.

Lucas curled his hand around the decorative cross that came out of the top of the throne. From where I stood it looked like a part of the seat. When he pulled it free, he held a sword out in front of him. The piece from the top of the throne was a hilt, and the blade was made from wood.

Grace, Charlotte thought in my head. *I think you should get out of here.*

We're not leaving you.

"We have to do something," I said to the others.

"Can't Michael use his light-wave thingy again?" Josh asked.

I looked at Michael, his forehead creased.

"You're going to let this happen, aren't you?" I said.

"You should have more faith, Grace."

"In what? A pack of angry vampires?"

"No." Michael shook his head and fixed me with his stare. "In Charlotte."

The vamps closed in until Charlotte was completely surrounded by the mob. Lucas stared at me over the crowd and snickered.

"Why aren't they attacking us?" I asked, watching the writhing mass of vamps.

"Because they want her blood." Michael stood with his arms folded.

Even though I was really angry with Charlotte and how she'd lied, it didn't mean I wanted any harm to come to her. I never wanted her dead.

"They're going to kill her," I whispered.

"We have to help." Archer started forward and Michael grabbed his shoulder, pulling him back. Seth slipped his arm around my waist, anchoring me so I couldn't run to help Charlotte.

She was out of sight, covered in a mass of vampire bodies all trying to feed from her. They writhed over each other, fighting for one purpose—to sink their teeth into her flesh.

Light emanated from the centre of the fray. A few of the vampires threw their arms up to shield their faces. A force so powerful shot outwards, making the walls shake, and the vamps scattered. Those closest to the centre copped the full impact, and some turned to dust instantly. Others sprawled onto the ground or fled back into the tunnels.

The light surrounding Charlotte blinded me, and it took my eyes a moment to adjust. When they did, they almost fell out of my head. Charlotte rose from a crouch and a pair of bat-like wings unfurled behind her. She beat them twice and took to the air, flying up to the high ceiling of the cavern. I thought Seth's and my own feathers were beautiful, but Charlotte's wings were something else altogether. A delicate membrane stretched between the slender finger-like bones. They were unlike any wings I'd ever seen. All the bats I'd ever come across had black wings, but Charlotte's were pure white, and when she beat them they rippled with a silver sheen. It was as if a precious metal was embedded below the surface. Where her pale skin wasn't concealed under black jeans and top, it shimmered with the same silvery light, and her strawberry-gold hair pooled onto her shoulders.

She was as glorious as any angel.

"How ...?" I couldn't finish the question.

"Look at her hands," Michael said.

On her right hand, Charlotte wore a silver ring—a ruby, as red as fresh blood, sat between two sweeping feathers.

"Her creation ring," I said. "But she's never worn it before."

"Secrets," Michael said. "She's good at keeping them."

Seth released his hold on me and I stepped out from the comfort of his arms. From the corner of my eye I saw Archer's mouth hang open as Charlotte conjured a ball in her palm. At first I thought it was light, like I used to conjure before I became fallen, but when I looked closer I saw it was actually blue and silver fire. The flames licked upwards as if searching for oxygen. Charlotte twirled the ball on her fingertips before releasing it at the remaining vamps inside the cavern. The fire swept from one to the next, a blue and silver wave of flame. It took out all the stragglers who hadn't gone into the tunnels, before dissipating into the air.

I felt as if someone had knocked the wind out of me. I gazed up at Charlotte in disbelief, and she stared back with her charcoal eyes. A crack echoed through the cavern, and my wings broke free, shredding the back of my top. I hadn't released them for a while, and seeing Charlotte in the air gave them a mind of their own.

I rose to meet her, hovering above everyone. My black and grey wings beat in time with her white ones. She stretched out her arm with her palm facing me, and I did the same. When our hands met, warmth flooded my heart, and I wanted everything to be right between us again.

"It will be," Charlotte said.

She descended slowly to the ground and retracted her wings. As they folded in behind her, the shimmering silver light also faded. She looked the way she always had.

Lucas stared at her from his position behind the throne.

I landed beside Seth, folding my wings close to my body.

"Well," Charlotte said, facing her brother. "Are you ready to face me on your own now?"

Lucas raised the wooden sword as his answer. His face clouded with anger and he bared his fangs.

Grace, Charlotte's voice invaded my mind. *You'll have to finish this for me.*

What are you talking about? You're going to finish this.

Promise me, Charlotte thought.

I stared into her eyes, the edges of them laced with fear. Something I'd never seen in them before. *I promise.*

Charlotte adjusted her stance, and raised her chin towards Lucas, her hands at her side. "If I let you kill me, this is all over. No more blood. No more chances to walk in the sun."

I wanted to scream at her. To ask her what the hell she was doing. A moment ago she wanted him dead. She could kill him easily. Why was she laying herself out in front of him to be slaughtered?

"What option do I have after your little display?" Lucas said. "We both know no matter what happens, I'm as good as dead anyway. You and your friends are too powerful for me. You've disappointed me, actually ... I thought you'd put up more of a fight."

"I'm done fighting." Charlotte moved to stand against the wall behind the throne, her arms by her sides, her head slightly back. "I let you make me, Lucas, but it was the worst decision I've ever made. You created a monster in me far worse than the hungriest vampire. Now you need to undo it. *You* have to destroy the one thing you're fighting so hard for. This way, my blood is on *your* hands … no one else's." She closed her eyes.

"No. We have to help her." Archer ran towards the base of the platform.

I misted and landed in his path. He crashed into me and we fell to the floor. The footsteps of the others were close behind, but all of us were too late.

The moment the sword entered Charlotte's chest, I screamed.

I didn't want her to die. We had too many things to talk about, and too much had happened between us for me to let her go. But it wasn't anyone's choice but hers.

I'm sorry. I stared at Charlotte. *For everything … for … everything.*

It's okay, Grace. This is what was always supposed to happen.

I scrambled to get to my feet, but my arms and legs were caught up in Archer's. Strong hands pulled me up and held me tightly. Charlotte exploded into a cloud of white dust. It burst outwards like the sun's rays, filling the cavern with light that washed away the yellow hue from the lamps behind the grates. Then the rays imploded, drawing back into themselves, exploding again—only this time the light swirled around itself, forming tiny orbs. Blue glittered around the edges. The orbs formed a huge mass of light that spread out above us like a blanket. They rained down on top of us like blue, falling stars, disappearing before they hit the ground.

Charlotte was gone.

Archer flopped back onto the ground and covered his face with his hands. Then he let out a scream louder than anything I'd ever heard come from his mouth. I could feel his heart being ripped from his chest, because mine was right beside it.

36

JOSH

Grace looked as if every ounce of energy had been drained from her body. She leant against Seth, her wings wrapped around them both, and her closeness to him made the anger inside me swell again.

"Where did she go?" Grace asked.

"Where she belongs," Michael said. "Where you were supposed to put her months ago."

Archer hadn't moved from the floor. His hands covered his face, as if he didn't want to look at anything anymore.

I knew how he felt.

"Heaven?" Grace asked.

Michael nodded. "Just think, if you had have done this when the Council asked you to, none of this would've happened."

"Don't throw that in my face now!" Grace said, the anger in her eyes burning like fire.

"You never did like to be told what to do," Michael said.

"And I still don't. But I have to finish this. I promised Charlotte." She headed straight for Lucas.

All eyes were on him. He stood on the platform with his back to us, the sword dangling in his hand. White dust littered the floor at his feet. His shoulders shook with laughter, and he turned to face us.

"Which one of you is next?" he said.

Every single person there wanted a piece of Lucas for one reason or another, even Lilith.

Grace reached the base of the platform. "I'm going to make you wish you'd never been created."

"Don't you think I wish that already?" Lucas asked. He towered over her small form from the height of the platform, the wooden sword in his hand. The light from the lamps reflected off the intricate carvings on the hilt.

Grace faltered, her face clouded with confusion, which then morphed into anger. "Where's your army now? Who is left to protect you?"

Lucas shrugged. "No one. It's just me and you."

"I won't give in as easily as Charlotte," Grace said.

"I don't expect you to." Lucas adjusted his grip on the sword.

Grace fluttered her wings, retracting them as she landed on the platform. In a split second, Seth was at her side, ready to fight, followed by Hope and Justice.

Michael looked on with a grin on his face.

Lucas was a goner.

"You used to fight for the right reasons," Grace said. "Now you fight for nothing but yourself."

Lucas gave another half laugh. "You have no idea how

hard it is. Do you? Of course you don't. You're the Protection Angel. Ask your brother what it's like to live in your shadow, to be the one without the power. Just a hunter."

"Have you ever thought about what it's like for us? Doing it over, and over again? Watching your brother die every generation?" Grace said. "The hunter is better off. At least it ends for you."

Lucas circled the sword through the air, bringing it around to a fight-ready pose. "All I wanted was to see the sun again. Charlotte could've given me that."

Grace shook her head. "All you wanted was the world, but the world doesn't want you."

She charged him, her arm poised with a stake at the ready, and it was as if she were putting every ounce of anger she possessed into that strike.

Lucas raised the sword in an arc, bringing it around to connect with Grace's side, but she was too quick. She misted, turning to a cloud of black smoke as the sword passed through her. She materialised again at his right side, ready to drive her stake home, but Lucas dodged the attack, rolling to the left. Justice was ready and planted a punch on Lucas's jaw, sending him reeling backwards. Lucas stumbled into Grace and they both fell heavily to the ground.

"Should we help?" I asked Michael. He stood beside me with his arms folded, a crooked smile on his face.

"I think they've got it under control."

"I want to help," I said.

Michael stared down his nose at me. "The best thing you can do is stay out of Grace's way."

Grace hooked her arm around Lucas's neck, and flipped

him onto his stomach. She had the perfect opportunity to bury her stake in his back, but she crawled off him and got to her feet.

"Stand up and face me," she said.

Lucas slowly got up. Hope and Justice circled him, stakes raised. We were all waiting for Grace to finish Lucas off. Seth stood at Grace's side, and I cringed at the fact that he looked so perfect there. I didn't want to think about it, but they had a history I could never understand, and they were connected in ways Grace and I could never be.

He was meant for her, and I wasn't. It was that simple.

Lucas stared at Grace, and she licked her lips. I'd never seen her so worked up before.

"Fight me!" she said. "Fight like you mean it."

It was like she was talking to me.

Lucas lunged at Grace, his lips pulled back in a snarl. His sword slid past her as she dodged his attack, the tip of it glancing off the stone floor. They faced each other, ready to go again.

Archer moaned. He hadn't moved from where he lay on his back; his hands still covered his eyes.

Grace took a few steps towards Lucas, adjusting the grip on her stake. "You have made my life hell since Charlotte walked into it, and I wish there was a way to make you pay. Killing you is giving you the easy way out."

"What other way is there?" Lucas asked.

"I could think of a few," Archer said through his hands.

Seth misted and reappeared behind Lucas, grabbing him in a headlock. Lucas swung his sword in an arc and it narrowly missed Grace's stomach. She lunged forward and planted her stake in his chest, but Lucas had brought the sword around again, and he drove it into Grace, the tip of the wood poking out through her right side.

Lucas exploded in a cloud of ash, and Grace fell forward onto her knees, clutching at the hilt of the sword. I kicked Archer and he finally took his hands away from his face. It was a fight between the two of us to see who could reach her first.

Blood dripped from Grace's wound, staining the stone floor. Within seconds the group surrounded her, and I was pushed to the edge. I should have been used to it by then, but it only made me angry.

Seth cradled Grace from behind, and she fell into him, her eyes half closed.

"She can't die," I said, more to convince myself than anyone else.

"Of course she can't, you idiot," Archer said. "But she can still get hurt." He stood over her, his hands fumbling with hers at the hilt of the sword.

"Pull it out," Grace said. "I'll heal."

"Not quick enough. Michael can fix you." Seth looked up at the archangel.

Michael nodded.

Archer wrapped his hands around the sword and Grace grimaced when it moved slightly. He waited for her to settle again, and then he pulled in one quick motion. Grace screamed, and the sound filled the cavern, cutting through the air like a razor blade.

Michael placed his hands over Grace's side. Seth fixed him with the meanest stare. Light from Michael's hands flowed into Grace, and wound itself into the hole in her flesh. The blood began to dry up, and it stopped dripping onto the floor.

All I could do was stand back and wait for her to be healed.

There were so many things I wanted to say to Grace, but I didn't know where to start. How could I apologise for the world turning to shit? How could I tell the girl I loved that she'd made the wrong decision—that I wanted her to choose me?

How would I go on existing without her?

You have to, Grace said in my head.

Her silent voice shocked me. It had been so long since she'd forced me to hear her; it felt weird having her invade my thoughts. Even though she could hear what I was thinking, it surprised me when she spoke to me.

I don't know if I can, I thought. *I've missed you.*

Grace opened her eyes and sat forward, the wound in her side better, but not completely healed. I followed her gaze over my shoulder to the floor of the cavern below the stage. When Grace was wounded, I'd forgotten about Lilith, she'd been so quiet.

Now I knew why.

Ryan.

37

GRACE

Ryan lay limp in Lilith's arms, like a rag doll waiting to be played with. She stood with his back against her chest, his head tilted to the side and his neck exposed. Blood smeared Lilith's lips, and her eyes burned with the passion of the blood frenzy.

I misted to her, but my wound wasn't completely healed, and I ended up being slower than Josh. He streaked across the cavern and grabbed Lilith around the throat mid-run. I caught Ryan as he fell from Lilith's arms. Josh didn't stop until Lilith's back hit the wall of the cavern. The rock above her head cracked from the impact.

Ryan wasn't conscious or breathing. Blood trickled down his neck from the gash under his chin. It seeped into the collar of his T-shirt, staining it a rusty red.

I pressed my hand to his neck, sobbing over his limp body. The scene was all too familiar, and memories of the night Josh had been turned flooded my mind. I couldn't let the same thing happen to Ryan. I wouldn't make the same mistake twice.

Ryan's blood stuck my fingers together, the tacky liquid covering my hands. I couldn't heal him.

Michael took Ryan from my arms.

"Please," I said. "You have to help him."

Michael nodded.

I cautiously followed Josh's path across the floor of the cavern. Rage had taken over him, and he screamed into Lilith's face, squeezing her neck so tightly I thought her head might pop off.

I was angry, too.

"I trusted you. He's my best friend." Josh hung his head. "I promised him I had his back. How could you?"

Lilith's eyes held no hint of remorse. Why would they? She ate people to survive. Josh and Charlotte were the only vampires I'd met that ever felt bad about what they were. Feeling sympathy or empathy wasn't in a vampire's nature. They survived on instinct.

"You can't be mad at me for doing what I'm supposed to do." Lilith clenched her teeth, and attempted to prise Josh's fingers away from her neck.

Josh punched the wall beside Lilith's head with his free hand. Bits of rock crumbled to the floor, and blood bloomed on his knuckles.

"Josh, baby?" Lilith said.

I'll do it if you can't, I thought. *But either way, you know it has to be done.*

Josh's eyes were vacant. He stared at Lilith, but at the same time he looked straight through her. Her mind was a jumbled mess, full of fear and resentment. His was full of anger at her, at me—at everyone.

Josh released Lilith and his hand fell to his side. A wicked smile spread across her face, and she stepped towards him, wrapping her arms around him. He ran his hands up her spine, and I moved away from them, watching as Josh positioned the point of the stake on Lilith's back.

"I didn't think you would—" But before Lilith could finish, Josh pushed her towards the wall and she exploded into a cloud of dust.

Josh let the stake drop to the ground. It rolled along the uneven surface until it hit my boot. He put his forehead against the wall and closed his eyes.

A hand squeezed my shoulder and I looked up at Michael. He shook his head, and it was as if the ground had fallen out from under me.

Ryan lay on the floor of the cavern. Archer knelt beside him, his shoulders shaking with silent sobs. Seth crouched beside him, a hand on his shoulder. Hope and Justice watched, their faces masked with stony expressions.

"No." The word puffed from my mouth. I stumbled.

Michael caught my arm. "He lost too much blood."

"No!" I shoved him away from me, but Michael held on and pulled me to his chest. I pounded his arms, trying to escape from his suffocating embrace. "No."

Josh punched the wall again, and more bits of rock clattered on the ground.

Seth misted to my side and took me from Michael's arms.

"We need to get the body out of here," Michael said.

"He has a name," I whispered.

Michael stuffed his hands into his pockets, an unread-able expression on his face. He had the wall up in his mind, so I couldn't tell if he was pissed off, or looking at me in that sly way he always did. I wanted to ask if he was angry with me, but I couldn't. Our problems were obsolete in the face of Ryan's death. At that moment, it didn't matter.

Nothing mattered.

I should have made him stay home.

He never would have accepted that. Archer raised his head. Tears lined his face.

Michael moved towards Archer. Justice picked Ryan up, cradling him in his arms.

Seth reached out and wiped a tear from my cheek, and as he moved away to join the others, a white butterfly appeared and flittered around Ryan's head. It landed on his chest where it stayed, beating its wings slowly.

I hoped he was with Emma, and that they were happy.

"Come when you're ready," Seth said.

"I'll meet you at the terrace?"

Michael nodded. *We need to talk about Josh.*

What about him?

He can't live.

You can't be serious, I thought. *No one touches him.*

He's killed, Grace. It changes things.

He didn't know who he was.

We can't be sure he won't do it again. Michael frowned.

Angelica's the one who's responsible. Make her answer to you.

"Michael, we can sort this out later." Seth gritted his teeth.

Both angels stared at me. I was thankful to Seth for stepping in. Michael nodded. The group orbed and misted, leaving me alone with Josh.

When he turned around, the anger in his eyes had been replaced with pain. I hated what he had become, and I hated myself for being the one to help him get there. But I had to find a way to walk away. If I didn't, we would keep coming back to the same place. I would keep questioning if I'd made the right decision, and my friends would continue to get hurt.

We stood in the silence of the cavern, surrounded by death and destruction. I stared at Josh's hand, at the ring that had my name engraved into it. I fiddled with the ring on my finger, the one Josh had given me, and I thought about the day I'd put it on. He was thinking about that day, too.

"It all seems so insignificant now, doesn't it?" Josh said.

"I don't know how to deal with any of this." More tears spilled onto my cheeks.

"In every battle someone has to die." Josh's words sounded hollow, and his dark gaze bore into me. "How did we get here?"

"I keep asking myself the same thing."

"It looks like our pieces still don't fit properly," Josh said. He reached up and touched my cheek. "I will always love you, no matter who dies, or where we go, or what happens."

"I know you will."

We stared at each other, and I wanted to tell him. The words were right there in my mouth, waiting to come out. If I said them, would it change anything? I didn't think so. But maybe if I told him, he'd believe me, and it might make things easier. Maybe we could share the pain, and make its burden less heavy.

Was it possible to love someone, but to love someone else more?

"I love you, too," I said. "But it isn't enough."

"It doesn't matter." Josh smiled. "What matters is you finally said it."

38

GRACE

I convinced Josh to come to the terrace with me—after all, it was his place—but when we got there he went straight upstairs.

I scanned the room, taking in the expressions on Archer, Abby, and Seth's faces.

"Where is he?" I said. "Where's Ryan?"

"Michael took him," Archer said.

"What? Where?"

"Home, Gracie. He took him home."

Archer stared at me with red-rimmed eyes, his conversation with Michael playing through his head like a movie. I turned to Seth. My mouth opened to say something, but I had no words. Abby sat on the edge of the couch, pressing her hands between her knees. Her shoulders shook, and she squeezed her eyes closed.

"It's for the best," Seth said. "Easier this way."

A painful sigh rushed out of my mouth, and I leant forward, resting my hands on my knees.

"Easier for who?" I said. "He can't do that, can he? He can't wipe him off the face of the earth, so no one remembers him."

"He can and he will … Michael's taking Ryan to our cemetery," Archer said. "We won't forget him."

"What about Abby, will she forget?"

Abby stared at me with vacant eyes, a tear lining her cheek.

Archer shrugged. "Michael agreed. Some of us need to remember. She promised not to talk about him. No one would know who she was talking about anyway."

"His parents?" I asked.

"It will be as if he never existed." Archer hung his head and stuffed his hands into his pockets.

I had something else to be angry with Michael for. If he'd stayed around a bit longer, I probably would have given him an earful.

"He also said Josh is safe—for now," Seth said. "Only condition is he doesn't feed, or take a life. If he does, Michael will personally kill him."

I picked up a note Hope had left on the kitchen bench and stared at the phone number. I programmed it into my phone before sticking it to the fridge. Maybe Josh would need it someday—not that she'd be thrilled to help him.

"Justice said to say bye. Hope frowned a lot." Archer grabbed our bags and lugged them down the hallway, his head hanging low and his eyes searching the floor. I helped Abby up and we followed. I stopped at the foot of the stairs.

"You ready?" Seth asked, placing his hand on my back. "Take Abby outside. I'll be a minute."

I climbed the staircase before he could say anything. When I reached Josh's room, I stopped outside his door. He stood at the window, looking out at the dreary day. The weather seemed to know exactly how we all felt. A fine mist of rain fell over everything, turning the city grey.

"We're heading off," I said.

Josh turned to face me. He leant against the windowsill and folded his arms.

I didn't know what to say.

There was so much pain hanging between us. Josh had lost his best friend, and now he was losing me.

I didn't want to say goodbye.

He stared at his feet. "This sucks."

A sigh whistled through my teeth. "I'm sorry for everything. For Ryan. Even for Lilith."

"Killing vampires is what we do." He looked up, and a new determination filled his eyes, as if he had a purpose. "I've done some bad things, and I think after all this time, Angelica didn't take my memory just to get to you. She took it knowing that one day she'd give it back, and I'd remember everything I'd done. She's punishing me for being what I am, and by punishing me, she's punishing you, too."

He was right. Angelica had thought about all of this far too much. I only hoped Michael would pull her into line somehow, and that he'd leave Josh alone as he'd said he would.

Josh was one vampire I didn't want to kill.

"I don't want to think about her," I said. "She's gone."

"For now." Josh glanced out the window.

"It's over," I said. "It has to be."

We both knew I wasn't only talking about Angelica, and Lucas. I was talking about us.

"It will never be over," Josh said. "As long as I'm walking this earth, I will always be looking over my shoulder."

"I can protect you if you come home." I couldn't believe I'd said that. I wanted Josh safe, but having him around all the time would complicate things again.

He pursed his lips. "You don't need to babysit me."

"I wish things were different."

"But they aren't."

We stared at each other for a long time. So many things had gone unspoken between us, but so much had been said as well. It was time for me to walk away, time to go home and get on with it, whatever *it* was supposed to be.

I fiddled with the ring Josh had given me, twisting it around my finger before sliding it off. I stared at the sapphire then went to Josh and placed the ring in his hand. By taking it off it felt as if I was breaking a promise, but I wasn't. Not really. Still, I couldn't keep wearing it.

"I can't keep this," I said.

Josh nodded, closing his fingers into a tight fist around the ring. He walked to his chest of drawers and opened the top one, dropping the ring inside. He pulled the silver band from his own finger and dropped it in next.

"You have to be careful," I said. "Michael is watching."

"If you're telling me not to kill anyone, don't. I know the consequences, and the guilt is enough to remind me."

"Just ... don't do anything ..." I sighed. "If you need me ..."

"Goodbye, Grace," Josh said without turning around.

I left without replying. There was nothing else I could say. I couldn't fix things between us because I couldn't give Josh what he wanted. I understood why angels were forbidden to fall in love with humans, or at all.

It hurt too damn much.

Abby stood on the footpath, wringing her hands.

"Can you get home?" I asked.

She nodded. "My car's at the end of the street. I'll follow you?"

I watched Abby walk up the footpath then got into the car where Archer and Seth were waiting for me.

Take us home, Arch. I stared out the windshield.

He glanced at me before turning the key in the ignition. The Defender roared to life, and he pulled away from the kerb.

"Will Josh be okay?" Seth asked.

"I hope so," I said, not having the energy to be surprised that Seth had asked. "But I really don't know."

"Call him in a week or so. See how he's doing." Archer stared straight ahead, driving slowly and waiting for Abby to pull out behind us. "I'd be happy if I never set foot in this city again."

I agreed.

Seth squeezed my shoulder. We hadn't had a chance to talk about anything at all since he'd appeared in the park wrapped in celestial fire. I knew nothing about where he'd been and what he'd been through. I wanted to know everything, but I was exhausted. It was like I was in a state of numbness nothing could penetrate. I wanted to be happy that Seth was there with me, but a shroud of sorrow hung over all of us, and I had no energy left. My mind and heart wanted me to throw myself at him, but my body had other ideas.

We have plenty of time, Seth thought.

The streets passed in a blur, and once we reached the other side of the iron bridge, putting Wide Island City behind us, I breathed a little easier.

So much had happened in such a short space of time. There were so many things to think about, and so much to consider when we finally got home. I wrapped my arms around myself, wishing they were Seth's arms.

Archer squeezed my leg. *Gracie, get in the back.*

You don't have to chauffeur.

You need him. He smiled. *And he needs you.*

I unclicked my belt and climbed through the middle of the car, drawing the centre lap-sash across my waist. Seth wrapped me up, and I rested my head on his chest. My heart ached with the loss of Ryan and Charlotte, but right then all I could do was focus on the moment, and take comfort in the feeling of Seth's arms around me. If I didn't, I'd crack a little more than I already had.

I never really knew what I'd had in Seth before he was taken away from me. I'd lost him twice already, and I was determined not to lose him again. It had taken quite a few mistakes, some bad choices, betrayal and heartbreak, but for the first time since Seth had taken his fall, in his arms I finally felt safe.

39

SETH

Two weeks later

The tree looked exactly the same. Nothing had changed in the ten years since I'd made my deal with Michael. I ran my fingers around the edge of the split in the trunk, and wondered how I'd gotten to where I was.

I'd made so many wrong decisions.

No matter what I tried to do, I couldn't seem to set things completely right.

Grace had always been beyond my reach.

"Reminiscing about old times?" Michael spoke, but I didn't turn around.

My hand fell away from the tree and I stuffed it into the pocket of my jeans.

"What do you want, Michael?" I asked.

"To collect the debt you owe me."

I faced him and squared my shoulders. "I owe you

nothing. Grace made her decision."

Laughter filled the small clearing, but it didn't touch Michael's eyes. "You'd be wrong about that. She may have chosen you, but has she given you her heart? That was the deal."

"You said I had this generation. It isn't over yet."

"It may as well be." Michael folded his arms and leant against a thick Tallowwood. "The rules have changed."

I sniggered. "Of course they have."

Michael stared at me, his brown eyes digging deep into my soul. "They changed as soon as Grace fell. There are no future generations."

"Well, since Grace can't die, I should have eternity."

My fingers itched to plant a fist on Michael's face, but to stop myself I pulled my hands from my pockets and folded my arms, mimicking his stance. We'd played this game before, and I was growing tired of him. Still, I couldn't win, and he knew it.

"You can't fight this," Michael said. "The original agreement is null and void. It was made when Grace was on the right side."

"She's still on the right side." I took a step forward. "After everything she's been through, why can't you leave us alone?"

Michael pushed off the tree and stepped towards me as well. We were close enough to take a swing at each other, but I waited to see what else he had to say.

"The Council won't let me leave her alone. I'm not the one calling the shots anymore," Michael said. "They want her back."

"Well, they should have thought about the consequences

when they asked her to kill someone she cared about."

All the thoughts I'd had about hitting Michael expanded ten-fold when his fist connected with my face. I stumbled backwards, the tree breaking my fall. My hands exploded with heat, and I threw two fireballs at Michael. He orbed and they passed through his lingering spheres, landing on the ground, where they set the undergrowth on fire.

Michael reappeared on the other side of the clearing. "For once, this is not about you!"

"If it's about Grace, then it's about me," I said. "What makes you think she'll want to go back?"

"She won't," Michael said. "That's where you come in."

I flexed my fingers at my sides, the heat in them making my palms glow red, but the fire stayed beneath my skin.

The undergrowth crackled as the fire spread. Michael opened his hand and threw light from his palm. It landed over the flames in a thin blanket, putting them out. Tendrils of smoke drifted into the air, rising from the mass of charred leaves.

"I'm not going to force her to do anything," I said.

"Then you'll end up in the In-Between, and I'll be a very happy arch."

"Why don't *you* ask her to come back? She listens to you. I'm sure you can convince her."

"I have other matters to attend to, and it isn't as simple as asking her to return."

"Nothing is ever simple," I said.

I regarded Michael for a few moments, probing the walls inside his mind to try and get a glimpse at what this was all about. If I knew him as well as I thought I did, anything I agreed to would come with conditions. And everything

I didn't agree to would also come with conditions.

"You want what's best for Grace, don't you?" Michael asked.

"I'm pretty sure Grace can make her own decisions."

"By now I'm sure you've noticed that both of you are pretty bad at decision-making."

"Screw you," I said. "The moment she tells me she loves me, everything will change. And you'd better not be anywhere near me."

Michael's shoulders shook, and he pressed his lips together into a thin smile. "This was never about her telling you she loved you. Any idiot can see that she does. It's about you realising the difference between right and wrong, and how things are supposed to be."

"And how's that? How *you* say?" I ran at Michael and shoved him as hard as I could. It didn't do much.

Michael shoved me back, only he put an orb of light behind his push, and it sent me reeling backwards. I wanted to lash out again, but it would get me nowhere with him. He was too strong. I also didn't want more cuts on my face. Grace would ask questions about the one that was already there. It seemed that every time Michael hit me, my wounds didn't heal as quickly.

"Stop fighting me, Seth. Either you do what needs to be done, or you end up in oblivion. I'm sure you don't want to spend eternity with Angelica watching over you."

I scowled. Oblivion I could probably handle. Angelica for eternity was a different story.

"What do I have to do?" I asked through clenched teeth.

"Grace's days are numbered." Michael stared at me, his eyes more serious than I'd ever seen them.

"I thought we'd established that she can't die, not easily, at least," I said.

The smile I hated so much crept onto Michael's face. "I told you, the Council has changed the rules."

"First, you tell me I'll be free once she gives me her heart. Now, and correct me if I'm wrong, you're saying to send her home, I have to kill her? It's Charlotte all over again."

Michael shook his head. "You don't need to kill anyone. This time, Grace is the one who needs to make the sacrifice."

"I won't let her die for me."

Michael's orbs began to spin from his feet up. They circled around him until all I could see was his face. "Who said she needs to die for *you*?"

"But she needs to die for someone?" I may as well have been asking the trees.

Once Michael was gone, the silence of the forest filtered into the clearing. My shoulders heaved with a heavy sigh. The darkness inside the split in my tree stared at me, and for a moment I wanted it to swallow me whole. Michael was right when he'd said the rules had changed.

Grace could die.

She wasn't indestructible anymore, and because of a deal I'd made with Michael ten years before, it was my fault.

In the past I'd always had eternity stretching out before me, with all the time in the world to try and make things right. Now, time was running out.

Grace could die.

I ran through the forest towards the shed and the clearing. The sound of Grace's laughter travelled on the breeze, and I stopped at the edge of the shadows, watching. Laughing was something she didn't do much anymore, and I wanted to savour the sound.

Abby stood, arms folded and a smile on her face, watching Grace twist and turn through the air. She jumped on the trampoline with Archer at her side, both of them moving in perfect unison. She was so graceful. If only I could stop time, we could have forever together, like I'd always wanted.

There was no way I could tell her that she was marked. If Grace knew she could die, I didn't know what would happen. She wouldn't want to be treated differently. I'd have to keep her out of trouble.

I took a deep breath and stepped into the clearing, checking my defences were up so Grace couldn't pick the details out of my head.

"Tell me again why you needed a trampoline?" I asked, chuckling.

Grace came out of a summersault and jumped off onto the grass. She ran to me and threw her arms around my neck. I picked her up and gave her a tight hug before setting her feet back on the ground. I would never get enough of holding her in my arms.

"Because Archer wanted one," she said. "It's good for training."

I tried to keep my expression neutral, but Grace knew me better than anyone. She saw the difference in my eyes, and hers changed to match.

"Don't worry," I said before she could ask what was wrong. I gently rubbed her back between her wing scars, and she let it go.

School's back tomorrow. I continued to rub circles on her back.

We watched in silence as Archer jumped for a while longer. Abby edged closer to us, and I offered her a smile.

A lot had happened over the break. We'd mostly adjusted to Ryan not being around, but Grace had admitted she wasn't looking forward to no one remembering him. He should be remembered, and I'd try my hardest not to let her forget.

Abby had found everything hard to deal with after Ryan died, but Grace helped her as best she could, and I think they may have found good friends in each other. Grace's strength amazed me.

I kissed her temple. *Are you ready to face everyone?*

There was also the issue of walking through the school gates with me at her side. Most of Hopetown Valley High didn't like me, and they would think it strange I'd decided to come back after apparently dropping out.

Grace stood on her toes and pressed her lips to mine. When she pulled away, her eyes glinted in the winter sunlight, and the corners of her mouth turned up.

As long as I'm with you, I'll be ready for anything.

The chain around her neck had slipped free of her top, and the diamond on the end sparkled in the sunlight. The sight of her wearing my tear reminded me where our journey began. For a while we'd lost each other, and my heart ached with the memory of giving her up. Finally, I'd found my way back to her, and losing Grace was something I vowed never to do again.

293

FIND OUT WHAT HAPPENS IN

DIE FOR ME

THE FINAL INSTALMENT IN
THE TATE CHRONICLES

READ ON FOR
A PREVIEW

GRACE

Leaves and sticks crunched beneath my feet as I ran. Branches whipped my face, and I drove deeper into the forest, refusing to give up the chase. The moonlight caught the vampire's pale skin as he flashed between the trees.

He was fast!

I misted to try and get closer to him, but I couldn't get close enough. The vamp dummied to the left then switched quickly to the right, leaping into the air and grabbing the closest tree trunk like a cat with its claws out. He glanced over his shoulder before shimmying into the canopy above.

I stopped at the base of the tree and put my hands on my hips, craning my neck.

"Good escape plan." I watched him move through the branches.

"Come and get me. Then you'll see how good it is." The vamp jumped from an outstretched limb and landed in another tree, sending leaves tumbling to the ground.

Great. A smartarse vamp. Just what I need.

I was sick of it—sick of chasing them, sick of fighting them. Sick of everything my existence had become. It had been more than three months since I'd gone to the city to find Josh. I'd found Seth as well, and Ryan had ended up dead. I'd done the wallowing thing, and tried the happy thing, but now I was at the stage where everything was all too much. In my line of work, I had to take the good with the bad, but when the bad outweighed the good—why did I bother?

Because it's what we do, Archer popped into my head. *We keep going, no matter what.*

I glanced around the forest but couldn't see him. *Where are you?*

In stealth mode, he thought.

I resisted the urge to roll my eyes, looking again and spotting him behind a tree about ten metres away.

Yeah, really stealthy, Arch, I thought. *Bet I can beat you to him.*

My brother moved from the base of the tree, taking a few steps back then running up the trunk until he caught a branch a little way above his head. He swung himself up with ease, but before he'd made it any farther, I misted and landed on the next branch above him.

"Hey, that's cheating!" he said.

"No, it's resourceful."

I searched the trees from my higher view point and spotted the vamp making a getaway through the canopy, jumping from tree to tree. He wasn't far enough away that I couldn't catch him, but when I went to mist again, I heard something else coming through the forest.

The undergrowth rustled with the sound of running feet, and I estimated maybe two pairs of boots pounding the ground. Two vamps burst through the trees in a blur, followed by a cloud of black mist. Seth materialised below us long enough to shout at Archer.

"Get your butt back in the game!"

Then he was gone again.

"Go," I said. "I've got this one."

Archer dropped to the ground and took off into the trees after Seth, no questions asked. That was what I loved about him. He got in there and did the job. No questioning the meaning of everything, like I'd been doing lately. Archer said we should keep going like we always had, because that was how you dealt with the loss and the grief. If we didn't stop, then we didn't have to think about it. But I was over people dying, and having to be the strong one through all of it. After so long fighting, maybe I'd reached my breaking point.

I sighed and scanned the forest again for my runaway vamp. I caught him clinging to a tree trunk near the path that wound through the forest. It took less than a second to mist to where he was. I landed on the path as he was about to drop to the ground.

"Hi there." I pulled a stake from my belt and curled my fingers around it. "Fancy seeing you here."

The vamp grunted and headed back up the tree. I conjured a fire ball in my free palm, rolling it between my fingers for a moment before letting it loose. It sailed over his head and landed in the top of the tallowwood. The leaves crackled and burned, raining little pieces of ash onto his head like black confetti.

I pulled my arm back to throw another fire ball, but I'd barely conjured it before Seth appeared at my side and grabbed my wrist.

"What the hell are you doing?" he said. "You'll burn down the forest."

I let a breath out slowly, then gave him the meanest look I could manage. "I'm fighting the only way I know how." And I didn't just mean physically.

"Think … before you make stupid decisions."

"What's up your butt?" I pressed my lips together and yanked my arm away from Seth.

When we'd first come back from the city, everything had been fine. He'd done a great job of keeping me smiling. But in the past month or so, everything between us had started to fall apart; Seth had become overprotective and annoying. I couldn't help thinking it had something to do with Josh. It always did. But I hadn't chosen him, I'd chosen Seth, and for some reason he couldn't be happy about it. He was angry about something but he wouldn't share it with me, and I was angry at him for being angry.

"Don't do anything stupid," Seth said.

"Yeah, because we both know that never happens."

I focused on the vamp up the tree. The fire had gone out, but he was trying to make himself invisible by keeping still. It wasn't working.

I misted and landed on a branch next to him. He whipped his head around and glared at me, right before I punched him in the face. The impact jarred through my knuckles, making them ache. It was weird, because it had never hurt like that before. He growled and lunged at me. *Finally! He's going to fight back.* They were no fun when they didn't fight back.

The vamp grabbed me around the throat and shoved me against the tree trunk. My foot slipped, and I fell onto the thick branch beneath me, crying out as my body connected with the wood. A sharp pain pinched my side. I wasn't sure if the cracking sound was the branch or my ribs breaking. The vamp fell on top of me, and I cried out again, clenching my teeth against the pain. His legs and arms flailed as he tried to scratch my face, but at least he'd let go of my throat.

"Need any help up there?" Seth asked.

"No. I got this." I wrapped my arms around the vamp's neck and squeezed.

We rolled off the branch, and I ended up on top, my body slamming into him as he hit another branch below. This one snapped and we kept falling, bits of tree scratching my face and arms. I pushed him away and misted, landing on the ground a few seconds before the vamp fell into a heap in front of Seth. I raced forward and staked him in the chest before he could get up. The dust flopped to the forest floor and mingled with the leaves and debris.

When I straightened up, I winced and put a hand over the wound in my side. My palm came away bloody, and I wiped it onto the leg of my jeans, hoping Seth wouldn't notice.

"You okay?" he asked.

"Fine." I clenched my teeth and forced a smile. I didn't

want him to know how much it hurt. "Are we done for the night, or do you think there's more?"

Archer barrelled through the trees and onto the path, stopping to catch his breath. "Definitely more … maybe two or three." He panted, resting against a tallowwood.

A possum scurried along a branch overhead, and a twig snapped in the darkness. Something moved behind us, and then a flash passed through the trees straight ahead.

"Looks like they've split up," Seth said. "Let's go." He moved towards Archer who pinched the bridge of his nose with his thumb and forefinger.

"Don't you ever just … let it go?" Archer said.

"What happened to, 'we keep going'?" I asked.

"That's only when I haven't covered myself in the dust of five vamps. And I'm really, really tired."

Seth clapped him on the shoulder. "Toughen up, Tate. You coming, Grace?"

Pain burned my side in fiery licks, and I tried to stand normally, hoping Archer and Seth wouldn't notice.

"I'll take that one." I thumbed towards the shed, looking for a reason to head towards the clearing. "I'll meet you back at home."

Seth stared at me for a long moment, and he tried to penetrate the edges of my thoughts with his mind. But I had my wall in place like I always did. It wasn't because I didn't trust him; I wanted to be able to share things with him on my own terms.

Sure you're okay? he asked in my head.

I'll heal, I thought. *Go and kill some vamps.*

He eventually turned away and Archer followed, both of them jogging along the path and disappearing into the darkness.

When they were out of sight, I relaxed against a tree and took a look at my side. A coin-sized hole marked my top. Blood had seeped into the fabric, pasting it to my skin in a dark, sticky mess. When I peeled the fabric away, a piece of tree branch stuck out of the wound by about a centimetre. I hoped the other end of it wasn't in me any farther than that. The last thing I needed was the stick pretending it was an iceberg.

Blood slicked my fingers as I tried to grip the end of the piece of wood. My jaw ached from clenching my teeth, and I realised after trying for a few minutes to pull it out, I needed something to grab onto the stick with. Poking it made it hurt more. I had to get home.

My vision clouded and I rested my head against the tree. My stomach clenched, and a sick feeling washed through me. I hadn't felt woozy like that since I'd made the decision to tell Josh what I really was, and the sensation was not one I favoured. My hair clung to the rough bark when I pulled my head away from the trunk, and I blinked a few times to focus. Someone stood in front of me, smiling. The man's face split into three blurry masses, and then he bared his teeth.

Great. He wants to eat me.

I was about to pass out on the forest floor, but before he could lunge and sink his teeth in, I misted back to the clearing. I needed to work fast if I wanted to clean myself up before Archer and Seth got home. The first-aid kit was in the cottage, so with my last bit of strength I pulled myself up the steps and through the front door.

Fifteen minutes, a pair of tweezers, several gauze

pads, some iodine, and two Panadol later, I'd patched myself up as best I could. My wound should have healed by now, but it hadn't, and there had never been a time when my bumps and scrapes hadn't healed themselves. I wasn't sure what scared me more—how much it hurt, or not knowing what the hell was happening to me.

GRACE

Two weeks later, Tuesday afternoon

A knock sounded on my bedroom door and I rolled my top down to cover my side.

"Come in." I flopped onto my bed and winced at the dull ache from my injury a couple of weeks before. Why was it still bothering me? I was an angel. It should have healed fast, but it hadn't, and I was confused as to why.

The door swung open and Seth leaned against the frame. "How was your last exam?"

I smiled. "Archer cheated the entire time."

He laughed. "No one will ever know."

"I'm glad school's over. We never have to go back."

"Abby might think differently ... the formal ..."

I groaned. "I told you, I'm not going."

Seth stared at me and didn't reply. He'd never force me to do something I didn't want to do. Abby was a different story, and I wasn't looking forward to making her listen the next time I told her I wasn't going. So far, every time I'd said no she'd ignored me and changed the subject.

I pressed my lips together and crossed my legs on the bed. Seth had something he wanted to say; I could tell by the way he looked at me. I could also tell it was something I probably didn't want to talk about.

He came over and sat on the edge of the bed, gently grabbing my ankles so he could unfold my legs and wrap them either side of him. Leaning in, he kissed me softly, letting his lips linger for a second.

"You okay?" Seth tucked my hair behind my ear and ran his thumb over my cheek. "The formal could be a good distraction."

"I'm ..." I nodded and rested my cheek on his shoulder, hiding my face. I'd been telling everyone I was fine. He wrapped his arms around me and I tucked my face into the crook of his neck. Seth fell onto the bed, pulling me with him. I cried out then winced, thankful Seth couldn't see my face and that he probably took my little yelp of pain as surprise.

Seth pulled me on top of him and I straddled his waist, leaning down to kiss him again. He rested his hands on my hips and I tensed, not wanting him to touch the tender wound on my side, or see the patch covering it. It was a miracle I'd made it this long without him finding out about my non-healing abilities. I should have told him about it when it had happened, but it scared me. I didn't want him and Archer worrying about me. And besides, I'd always looked after myself. I wasn't the kind of girl who needed help, or who asked for it.

Seth squeezed my hips and ended our kiss. "When are you going to tell me what's bothering you?"

I sat back and ran my fingers through my hair. "Nothing's bothering me."

He regarded me with dark eyes. "I know you, Grace. Don't say it's nothing."

"Yeah. Well, I know you, too." I flung one leg over him and jumped off the bed. "You've been hiding something from me since we came back from Wide Island."

The mention of our time in the city threw a heavy shroud of silence over us. Seth took a deep breath and ran a hand down his face, staring at me from where he lay on the bed. I crossed my arms and waited out the silence.

"I liked it better when you were over here," he finally said.

I moved back to the bed and sat on the edge, hugging myself, careful not to put too much pressure on my right side.

"I miss him." I stared at the scuffed toes of my boots.

Seth touched my back and trailed his fingers down my spine. "Do you mean Ryan, or—"

"Of course I'm talking about Ryan."

After everything that had happened, Josh's name was not a word I could freely say around Seth. He sat up and nestled in behind me, pressing his chest to my back and wrapping his strong arms around me. I slipped my arms around my stomach, under his, to relieve the weight of his embrace.

"I wouldn't be upset if you ... wanted to talk about someone else."

I snorted, turning to look at him. "Yeah, you would."

"Grace ..." Seth sighed and pressed his lips to my neck. "The past is in the past. And no matter what you do, I will always love you. Always."

I rested my cheek against his and closed my eyes. "I know." And I also knew what he wanted me to say back to him. I did love him. I'd shown him that many times. I'd fallen apart over him, and that was the main reason I hadn't told him yet. I was scared if I did that it would all disappear. That somehow he'd leave me again. The last time I'd told someone I loved them, I had to be the one to leave. The word love and I didn't have a good history. I tried every day to show Seth as much as possible how strongly my heart beat for him, but I couldn't say those three words. I was waiting for the right time.

Seth hitched my leg and spun me around to face him. *And you don't think now is the right time?*

You snuck into my head! I thought.

He stared at me, his mouth set into a firm line. He wasn't angry, but he was hardly smiling either. *You haven't let me do that in a long time.*

I reached up and ran my thumb over his lips in an attempt to relax them. *Maybe I do want you to hear me say it.* "But in here," I said aloud, placing my palm over his heart.

His lips parted and my gaze dropped from his eyes to his mouth. Heat rose into my chest, consuming me with a powerful desire laced with panic. What if something happened to me, and I never got to tell him how much I loved him? What if my inability to heal myself meant that losing him was also a possibility? The panic over the thought consumed me, and I grabbed Seth's face with both hands, pulling his lips to mine, crushing them with desperation. I couldn't get enough of him, and something inside me snapped. I tasted the salt of my tears as they ran over our lips and into our mouths.

Seth broke our connection, his lips moving to speak.

"I love you," I said, before he could form words. "I love you so much it hurts."

He leaned forward and rested his forehead on mine, stroking my cheek with the tips of his fingers. I clung to him like he was my life source and without him I'd die.

"Why are you crying?" he whispered into my hair.

Because I'm scared, I thought. *I've already lost you twice. I promise you won't lose me again.*

We sat on the bed in each other's arms, and I spent a few minutes wandering what else was wrong. When he'd first come into the room he'd wanted to talk about something, and it seemed we'd gotten side-tracked.

"I know there's something else you want to say," I said.

Seth loosened his embrace and I stood, hoping I could keep my feet after riding the emotional roller coaster.

"You need to come downstairs. Archer wants to have a meeting." Seth looked up at me and half-smiled.

"Since when did he become the boss?"

"Since you decided to give up the fight." Archer stood in the doorway, his hands stuffed into his jeans pockets. "You were taking too long." He glared at Seth.

Seth stared him down, raising an eyebrow. "Tactful."

"It's my middle name. Come on. I'd rather not talk in a room with you two and a bed."

Seth slipped his hand into mine and we followed

Archer down the metal stairs to the bottom floor of the shed. I already knew what this was going to be about. Archer wanted me to fight again, and like every time he'd tried to put his foot down for the past two weeks, I'd do the same and say no. I had a wound that wouldn't heal, and I didn't want another one before I could work out what was wrong with me. Still, I gave him points for persistence.

Archer stopped in front of the kitchen table and turned to face us, leaning back against the edge and crossing his legs at the ankles. I sat on the arm of the couch and tucked my foot behind my knee. Seth flopped onto the couch and put his hand on my back. I wasn't a hundred percent sure where he stood with the situation. Whenever Archer called one of these meetings, Seth said he wouldn't force me to do something I didn't want to do.

"Before you say it, Arch, the answer is still no."

He scowled. "Come on, Gracie. Fighting. It's what we do."

"Did," I said. "I've told you, I don't want to do it anymore. I'm fallen now. There's no rule that says I have to keep the mission."

"What about doing the right thing?" Archer waited for an answer, but I wasn't playing the game. "What about protecting me?"

"I can't heal you anymore," I said. "And you have Seth, who's willing to fight in my place."

Archer's gaze flicked to Seth then back to me. He licked his lips and shook his head. "I can't believe you've given up."

I closed my eyes and counted to five. The speech was

getting old, and I wanted to tell them why I'd decided to stop fighting, but it didn't seem like a good idea. They'd treat me differently if they knew I could get hurt. I was the same Grace, and I refused to become the main guest at their pity party. They were doing fine without me.

"I think what Arch means," Seth said, "is the situation is getting worse."

"Really? Because I thought he was trying to make me feel guilty," I said.

"I can try harder." Archer glared at me and pushed off the table. He clenched his fists and the sudden display of anger caught me off guard.

"What are you going to do, beat it into me?" I asked. "I've made my decision. I don't want to fight anymore."

"Things are getting out of hand, Gracie." Archer took a step forward. "You need to suck it up, get over whatever it is that happened, and get your arse back out there."

"What I need," I said, as calmly as I could, "is for everyone I love to stop dying around me."

"Well, one day I'm going to end up dead," Archer said, "because you don't have my back anymore."

"Calm down," Seth said. "I told you she wouldn't have changed her mind."

I couldn't believe what I was hearing. Archer had never used this tactic before. It was usually the *please tell us what's wrong* card. Maybe he thought it was time to try something else.

I stood from my perch on the arm of the couch and walked towards the shed door. "I'm done listening to you, because you don't seem to be hearing me."

When I reached the door, I grasped the knob and

turned, but I only got it halfway open before Archer was at my side shoving it closed. Seth was at my other side in an instant, but I ignored him. I wasn't entirely happy with the fact he wasn't arguing for me. He seemed to be sitting on the fence a bit too much, which made me think he agreed with Archer more than I wanted him to.

Slowly, I turned to face my brother. "Angry doesn't suit you, Arch." I opened the door again, and this time he didn't stop me from walking out into the warm afternoon sun.

"Why won't you tell us what's going on, Gracie?" Archer yelled after me.

Because it's none of your business, I thought. And I was too scared to tell them.

Neither of them replied.

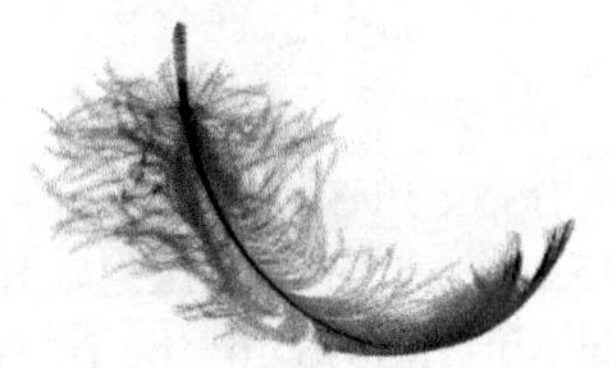

ACKNOWLEDGEMENTS

As with every book I've written, there are always so many people I need to thank. I'd be crazy to think that I could ever do this on my own. Writing itself is a very solitary exercise, but the journey is filled with people from every aspect of my life.

To my husband and children, thank you for putting up (again) with my zone outs, and all the times I haven't listened because I've been thinking about Grace, Josh, and Seth.

To my mum and dad, thank you for being there for me—all the time. To my brother, for showing interest in something that you're really not interested in.

To Kylie, thank you for finally reading the first book, and saying it was okay.

Thank you Katrina—a million times, thank you. There are no words in the English language that can describe how thankful I am to have you in my life. You never complain, even when I asked you to read this story again, and again. I think you've read it more times than I have. Your opinion and especially your friendship are highly cherished, and like I said—there are no words.

Cass, thank you for dropping everything to beta read for me. You are always thorough, and I love all your comments that make me laugh out loud. Your willingness to help is greatly appreciated. I've found a valued writing friend in you, and I hold our friendship close to my heart.

Thank you, Stacey, for your mad proof reading skills, but mostly for all the times you've let me chew your ear off about anything and everything—even the stuff that has nothing to do with books. I'm so glad to have found a friend in you. I hold your opinion and advice in the highest regard.

To Lauren, well, what can I say? Editor extraordinaire, awesome writer, beautiful soul, and cherished friend—you are the most awesome of awesome. Thank you.

Nikki, my OS writing friend, thank you for beta reading—your feedback and opinions are priceless. And thank you for all the wonderful email chats. Hugs.

My Aussie Owned and Read girls—thank you. I'm so grateful for the wonderful community I've found with you all, both online and in real life.

To my writer's group: Stacey, Lauren, Laura, and Selina. I love the support we give each other. Thank you for the chats, discussions, brainstorming, and awesome idea sessions, and, of course, the tea and biscuits. I'm looking forward to many more meetings in the future.

Thank you to my street team, Team Awesome. I treasure everyone who helps support me, my writing, and my books.

And finally, huge thanks to everyone who has read *Fall For Me*, and loved it enough to continue reading Grace's story.

ABOUT THE AUTHOR

K. A. Last was born in Subiaco, Western Australia, and moved to Sydney when she was eight. Artistic and creative by nature, she studied Graphic Design and graduated with an Advanced Diploma. After marrying her high school sweetheart, she concentrated on her career before settling into family life. Blessed with a vivid imagination, K. A. Last began writing to let off creative steam, and fell in love with it. She has a Bachelor of Arts Degree from Charles Sturt University, with a major in English, and minors in Children's Literature, Art History, and Visual Culture. She now resides in the NSW countryside with her family and a menagerie of animals.

CONNECT WITH
K. A. LAST

Scan the code to subscribe
to K. A. Last's newsletter.

Website www.kalastbooks.com.au
Facebook www.facebook.com/KALastBooks
Instagram www.instagram.com/kalastbooks
Pinterest www.pinterest.com/kalast
Goodreads www.goodreads.com/KALast
Twitter www.twitter.com/KALastBooks

BOOKS BY K. A. LAST

YA Fantasy Fiction
Sacrifice – A Fall For Me Prequel
Fall For Me (The Tate Chronicles, #1)
Fight For Me (The Tate Chronicles, #2)
Die For Me (The Tate Chronicles, #3)
Immagica
The Lovely Dark
Ella and Ash (Happily Ever After, #1)
Chasing Neve (Happily Ever After, #2)
False Princess (Happily Ever After, #3)
Dance of Wishes (Happily Ever After, #4)
Winter Flame (Happily Ever After, #5)

YA Contemporary Fiction
Something (All the Things: part one)
Nothing (All the Things: part two)
Everything (All the Things: part three)
The Other Side of Me (All the Things: part four)

Non-fiction
A Novel Idea! Colouring Journal for Writers
A Novel Idea Workbook for Writers